RICK PARTLOW

www.aethonbooks.com

HYBRID

©2018-2020 RICK PARTLOW

"Repent! Repent!" the naked man screamed. "You desecrate the perfection gifted to us by the Ancients! You sacrifice your humanity to the false god of technology!"

Ashton Carpenter watched the street preacher out of the corner of his eye, afraid to look straight at him for fear the man might try to engage him. The guy had balls to start haranguing crowds outside a Skin-ganger chop shop. The Skin-ganger cyborgs, "Evolutionists" they liked to call themselves, were already filtering out of the dingy, sheet metal building, their glowing red oculars glaring at the Predecessor Cult missionaries. The neon glow of the street signs glinted menacingly off the exposed silvery metal of their bionic limbs, and Ash walked a little faster.

Kanesh was bad enough without wading through a religious gang war. He hated the dank, claustrophobic chill of the tunnels and the thin sheen of condensation clinging to every metal or plastic surface, and the unshakable feeling that, with every step, he was descending deeper into the bowels of Hell. Docking at the asteroid's hub, the place had seemed a strange and almost quaintly bureaucratic cut-rate version of upscale pleasure stations like Belial in the Alpha Centauri system, except here they let you keep your weapons as long as you paid an exorbitant tax.

But then he'd traveled spinward in the lift, towards the outer levels of the rotating cylinder of asteroid rock with centripetal gravity closer to Earth-normal, and had to search each one of them, had to experience everything that people were willing to do to each other when there were no consequences for their actions. Kanesh had been built by the Pirate World cartels, far outside the jurisdiction of the Patrol, too remote for even the military to bother with it. Like Belial and other, smaller pleasure stations inside the bounds of the Commonwealth, it was a "blown" asteroid, cored with a high-power laser, filled with water, spun and then heated with solar reflectors until it expanded like a balloon, leaving a thick sheath of nickel iron shielding the empty space within.

Unlike Belial, though, Kanesh lacked even the semblance of law or restraint. The station had been built by criminals as neutral ground, a place to do business without the worry of another cartel crashing through the door or one side double-crossing the other. And that was the only order maintained on Kanesh: business was sacrosanct and anyone who interfered with it was dealt with swiftly and brutally, usually without even wasting a round of ammo on them. The bodies floated like debris in orbit around the station, more effective than any verbal warning.

Cartel negotiators, smuggler crews, assassins, bounty hunters, enforcers, fugitives and exiles flocked here, and so did those who fed on their appetites. There were restaurants and bars and hotels and dance clubs, of course, almost prosaic in how little they differed from businesses just like them on dozens of worlds. They seemed out of place here, obscene in their normality next to the other things, the things you wouldn't find on the Pirate Worlds themselves, because even a cartel boss wouldn't want to admit they sanctioned it.

Here, no attempt was made to hide their vices, no cosmetic veneer was thrown up as camouflage. Garish holographs advertised the attractions of each level, with little organization by types: gladiatorial combat to the death, with and without weapons, bettors welcome; chopshops where you could sell the limbs and organs stolen off of others, or have a suitable replacement grafted from the inventory, or have your own biological pieces replaced with cybernetics to chase the next step in human evolution; snuff shows where you could watch unwilling participants killed live in imaginative ways; drug dens that catered to whatever addiction might suit, from conventional chemicals such as Kick and Spindle to black market Virtual Reality that directly stimulated the pleasure centers of the brain.

And, of course, there were the older vices, the ones that were the great equalizer. No matter how powerful or dangerous or inhuman the client, nearly everyone shared the same hardwired desires. On Kanesh, you could enjoy them safely, cheaply, simply, with cybernetic pleasure dolls and Virtual Reality, the same as in any of the seedier establishments in the Commonwealth proper. Pleasure dolls felt no pain, had no pride, carried no diseases or psychological baggage; you could do to them whatever you wished, indulge whatever sick fantasy that appealed to you without worrying about hurting anyone else.

Which was why those *other* places existed. Because humans being what they were, there was always a percentage who *wanted* to hurt others, who *wanted* pain and psychological scars, who *wanted* to make victims. The advertisements and the glowing neon signs were blatantly honest in what they offered, and the open brutality of it struck Ash like a physical blow.

Sandi had warned him, but he'd thought she was exaggerating. He wished someone else could have gone, but there *was* no one else. Sandi didn't fit the profile of a customer who'd frequent this sort of business, and Fontenot wouldn't have been able to control herself; she'd have wound up shooting everything in sight and getting them all killed in the process. Kan-Ten, of course, was a Tahni, and he'd never be able to convince anyone that he was sexually attracted to humans.

He'd walked by a dozen different brothels before he found the right one; it was distinguishable only by the hand-painted mural across its front wall, matching the still capture on the screen of his 'link. The artist had been passionate about the subject, and given that the subject involved whips and chains and abject terror, that thought made Ash's skin crawl. There were two men leaning against the wall next to the painting, their craggy, lined features thrown into sharp relief by the garish lights illuminating the mural.

They were laughing. There was nothing good-natured or friendly about it; the laughter was cruel and harsh, the sort of laugh that came at someone else's expense, at the appreciation of someone else's pain. Ash remembered laughter like that very well; when he was a kid, laughter like that was usually a prologue for a beating, or the threat of a beating. He walked past them, smelling tobacco and marijuana and alcohol and sweat, then steeled himself and pushed through the front door and into the darkness.

There were no automated kiosks in a place like this, no holographic menus to look through. A slovenly little man with stringy, black hair and folds of fat hanging down his face to his neck sat on a metal stool behind a desk, tapping fat, dirty fingers against the cheap plastic and watching a video on a long-obsolete tablet. He glanced up at Ash's approach, looking annoyed at the interruption.

"What ya' want?" he muttered around a mouthful of chewing tobacco.

"A girl," Ash told him, trying to make his voice gruff and self-assured.

The old man giggled. "You're going to have to be a bit more specific."

Ash bit back a curse; he was screwing this up.

"I heard there's a new girl in," he said. "Young, blond. Pretty. I'd like her."

The old man grunted in reply, changing the screen on the tablet and scrolling through it.

"Yeah, okay, she's free right now." He looked up. "That'll be four hundred in Tradenotes for an hour." He cocked an eyebrow. "You can rough her up, but nothing disfiguring."

Ash felt his gut twist as he handed the bills over, wishing he could kill the greasy bastard. He had a pistol under his jacket, all it would take was a single squeeze of the trigger. Instead, he followed the man's gesture and was buzzed through the solid-looking door to the back rooms.

"Room number six," the older man supplied over his shoulder just before the portal to the next level of Hell closed.

There was a narrow hallway between walls of blood red, lined with doors of black metal, and everything was sound-proofed; all he could hear was his own, ragged breathing and the tap of his boot soles on the tile.

A door slammed open and a brawny, broad-bodied man stepped out, a grin splitting his shaggy, black beard as he fastened his jacket. The angle was wrong; Ash couldn't see through the door, but he heard the crying. It was the kind of sobs that wracked a body, that shook it to its core until your chest ached with it. The door swung shut and it was gone. Ash didn't look the bearded man in the eye as he passed, just kept walking.

Room number six was near the end of the hallway and he could hear the magnetic lock click in release as he reached for the handle. It swung open with a squeak of old and neglected hinges and he stepped through with the slightest of hesitations, afraid what he'd see inside. The chamber was small, with barely space for the bed and a single, padded chair, both fitted with shackles for hands and feet. A cheap plastic swinging barrier at the back probably held a small bathroom.

The girl sat on the bed, her legs drawn up beneath her, arms wrapped around herself. She was naked and he could see the faded bruises on her arms and legs, not fresh but not that old. Her blond hair was long and tangled, almost wild, and the look in her blue eyes was broken and hopeless and wishing for death. She wore nothing but a collar around her neck, simple and black and metallic; it was an obedience collar, designed to deliver painful electric shocks if she fought or tried to run. Or if someone felt like causing her pain just for kicks.

The door swung shut behind him and she flinched at the sound of it slamming.

Ash reached into the side pocket of his jacket and felt the small, ceramic globe there, comfortingly cold and solid. His thumb settled on the button in its side as he stepped closer to the bed.

"Chandra," he said softly. The girl's gaze snapped up to meet his, suspicion strong in her expression. "Chandra, your mom sent me. I need you to get ready to run."

Hope flared in her eyes and she began to uncurl, letting her feet touch the floor, but still she said nothing. Ash shrugged. It was the best he could hope for; at least she hadn't just started screaming. He pulled out the device Chandra's mother had supplied for them, held it above his head and pushed the button. There was a moment's delay, and then it hummed and vibrated in his hand and there was a pulse he felt rather than heard or saw, and the lights in the room went out, plunging it into the dim, green-tinted gloom of emergency chemical ghostlights long past their expiration date.

He grabbed at the collar around Chandra's neck and she tried to jerk away, but he caught it and yanked sharply. With its electromagnetic lock deactivated, it pulled free and he tossed it aside, sliding his handgun loose of its shoulder holster and moving toward the door. Chandra stared for a moment at the collar where it lay discarded on the other side of the bed, as if she thought this was a dream, or an hallucination.

"Come on, damn it!" Ash snapped at her. The door was creaking open, its magnetic lock lacking the power to keep it shut thanks to the pulse generator.

It wouldn't have worked in a military installation, or even in most high-end commercial stations back in the Commonwealth, where everything was shielded; but this was a cut-rate brothel on a cut-rate space station in the Pirate Worlds, and they'd taken the chance.

Chandra stood and followed him into the utter blackness of the hallway and he took a moment to slip on the enhanced optics glasses he'd retrieved from a case on his belt. *They* were shielded, and the hallway lit up with a computer amalgam of infrared, thermal and software interpolation. Other doors were swinging open up and down the corridor and he could see heads peeking out, men mostly.

"What the hell?" a high-pitched voice demanded. "I want my money back!"

"What happened to the fucking lights?"

"Where are we going?" It took Ash a second to realize that the female voice asking it was Chandra's.

"We have a ship," he told her reaching out a hand and grabbing hers. She tried to jerk away, but he held on and pulled her down the corridor behind him, moving quickly. "We need to get out of here," he warned her. "That pulse won't last forever..."

"I'm not going anywhere with you!" She pulled away from him and, through the goggles, he saw her squaring up in a combative stance, all of a sudden full of fight now that the collar was off. "How do I know you're not just like Carlito, that you're not just going to sell me off to another place like this?"

Ash recognized the name from the mission brief; Carlito was her former boyfriend, the one she'd met on Belial and followed here. The one who'd proceeded to abuse her and, when she'd tried to leave him, had sold her to the owner of the brothel on the condition that he not allow her mother to buy her back. Svetlana Breslov owned one of the largest night clubs on Belial station, and when her money hadn't been enough to buy the return of her daughter, she'd used it to hire them.

"Your mother said that you had a cat when you were like eight years old," he said quickly, using the information Breslov had given him. "You named him 'Carrot,' and he was killed when he climbed into a ventilation duct and the pest control systems electrocuted him. She said you cried for three days, then you pretended it had never happened and never talked about him again."

Her expression shifted abruptly, stubborn suspicion washed away in a wave of hope that nearly staggered her. She nodded, choking back a sob, and he offered his hand again. She took it, squeezing gratefully, and followed him to the end of the hallway. The door there was open as well, its magnetic lock disabled, a sliver of light streaming through from the street outside; for a moment, Ash thought they were just going to be able to walk right out without any trouble.

Then the two men he'd seen lounging outside by the mural burst through, the shoulder of the one in the lead slamming into the heavy door and banging it back against the wall with a thunderous boom that echoed back down the hallway. Their former sleazy good humor had been replaced by deadly serious expressions, along with matching sets of night vision glasses and handguns thrust ahead of them in a very professional looking stance.

Security guards, Ash thought, and he cursed himself for not realizing it from the beginning.

"He's got a gun!" the one in front snapped harshly, his aim shifting.

Ash was no sort of gunfighter; he'd been trained by the military as a pilot and that he was damned good at, but the only shooting with small arms he'd done in the service had been in the simulator or at the range. But he had been getting some tutoring lately from someone who'd been carrying a gun longer than the Commonwealth had been in existence, and she'd drilled home several key tenets of gunfighting.

The first one was movement. He pulled Chandra against the right-hand wall, then fell to a knee and brought up his own handgun, ignoring the shot that streaked down the hallway where his head had been a moment earlier. The malignant firefly of a miniature rocket engine made a hiss-crack above his ear, followed closely by a flash and a loud bang from somewhere behind him where the warhead had struck the far wall. The aiming reticle of his own weapon had popped up on his goggles the minute his fingers had wrapped around the grip, synched via a wireless connection, and he let it hover over the chest of the lead shooter before he touched the trigger pad.

Ash felt a shudder vibrating against his right palm as three shaped charges of chemical HyperExplosives ignited in quick succession in the reaction chamber of his pistol, pulsing the heat energy of the explosions through a semiconducting lasing rod and blasting it out the focusing lens of the emitter as a three-round burst of laser fire. The laser beams would have been invisible except as a refraction on dust or smoke in the hallway, but the pulses were powerful enough that they ionized the air around them in a flash of short-lived plasma that seemed to move in slow motion compared to the lasers themselves, drawing a sizzling, staticky line between Ash and the security guard.

There was a small steam explosion inside the man's chest, blood superheated to vapor doing more damage than the actual penetration of the pulses of coherent light, a sharp crack that seemed like an echo of the clap of the pulses wake through the atmosphere. The rocket pistol slipped from strengthless fingers and the guard pitched forward, dead before he hit the ground.

The second man, though…he'd been shielded by his partner, and he'd seen where the shot had come from, had an extra second to aim, and he was fast. His finger was tightening, just a fraction of a second and a fraction of a gram of pressure from firing the round that would end Ash's life, and then his head just wasn't there anymore. The crack of a metal slug breaking the sound barrier chased the splash of blood and brains and bits of skull and beat them to the wall behind him, punching a nice, neat hole through it and ending up God knew where. The body slid to the floor, feet kicking with one final, Galvanic response.

Ash had already been pushing up from his position on the wall and for a brief, confused moment, it seemed to him as if the man's head had exploded by magic, but then reality penetrated and he wasn't surprised to hear the gruff, scratchy voice that called out from the door.

"It's me," she said. "You're clear, come on out."

Ash glanced back at Chandra and saw less horror on her face than he'd expected, as if death in the abstract bothered her but not these two deaths in particular. Ash had to agree. He moved past the bodies, tugging Sandra along with him, skirting carefully around the growing pools of blood. The stink of burned flesh and boiled blood hit him just at the door and he clenched his teeth against the bile rising in his throat, but then he was through the exit and back in the reception area where the greasy old clerk had taken his money.

The clerk was sprawled on the floor, his eyes wide and unseeing, head cocked at an impossible angle, neck clearly broken. Standing over him was a tall, broad-shouldered woman with the lines of age and experience on half her face that matched her short, silvery hair. The skin on the other side of her face was smoother, less natural, and there was a flatness to her left eye that gave away what she'd finally attempted to conceal after decades of wearing it openly.

She held a heavy Gauss pistol at low ready in her right hand, the gunbelt partially concealed under the flaps of her dark-colored duster. The pistol was damned expensive, and damned hard to get out here, and he'd worried it might draw too much attention, but Fontenot had insisted on bringing it.

"Is she all right?" Korri Fontenot asked, tossing a handful of clothes to him that he passed awkwardly back to Chandra.

"*She* can talk, you know," Chandra bit off, grabbing the fatigue pants and t-shirt and slipping into them quickly. "Get me out of here and I'll be fine."

The look on the biological half of Fontenot's face told Ash she wasn't convinced of that, but she let it go.

"How many more you think are in there?" Fontenot asked, her tone casually curious, but the glint in her eye saying something completely different.

Ash hissed out a breath, knowing what she was thinking.

"We can't save them all," he reminded her. "We'd just get them killed if we tried."

She grunted noncommittally, but waved at him and Chandra to go in front of her. There were people out in the street, most of them too drunk or high to notice what was going on, but there were one or two who stared at them in open curiosity. No one challenged them, and by the time they reached Kan-Ten's position, Fontenot had signaled to Ash to holster his pulse pistol.

The Tahni was a gargoyle squatting in the shadows of a shut-down bar, his features hidden under a hood, his pulse pistol concealed under the folds of his cape. He unfolded as they approached, rising to his full height of nearly two meters, the odd configuration of his joints invisible inside his loose clothing.

"We are clear on this side," he announced in his sing-song accent, some of the consonants distorted out of a voice box that hadn't evolved to speak any human language.

He turned towards them and Ash could hear Chandra gasp. His face was humanoid but inhuman, the dark, beady eyes protected under ridges of bone, the nose nothing more than elongated nostrils flat against his skull, and his jaws as large and brutal as the shovels of a power digger.

"What," he asked her with a sense of humor learned from years among humans, "you've never seen a Tahni before?"

She probably had, Ash reflected. It had been nearly six years since the war with the Tahni had ended, and more and more of the aliens were integrating with the human Commonwealth, settling in human colonies or simply staying put on former Tahni colonies that the Commonwealth had taken during the hostilities. Belial was the Casablanca of the Commonwealth and Ash was sure there were at least some Tahni on the station, but maybe none had worked at her mother's club.

Kan-Ten didn't wait around for an answer, just fell into step with the others. Once they were around the curve of the cylinder and the brothel was out of sight, Ash let himself take a breath.

"It can't be this easy," he murmured as they waited at the lift station, eyes scanning 180 degrees around them.

"We're not fighting *La Sombra* bounty hunters," Fontenot reminded him, sounding a bit amused. "Just small-time scumbag slavers." She shrugged, more a motion of her head since both of her shoulders were cybernetic. "The three we killed were probably half their employees. They probably have a protection arrangement with one or another of the cartels, but by the time they figure out who did it, we'll be long gone."

The words were comforting, but Ash still sweated the entire ride up the lift to the docking hub, hand hovering over the grip of his pistol and tightening each time the doors parted at a new level. But the weight fell off of his shoulders the closer they came to the ship---literally, since the centripetal force that simulated gravity grew weaker as the lift approached the hub. When the doors slid open for the last time, they were in free fall and only the sticky plates on his ship boots kept him attached to what had been the floor. He felt Chandra grabbing at his arm to try to keep from floating upward as their lift car's motion abruptly halted.

The hub level was a buzz of activity as people surged this way and that like water bugs, some pushing themselves along the broad causeways in zero gravity with the ease of frequent flyers, some using hand-held propulsion units and more still walking stiffly with the aid of magnetic boots or sticky plates. They were a motley lot of smugglers, petty criminals in cheap, colorful flash, serious cartel heavy hitters in more practical and usually armored gear, and average workers dressed in stained and worn coveralls, mixed with those who considered themselves businesspeople and dressed the part. Each group moved with a natural flow, falling as if by design into lanes of purposeful speed, casual indifference or reluctant drag, some towards the lift banks, some back towards the docking bay and others to workstations right there in the hub itself.

Ash and the others fell in with the casual floaters, moving slow enough to avoid attracting attention but faster than the ones trudging along the deck with the speed of a garden slug. Moving in zero gravity was natural for Ash after years in Space Fleet, Chandra had been raised on a space station and Fontenot was old enough to be experienced at *everything*. Kan-Ten, however, flailed about like a drowning fish and wound up having to grab onto Fontenot to keep from drifting into oncoming traffic. Ash still couldn't read Tahni expressions well enough to know if Kan-Ten was embarrassed by the whole thing.

"We're two minutes out," Ash said in a conversational tone, speaking into the pickup of his 'link. "No one following that we can see."

The security zone was just this side of the docking bay, but it was for incoming traffic only; no one cared what you took *out* of the station.

Hell, they didn't care that much what you brought into it either, Ash mused. *They just want to make sure they charge you for it.*

The guards on either side of the security lock were big and armored and intimidating, fastened to the deck with magnetic boots and lugging around assault guns that would have been impossibly heavy if there'd been anything more than microgravity. Ash tried not to stare at them, and he could see that Chandra wasn't even trying; she watched them with eyes wide and face pale, as if she expected them to see who and what she was and try to take her back to a life of slavery. *That*, he decided, was *not* going to happen. He'd bring the whole station down around their ears before he'd let her go back to that.

Then the guards were behind them and they emerged out of

the darkness of the man-made cave and into the multi-tiered docking bay that stuck out of the polar hub of the station, a shiny, ornate decoration on the dull grey of the station's cylinder, matched by the silvery cooling vanes emerging from the opposite pole. Light from the nearby primary star streamed in through meter-thick transplas windows, reflected by the same mirror-bright polished shielding that protected them from micrometeorite strikes; and in between the windows, evenly spaced around the circumference of the cylinder, were the docking collars. Each was mated with the airlock of a shuttle or other small vessel; larger cargo ships orbited the station at a safe distance and sent shuttles in to transfer crew, passengers or cargo.

Their ship, the *Acheron*, wasn't a shuttle; she was a converted Fleet missile cutter, bought surplus by him and still mostly owned by the bank. He'd bought her while he was still a Fleet officer, using his pension as collateral, back before he'd had to go on the run with Sandi. He was still technically AWOL, though in a peacetime drawdown, that wasn't nearly as worrying as the trumped-up murder charge still hanging over them or the price that the *La Sombra* cartel still had on his and Sandi's heads.

Luckily, no one cared about that sort of thing out here, unless a bounty hunter happened to track them down...

"Shit!" That was Sandi's voice coming over his ear bud, and she didn't sound happy. "Ash, get everyone into the ship now! We have company."

He could tell by Fontenot and Kan-Ten's reactions that she'd included them in on the transmission, and Chandra was glancing between the three of them, noticing the alarm on the humans' faces.

"What is it?" she wondered, fear leeching back into her eyes.

"Hold on," he warned her, grabbing her arm with one hand and the safety rail that ran along the right-hand bulkhead with another and yanking them both forward.

The crowd parted around them as they flew through the sedate movers, jostling a few and earning muttered or shouted curses in return. The corridor seemed to blur on either side of Ash and he was starting to seriously worry whether he'd be able to stop, and then he saw the berth number for their ship lit up on the wall ahead only thirty meters or so away. He twisted his body around, dragging the side of his boot against the roughened surface of the rail, slowing both of them down enough that he was able to grab the railing without breaking his fingers.

He still left a layer of skin on the surface of the railing, but they jerked to a halt just a meter or so past the *Acheron*'s docking station. He glanced back and saw Fontenot braking abruptly, her bionic hand squeezing down hard against the railing with no worry for pain or injury. Kan-Ten had been riding her like a magic carpet and he barely hung on, his feet flying wildly out in front of them; Ash would have laughed had his gut not been too tight for it.

The inner and outer lock doors were already open and Ash pulled Chandra into the utility bay, letting her get a hand hold next to one of the passenger acceleration couches mounted in a corner by the utility lockers.

"Strap yourself in," he instructed tersely, then pushed off through the central passageway into the cockpit, trusting Fontenot to make sure she followed his instructions.

Behind him, he could hear the airlock hissing shut, and halfway up the passage, he felt a jolt and the accompanying bang of maneuvering thrusters pushing them away from the docking collar. Passing by the cabin hatches and the small galley, he could see Sandi already strapped into the pilot's seat, her short, red hair pulled back and interface jacks from the control panel plugged into the implant sockets at her temples. Her face was taut with concentration, her hands clenched on the armrests of the acceleration couch and, rather than distract her, Ash pulled himself into the copilot's seat and scanned the sensor display as he strapped himself in.

The system was laid out for him in the holographic projection of the main viewscreen, a white dwarf with no surviving terrestrial planets, only an ice giant so far out that you could barely tell it orbited the star at all. There were a dozen cargo ships in long orbits around the station itself, but none of them seemed particularly threatening at the moment. There was one ship boosting, probably just out of Transition Space, a fairly common looking freighter, but Ash couldn't see that it was any different than the others.

"What am I missing?" he finally asked her, feeling the ship swinging around away from the station.

"That's the fucking *Gitano*," she bit off, sounding more scared than annoyed.

"Shit," he swore, not having to ask anything else. The *Gitano* was a *La Sombra* cartel ship, and the last time they'd seen it... "It's Singh."

The communications console lit up with an incoming signal and the head and shoulders of a man were projected in a corner of the main screen. He had once been harshly handsome, with a hard-edged rakishness to his face, but now half that face was metal, matte black and obscenely bare, with the right eye grey and cybernetic while the other was dark and full of a rage for revenge.

"Carpenter, Hollande," he addressed them, "I'm going to give you one opportunity to surrender because I promised Jordi Abdullah I would."

"So he can have the chance to torture us to death instead?"

Ash snapped back. "Did you really think that would work, Singh?"

"Honestly, no," the bounty hunter admitted. "But a promise is a promise."

The hologram snapped off as the transmission ended, and Ash barely caught a glimpse on the sensor display of a flight of anti-spacecraft missiles launching from the *Gitano's* weapons bay before the *Acheron's* fusion drive ignited and slammed him back into his padded acceleration couch with the force of nearly six times his normal weight. His vision began to narrow into a tunnel as the pressure on his chest increased and breath became impossible; he tried to tighten his core muscles against the acceleration, but as it approached nine g's, he knew he was going to pass out...and he knew it wasn't going to be enough. The missiles could accelerate for twenty g's for a brief burst, and humans couldn't take that.

Spacetime ripped open around the nose of the cutter and the living nothingness of Transition Space swallowed them up. Ash sucked down a sweet lungful of air and relief as the weight of an elephant shifted abruptly to his normal ninety kilograms, pulling downward towards the deck. The artificial gravity worked in conjunction with the ship's warp field, and then only in Transition Space, for reasons he'd never been quite able to understand without an advanced degree in trans-dimensional physics.

He looked over to Sandi. She didn't look nearly as relieved as he felt. Her face was angular, with high cheekbones and a slightly imperfect tilt that lit up her blue eyes when she smiled, but she wasn't smiling now.

"That was too damned close," she ground out, yanking at the quick-release for her seat restraints. "If Kanesh massed another million kilograms, I wouldn't have been able to get out of its gravito-inertial shadow in time to make the jump and this ship and everyone in it would be a fond fucking memory."

He nodded, unsure of how else to respond.

"Thanks for keeping a look out," he said, attempting a smile.

She snorted, then gave in and returned it, leaning over to kiss him fondly.

"Next time," she warned, "I get to go risk my neck while you stay on the ship and play getaway driver."

"Deal," he promised, standing and unbuckling his gunbelt. "I'm not cut out for this gunfighter shit anyway."

"Did you have to use it?" She nodded towards the laser.

"Yeah." His face went grim and hard. "And this time, I don't feel a bit bad about it."

She closed her eyes and hissed out a sigh, obviously understanding what he was saying.

"How is she?"

"Better than I would be," was the only answer he could give without sounding trite. "I thought I was going to have to drag Fontenot out of the place, though." He restrained an urge to spit. "It's hell in there."

"A guy named Jean-Paul Sartre once said, 'hell is other people.' I don't know who the hell he was," she admitted with a shrug, "but he had a point."

"At least we got the girl out. We'll get her back to her mom and try to figure out how Singh found us...*again*." He worked at a kink in his neck. "We should be safe on Belial."

"With Singh after us?" Sandi shook her head. "We're not safe anywhere."

CHAPTER TWO

Sandrine Hollande watched Chandra sobbing quietly in her mother's arms and felt a sharp spear of pain in her chest. She hadn't had the chance for a tearful reunion with her own mother, and she wasn't sure she was as happy for the girl as she was resentful. Svetlana Breslov, however, was unequivocally happy. The woman was a slightly more weathered version of her daughter and looked nearly as young with the glow on her face at the girl's return. And the idea that she'd been a part of that made her feel worthwhile.

She'd felt the same when they'd managed to rescue Adam Krieger from the stronghold of a cartel boss who'd been trying to use him as leverage against his father, a corrupt Fleet Admiral. When Breslov had contacted them, she'd seemed to know everything about the whole business with Adam; it was why she'd sought them out to retrieve her daughter. She'd heard about it all, ironically enough, from Lena Brunner, the daughter of the cartel boss from whom they'd rescued Adam.

"Maybe we've found our new business model," Ash murmured softly by her ear, slipping an arm around her as they waited near the rear of the main dining room of the *Worlds*

Away, Breslov's massive casino hotel deep inside the mountain of asteroidal nickel-iron that was Belial Pleasure Station.

Sandi eyed him sidelong, wondering if he'd read her expression. Ash had always been good at that, all the way back to their freshman year in the Commonwealth Service Academy. He'd been her best friend for a long time before they'd become lovers, and the former was still more important than the latter. Still, looking into those soulful dark eyes and that square-jawed, boy-scout-earnest face, the latter wasn't a bad deal, either.

"*Acheron* LLC, finder of lost children?" she whispered back playfully. "You think there's money in it?"

"There certainly was this time." That was Korri Fontenot, standing sentinel-like behind them, her arms crossed, her face with an obvious look of satisfaction. "Don't know that we can count on every desperate parent to be quite as wealthy as Ms. Breslov."

"Do we require the money that badly?" Kan-Ten asked. He was propped on a stool at the high-top table the rest of them were standing beside. His alien face was cloaked in the hood of his cape for the same reason that Fontenot had taken to covering her bionics with synthskin: they were wanted, both by the law and, almost more significantly, by the *La Sombra* cartel, and anything that would throw off potential informants was worth trying.

At Sandi's frown, the Tahni clarified: "Does not the other funding we are receiving cover most of our expenses?"

Sandi scowled at the thought of their *other* source of funding. It was a sore spot for her, and even more for Ash.

"I'm not sure we should count on *that* money too heavily," Ash warned, his expression darkening.

Before they could discuss the topic further, Svetlana Breslov gave her daughter a kiss on the forehead and sent her off with one of her employees, presumably to clean up and change. Then she walked over to the four of them, unselfconsciously wiping away a tear that streaked down her right cheek.

"I cannot begin to thank you enough," she said in an accent that still spoke of a home in the Russian refugee camps of Fairbanks over a century ago. "The money, it is not enough."

"Honestly, ma'am," Ash told her, "having been there and seen what I've seen..." He shook his head. "I'd have done it free."

"I wish," Fontenot spoke up, a harsh, angry tone to her words, "that we could have gotten them all out."

"Ms. Breslov," Sandi cut in, "we need to ask you something. Did anyone come around looking for us after we left here to go get your daughter?"

The older woman's face lost the soft, parental look and transformed quickly into the hardened businesswoman that she'd been for decades.

"Yes. There was a bounty hunter," she told them, "a man with cyborg replacements. His name was Singh and he and some flunkies I recognized as low-level *La Sombra* operatives arrived before your ship had even left the dock. They began spreading money and threats around, and eventually they found one of my employees whose mouth and greed were both too big." She snarled. "I have dealt with the man, but the damage was done."

"It's all right," Sandi assured her. "We got out all right." *Barely.*

"Still," Breslov insisted, "you will stay in one of my suites for as long as you are here, and you will pay for nothing. I will not hear of anything else."

"Thank you, ma'am," Ash said, nodding gratefully. "And I hope your daughter is..." He trailed off and Sandi squeezed his arm, knowing what he meant and what a doofus he could be.

"She is a strong woman," Breslov said, keeping herself from breaking down, but only just. "She will get through this."

She left them, heading through the door to the back rooms where her daughter had preceded her. Sandi looked the others in the eye significantly.

"He's been right on our heels for months now," she declared. "He's a fucking mad dog, and he's got Jordi Abdullah's money backing him."

"We can't handle him by ourselves," Ash agreed reluctantly. "We need to contact Fox."

"God help us," Fontenot muttered.

———

"You're sure we haven't done anything illegal on this planet?" Ash asked softly.

Sandi snorted in dark amusement and nodded. It was a good question. They sure as hell couldn't go back to Borealis, not after they'd helped the Rif cartel break into the Fleet weapons depot there, and they couldn't just show up on Andalusia either, not after stealing a shipment of proton cannons from *La Sombra* on that world. Honestly, they were running out of Periphery planets where they could show their face without getting arrested or shot.

Sylvanus was still fairly safe territory, for now. And Dollabella, the capital, was actually a pleasant, bustling, mid-size city rather than a washed-out ghost town like some of the failed colonies on the Periphery. The buildings were restricted by code to a look that she thought of as a cross between early art deco and mid-Twentieth Century Western European, and the people seemed to revel in the anachronism as well, many going so far as dressing in throwback fashions. It looked, she thought, particularly pleasant and homey on a clear, summer night, and she was tempted to lean into Ash on her chair in the open-air café and sit back and look at the stars.

But they were here on business, and she had to remind herself to be vigilant. Just because the place had seemed safe previously didn't mean Singh couldn't track them here. She felt the comforting weight of the pulse pistol holstered under her flight jacket and wondered if there'd ever be a day she didn't have to carry a weapon and constantly look over her shoulder.

"He's here," Fontenot's voice said low and steady over her ear bud. "Heading your way."

She felt Ash shift his weight beside her as he heard the announcement, like he was instinctively getting ready for flight or fight.

"Relax," she whispered to him, putting a hand on his. "The worst that'll happen is that he'll be useless, just like every other spook we ever met."

That drew a chuckle, as she'd known it would, and Ash settled back in his chair, taking a sip of his espresso and waiting. It was another ten seconds before they saw him rounding the corner from the next street over, dressed inconspicuously in a brown formal coat and a narrow tie. Sandi couldn't remember the last time she'd seen anyone wear a tie anywhere but Dollabella, except in remastered copies of old movies. He was an average man, average in looks, average in height, totally unremarkable in just about every way. His face was rounded but not fat, his hair the same shade of dark brown as his eyes, his skin a generic tan and his looks a multiethnic blend that could have put him from anywhere on Earth or off it. The only distinguishing characteristic that she could put to him was his build, which marked him as someone who'd grown up on a world with a gravity around Earth-normal. Other than that, he could have gunned someone down in the street and not one person would have remembered his face.

"Hollande, Fontenot." He nodded to them, pulling out the third chair at their small table and sitting down unbidden.

"Good evening, Captain Fox," Sandi returned, forcing herself to be calm and casual. "Can we order you a drink?"

"Maybe later." The Fleet Intelligence officer smiled thinly, glancing around. "Aren't Kan-Ten and Ms. Fontenot going to join us?"

"Last time they sat down with you here," Ash reminded him, "you held them at gunpoint."

"Ah well, it was nothing personal." He leaned forward, forearms resting on the metal latticework of the table. "You called me all the way from Belial for a meeting; I assume this is important."

"It's Singh," Ash told him. "The bounty hunter."

"Yes, Commander," Fox interjected drily, "I assumed that was the Singh to which you were referring. Jagmeet Singh, former Fleet Marine Corps NCO, formerly married to another retired Marine NCO, Freya Rasmussen, until you, Commander Carpenter, shot her down over Borealis."

"It wasn't as if I had much of a choice."

"No, she would have killed you if you hadn't," Fox admitted readily. "But apparently Mr. Singh isn't quite as understanding as I am about the whole thing."

"He's tracked us down three times in just the last four months," Sandi cut in, trying to bring the conversation back to why they'd called him. "The last time, we jumped out about two seconds ahead of an assload of missiles. He's got *La Sombra's* snitches working for him, and we need some intelligence of our own working for us."

"If I recall our arrangement correctly," Fox said with a smirk Sandi would very much have liked to slap off his face, "Intelligence doesn't work for you, you work for us."

"How much work do you think we'll be able to do for you if

Singh kills us?" Ash pointed out. Sandi could see his jaw tightening, a sign he was getting angry but trying to control it. Ash, she thought, always tried to control himself, sometimes too much.

"Point, Commander Carpenter," Fox acknowledged. He waved at the human waiter and the man stepped over attentively. "Could I have a bourbon and soda?"

"Umm, we don't serve alcohol here, sir," the waiter admitted.

"Well, what the hell," Fox muttered, scowling. "No wonder I don't come here. Get me a coffee then, large and black."

"Yes, sir, we have the vente decaf blond roast, the Mountain High caramel..."

"Coffee," Fox repeated, his expression hardening. "Large and black."

"Of course, sir." The waiter scurried away and Sandi suppressed a laugh.

"All right." The Intelligence officer steepled his fingers, staring thoughtfully ahead. "I can work on it. If we had many resources inside the cartels, we wouldn't need you folks, would we? But I'll do some digging. Would more money help?" He raised an eyebrow. "Maybe some weapons upgrades for the ship? I'm always happy to spend the taxpayer's money."

Sandi shook her head. "We already have as much as we can fit onto a ship her size without attracting too much attention. And we appreciate it, honestly."

"It's not a gift, Hollande. In fact, you're about to earn it." He paused to nod to the waiter as the young man brought him a steaming mug of coffee, watching the server until he was out of earshot. "You're about to get a job offer from the *Novya Moscva Bratva*. I want you to take it."

"The *bratva*?" Sandi repeated, brow furling. "Aren't they

getting their asses kicked all over the Worlds by the Sung Brothers?"

"Oh yeah," Fox agreed readily. "They're fucking desperate. Desperate enough to stick a spy in the Sung Brothers organization, and now desperate enough to hire someone the Sung Brothers won't know so they can pull her out."

"You want the data she's smuggling out," Ash assumed, and Sandi could see the wheels turning behind his eyes as he'd already begun planning ahead for the mission.

"Just one little bit of it," Fox corrected him. His eyes danced around, making sure no one was within earshot. Sandi didn't bother to ask, but she assumed he'd already taken precautions against electronic surveillance. "Have either of you ever heard of a ship called the *Metaurus*?"

Sandi shook her head, but she saw Ash's eyes narrow, searching for a memory.

"She's that cruiser that disappeared during the push to the Tahni homeworld," he said, finally. "Back when we were retaking the colony worlds they'd invaded. She was assumed destroyed near Loki, I think?"

"That was a cover story," Fox informed him, awfully frank, she thought, about something that was undoubtedly top secret. "The reality is, she was tasked to the DSI."

Sandi grunted impolitely, sharing the universal military disdain for the civilian intelligence agency that had long competed with Fleet Intelligence for funding, influence and accolades. She didn't have much use for Fleet spooks; she had none whatsoever for the stuffed shirts at the Department of Security and Intelligence.

"Tasked for what?" she asked.

"Well, that's the million-dollar question, isn't it? It was top secret then, and by God, it's top secret now, and the DSI just doesn't like to fucking share. But..." He grinned. "We've heard rumors, I won't say where from, that a mineral scout working for the Sung Brothers spotted a Fleet cruiser way the hell out on the edge of the Cluster. He didn't stick around to figure out what she was doing there, but I happen to have a fairly good idea of the current locations of all the Fleet's active cruisers, and way the fuck out there isn't one of them."

"You think he found the *Metaurus*," Ash mused, sounding intrigued by the mystery. "What the hell would it be doing out there?"

"Well, that's just what you're going to find out for me."

"What?" Sandi snapped, blinking. "You want *us* to go way out there and do what, exactly? We're not damned Spaceflight Safety investigators, what do you expect us to be able to tell you about it?"

"Don't you have more qualified people you could send on a mission like that?" Ash wondered, spreading his hands in a confused shrug.

"Of course we do," Fox agreed readily. "And do you know what they all have in common? The DSI would know the *minute* we ordered any of them out that far, and it wouldn't take them too long to figure out why. You, on the other hand..." He trailed off, seeming confident they'd get the idea.

"Shit," Sandi hissed. At least the spook was being honest with them. That was something of a minor miracle in and of itself. She had a sudden thought that penetrated through everything else. "Hey, how the hell did the *bratva* hear about us, anyway?"

"I told them, obviously." Fox shrugged. "Well, not me personally, but it's in our interest to have you gain access to as much of the Pirate World cartel structure as possible, so I've used the contacts I have on places like Belial and out here in the Periphery to make sure the right people know about the sort of work you specialize in."

"What sort of work is that?" Ash blurted.

"Getting people out of trouble." Fox took a long sip of the coffee and made a "not bad" face. "Look, I know this is quite the task I'm setting out for you, probably a bit more than you expected when you took this job. I'll tell you what, if you do this and do it right, I'll make sure this Singh asshole doesn't bother you anymore." He cocked an eyebrow. "Deal?"

"Korri?" Sandi called over her 'link's pickup. "Kan-Ten?"

"Sounds interesting," Fontenot offered.

"One place is as good as another," the Tahni said. She couldn't decide if he was happy about that or disgusted.

She caught Ash's eye and he tossed his head slightly as if he were weighing the situation, then finally nodded.

"All right, then," she said, shrugging her assent.

Fox smiled, fishing in the pocket of his jacket and coming up with a crystalline dataspike. He handed it off to Sandi and she turned it over in her fingers, glancing back at him curiously.

"That spike," he explained, "will get you access to the *Metaurus'* computer systems. I need you to download the ship's log onto that and bring it back to me."

Sandi slipped the storage crystal into a pocket of her flight jacket.

"If the ship's really out there, we'll find her."

"And figure out what's so important about her," Ash added. He frowned suddenly. "What do we do if we run across her crew?"

"It's been six years, Carpenter," Fox reminded him grimly. "If any of her crew were alive when they got to that system, they're certainly dead by now."

CHAPTER THREE

I SPEND, SANDI THOUGHT RUEFULLY, *WAY TOO MUCH TIME IN bars.*

The *Winter's Heart* in Shakak wasn't horrible as bars went, particularly bars in the Pirate Worlds; it was a bit impersonal, with automated drink dispensers and digital menus, but that was probably an affectation to make themselves seem more like the bars and restaurants in the Periphery, more modern and mainstream. The dance floor was psychedelic and perhaps overly busy, with multiple rotating platforms, some of them also moving vertically in ways that, when combined with the free-flowing drugs and alcohol, seemed like a recipe for broken bones.

"She's late," Fontenot murmured over the earbud for her 'link.

From her table in the dining room, Sandi could see her cyborg crewmember leaning heavily on the plastic bar, pretending to fiddle with the drink menu. Fontenot was dressed in the leather duster she'd taken to wearing ever since she'd had her bionics covered with synthskin; prior to that, she'd leaned towards sleeveless vests that showed off the bare metal. She'd done that to keep people at arm's length, to keep from having to deal with them, and Sandi liked to think that the change in styles represented more than just an attempt at greater anonymity and a need for something to conceal the pulse carbine hanging off her shoulder.

"This is taking too long," Sandi opined under her breath, sipping the beer that was all she'd ordered. It was hard being in a place like this and not drinking something stronger, but she was fighting a history of sinking a bit too far into the bottle. She reached under her jacket and shifted the pulse pistol in its holster, a nervous tick she'd picked up since she'd started carrying the gun.

"I think I see her," Kan-Ten announced from his position near their rental groundcar, out in the street and in the harsh winter of Peboan's southern hemisphere.

He definitely drew the short stick this time. It's damned cold out there.

"You *think* you see her?" Fontenot demanded critically.

"You know you all look alike to me, sister."

Sandi had been taking a swallow of beer and she nearly shot it out her nose with a suppressed laugh. For someone who claimed to not understand their humor, the Tahni could play a damned good straight man.

She surreptitiously glanced around the bar and dining room, checking the display screen of her 'link one more time to compare the still photo they'd been given by their *bratva* contact to incoming customers. There were a half a dozen of them coming in from the airlock-style doorway, shaking stray clumps of snow off their jackets, most of them with the look of spacers. One was dressed like a local, and a well-to-do local at that, her clothes pragmatic yet still stylish, even to the cut of her garnet cold-weather jacket.

She threw back her hood and ran her hands through her

long, jet-black hair, shaking off drops of melt-water, and Sandi immediately recognized her. The lean, narrow face, the amber skin, and the dark, hooded eyes matched the picture she'd been given exactly. Her hair was jet black and cut short, revealing a set of interface jacks implanted at her temples, similar to the ones Sandi and Ash had, though perhaps a bit larger and clunkier for being manufactured and installed out here in the Pirate Worlds.

The woman's gaze flitted around the bar to the dining room until Sandi caught her eye, nodding slightly, almost imperceptibly. She moved slowly and nonchalantly across the room, slipping off her coat and hanging it on the back of the chair opposite Sandi's before sitting down.

"Prya Shaw?" Sandi asked. At the woman's silent nod, she went on. "I'm Sandi. Mr. Standish told me to say hi if I was ever in town."

At the pre-arranged code-phrase, Shaw's eyes widened slightly for just a moment, but she managed to keep her reaction subdued.

"It has been a long time since I spoke with Mr. Standish," she responded, her accent clipped and hard, like some she'd heard from those born in the Periphery. "I did not expect to hear from him until he returned from his business trip next year."

More code phrases, and Sandi sighed inwardly as she mentally translated that Shaw had thought her assignment wasn't going to be over until after the first of the year. She searched her memory for the right response.

"He came home early because of a business opportunity." *In other words, the* bratva *think your cover's blown, so stop screwing around so we can get out of here.*

Shaw *did* react to that; just a small gasp and a quick, paranoid sidelong glance.

"They're watching the spaceport," she said, abandoning the

charade and the code. "They keep track if anyone with access to sensitive materials tries to fly out unauthorized. I'm the senior netdiver, they'll never let me leave."

"We've arranged to rent a hopper," Sandi explained. "We'll fly you out to Moreau Island and our ship can land there and pick us up." Moreau was out in the middle of the inland sea northwest of Shakak; it would be an hour-long flight in a ducted-fan hovercraft, but it wouldn't attract too much attention.

Prya frowned. "Won't orbital traffic control get suspicious about a ship landing out there?"

"Not after the bribe we dropped." Sandi grinned. "Don't worry, we're professionals." *Sort of.* "Do you have anything you want to bring with you?"

"Shit, no." She shook her head sharply. "Just get me the hell out of here."

"Kan-Ten," she said, keying her 'link. "Bring the car around. We're leaving."

———

"What the hell is taking so long?" Ash wondered, asking the question out loud and getting no answer except the rhythmic vibration in the deck from the turbines idling.

He'd had the ship's reactor powered up and the turbines running for ten minutes, and was only waiting for the word from Sandi to call Orbital Traffic Control for the clearance to take off. Looking out the viewscreen at the open, fusion-form landing field they called a spaceport here, lit up almost to daylight in the harsh glare of the security floodlights, it seemed a bit odd to be following prosaic regulations like they were back on Eden or Hermes or one of the other Core colonies, but the Sung Brothers liked things orderly and businesslike. If you tried to take off without clearance, they had batteries of anti-spacecraft missiles they were more than happy to share with you, and not even the new avionics and ECM hardware Fox had provided would be able to avoid all of them.

His finger hovered over the communications panel as he debated whether to call Sandi again. She'd probably be irritated; she hated him jiggling her elbow.

"Fuck it," he mumbled, touching the control. "Sandi, did she show up yet?" He waited for a reply, but got nothing. He frowned. The least she could do was tell him to go to hell. He switched over to Fontenot's 'link address. "Korri, what's the status? Did the subject show up? Are you guys in the air yet?"

Nothing.

"What the hell?" He tried pinging their 'links to get a position, but received no return signal. A bad feeling began to crawl out of his gut and he muttered a string of curses in English, Spanish and Tagalog as he switched over to the Traffic Control frequency.

"Peboan Control," he called, trying to keep from yelling it, "this is the independent freighter *Acheron* calling for clearance to take off from Shakak spaceport."

More nothing, not even an automated acknowledgement. They were being jammed, broad-spectrum, high-energy. And any jammer close enough to do that...

"Shit!" He yanked the manual control stick and slid his fingers up the touch-screen for the throttle, then felt the hand of God pushing him back into the acceleration couch as the belly jets screamed to life.

Everything seemed to be happening at once and he was left with not enough hands to strap himself into the seat restraint and plug the interface cables into his implant sockets and still maintain control of the ship *and* try to evade the flight of two air-to-air missiles that he could see on the screen accelerating towards him at twelve gravities. He'd been berthed fifty meters from a patched-together cargo lifter, and the missiles sliced through the space the *Acheron* had occupied only half a second before and struck the shuttle.

A fireball climbed forty meters into the night sky and a blast of superheated air nearly set the cutter into a spin; Ash clenched his teeth and yanked back on the stick, boosting out of the turbulence, then cursing and taking the half-second to secure the flight harness. He could see the two assault shuttles burning in over the horizon about six kilometers out and the time it took him to fasten his restraints seemed to be enough for them to halve the distance.

He switched to forward thrust and the view on the front screens blurred as the cutter shot out over the city, putting more distance between him and his pursuers. Desperately, he clawed one-handed at the spools of interface cable, yanking the leads out and plugging them into his jacks. The virtual world of the interface began to swallow him in streams of data, but one piece of knowledge shone through the others: there was no activity from the Shakak air defenses. If this was *La Sombra* tracking them down again, they'd made a deal with the Sung Brothers, and they were killing two birds with one stone.

"Sandi!" he yelled into the communications pickup, knowing it was futile. "It's a trap!"

———

"Remind me again," Fontenot grumbled from the backseat of the groundcar, "why we didn't get the hopper to start with and just park it in front of the *Winter's Heart*?"

"Because landing a hopper in front of the restaurant would have attracted attention," Sandi explained with exaggerated patience, not taking her eyes off the snow-covered gravel road. "And we're trying to avoid attracting attention."

It was starting to snow again, and the large flakes flared white and distracting in the car's headlights and Sandi's knuckles were white where she clutched the steering wheel. There was no auto-drive or Heads-Up Display or even a night-vision filter in the windshield, not in a cheap piece of junk slapped together from fabricated parts here on Peboan, but that didn't stop idiotic pedestrians from stepping out into the street blindly, not even checking for oncoming traffic. She felt as if she was stuck in a period piece about life on antebellum Earth, and she didn't even *like* those kinds of movies.

"People would have noticed me climbing into a hopper with a bunch of strangers," Prya Shaw declared, sitting next to Fontenot in the back seat, her hood up to cover her face as much as possible. "The Sung Brothers have been paranoid about retaliation from the *bratva* ever since they finally kicked them off Peboan last year."

"The two cartels shared this place?" Kan-Ten asked, twisting around in the front passenger seat to meet the netdiver's gaze. "How did that work?"

"About as well as you might expect. Both sides hired mercenaries and the city was nearly destroyed." The woman sounded disgusted. "They're still rebuilding. Look." She pointed out the front windshield at a row of burned-out buildings, charred and blackened beams of local wood all that remained of what had once been urban townhouses. "We had refugees living in hand-built lean-to's right in the city up till a few months ago."

"You sound like you find this wasteful," Kan-Ten commented, showing a remarkable comprehension of human intonations, Sandi thought. "If that is so, why do you work as a spy to continue the conflict?"

Sandi couldn't spare the attention to turn around and look at Prya's face, but the silence that answered the question didn't seem entirely comfortable.

"I have relatives who work for Alexi Putschin, the head of the *bratva*," she finally said, sounding as if she had to yank the truth out of herself. "My uncle asked that I do this for the sake of the family."

"Well, I guess we all know what a pain in the ass family can be," Sandi told her. She leaned forward, trying to get a better look at the next intersection, which was taking them towards the more industrial section of the city. "I think we turn right up here, then the hopper was parked maybe a half a kilometer down the road in an open lot. Korri, call Ash and tell him to go ahead and get clearance for take-off."

She'd barely finished the sentence when she saw the cargo truck pulling out of the side street only ten meters ahead of them, directly in their path, its covered bed blocking out the streetlights. Cursing reflexively, she jammed on the brakes and felt her safety harness biting into her shoulder as the car skidded to a halt less than three meters from the driver's side of the truck, hearing the pinging clatter of gravel thrown up by their tires ricocheting off the larger vehicle's wheel well.

"Reverse!" Fontenot was yelling, but she was already shifting the car, slamming her foot on the accelerator as it went into gear.

The groundcar jerked backwards with a rush of power from the decades-obsolete alcohol-burning engine and Sandi grunted, twisting around to look behind them. There was another cross street only twenty meters back, on the opposite side, and their car had barely begun to reverse when another truck, this one a flatbed, roared out of the alley to block their retreat. Sandi let off the accelerator and looked back forward to see a familiar face staring at her from inside the cab of the cargo truck there. It was Jagmeet Singh, smiling coldly with half his mouth.

The canvas flap was thrown off the back of the truck and armed and armored men and women began jumping off the back, dressed in the characteristic khaki and brown of the *La Sombra* cartel.

"Korri!" Sandi yelled, ripping her pulse pistol out of its holster, but Fontenot was already yanking her safety harness loose and throwing open the door.

Behind them, she saw with a quick glimpse in the mirror, more troops were piling off the back of the flatbed, and she hit the accelerator again, feeling a hollow thump and hearing the impact of the rear bumper on at least two of them as they were crushed between her car and the truck's loading gate. Then Fontenot was hanging out her open door, cradling the oversized bulk of an old assault gun, a weapon that had been obsolete for a few decades in an age of mobile battlesuits but still held a lot of value when dealing with lightly-armored opponents.

The dual-drum-fed support weapon belched out a sustained fusillade of proximity-fused 25mm warheads that burst like fireworks in the midst of the oncoming cartel soldiers, the powdered metal payloads transformed to spears of plasma by the heat of the shaped-charge HyperExplosives. Four of the attackers collapsed into nerveless heaps, their helmets smoking where the plasma had burned through, and the rest scattered, firing back blindly. Sandi flinched as mini-rockets glanced off the roof with thunderous bangs, then she cursed aloud when one cracked through the front windshield. She looked back for just an instant and saw that it had passed over Prya's head. The woman was crouched on the floor, hands clenched on top of her head and terror written on her face, while Kan-Ten fired off a steady barrage of laser fire from his pulse carbine over the top of the back seat through what was left of the rear windscreen.

"Hang on!" Sandi yelled, leaning out her window and shooting left-handed at the cab of the truck in front of them.

Singh and the driver ducked as laser pulses punched through the heavy plastic of the windshield or spalled melted or vaporized metal off the body of the cab, and Sandi used their distraction to shift back to drive and stomp down on the gas pedal once again. The groundcar lurched forward and she jerked the wheel to the left, steering around the front end of the cargo truck.

They barely made it past: the driver tried to slam into them broadside and managed to clip the rear bumper, tearing off the rear quarter-panel on the passenger's side of the car, but then they were around it and she was gunning for the next intersection. She tried not to hyperventilate, tried to keep herself steady, pretending it was a space battle during the war and she was plugged into the interface. But this was so much less controlled and yet so much more overwhelming even than the full immersion of the interface, and she could feel her fingers cramping as she yanked the wheel over in a sharp right turn. The rear of the car fishtailed and she felt the solid bump as it grazed the edge of the sidewalk before she could straighten it out.

The tires dug into the dirt beneath the snow and gravel and they were heading down the dark, narrow street at seventy kilometers an hour, their headlights sweeping over the empty, burned out buildings on both sides of what had once been a thoroughfare. She wanted to look behind them, but the rearview camera had busted when she'd backed into the truck behind them and the physical mirror had been shot off along with the top right quarter of the windshield. Wind was whistling through the car and snow was pelting her face and it was all she could do to stay between the sidewalks.

"They're behind us," Fontenot yelled, seemingly sensing her thoughts. "Thirty meters back, both trucks."

"You've got that fucking cannon," Sandi said tightly. "Can you discourage them?"

"Not with this door in the way."

Sandi didn't look back, but she heard the rending squeal of

metal and plastic tearing and the uneven roar of air rushing in from only one opening, and then a shifting of weight on the suspension as Fontenot hung out the side of the car by one unyielding metal hand, the other filled with the grip of the assault gun. There was a deep-throated thumping that was partially carried away by the wind, and then the squeal of tires behind them as the truck swerved away from the gunfire.

For a second, Sandi thought Fontenot was going to take the pursuing trucks out all by herself, but then the deep thumping of the assault gun was answered by a string of crackling bangs across the roof of the car and a terrified scream from Prya Shaw. An incandescent stream of molten metal speared through the dashboard only centimeters from the steering column, making Sandi flinch and jerk away and nearly run off the road. She heard an intake of breath from Kan-Ten and saw that another shot had burned a nasty groove across his right shoulder; she didn't think it had penetrated the armor they all wore under their jackets, but it had to have hurt just the same.

"Shit!" Fontenot cursed, ducking back inside. "They hit the damned ammo drum! The gun's jammed!"

Another burst from behind them sliced across the passenger's side of the car and Kan-Ten ducked down in his seat a half-second before a round blew his headrest apart in a flash of vaporizing plastic. Sandi saw an alleyway off to the right and turned into it with a desperate twist of the wheel, sending the groundcar up on its left-side wheels and nearly flipping it over. She felt her teeth clack together as the vehicle slammed back down onto all four tires and gunned the engine to take the car into the alley...and then cursed and hit the brakes.

Half of a burned-out warehouse had collapsed across the alleyway about ten meters into it, clogging the street with tons of brick, cement block and fire-charred wooden support beams, all partially covered with the recent snow. Sandi shifted the groundcar into reverse, the transmission clunking into gear roughly, then twisted around in her seat, trying desperately to get back out on the road before their pursuers overtook them. She'd barely touched her foot to the accelerator before the flatbed cut them off, pulling so close to the end of the alley that the edge of the truck bed scraped across the still-standing front faces of the buildings.

Sandi's brain locked up for just a heartbeat, bereft of ideas and hurting for options.

"Everybody out!" Fontenot yelled, jarring her out of her fugue.

She unfastened her seat harness and slammed a shoulder into her door, tumbling out onto the dirt and gravel of the alley, barely remembering to reach back inside to retrieve her pistol off the seat where she'd dropped it. Snowflakes slipped down the neck of her jacket but she barely felt it, adrenalin coursing through her right alongside the conviction that they were about to die.

She'd thought the roaring in her ears was her own pulse until the flatbed truck exploded.

The concussion laid her out flat on the street, the breath gone from her in a blast of blistering-hot air and her vision full of flaring after-images. She squeezed her eyes shut, trying to clear her vision and her head, and when she opened them, she saw Fontenot standing over her, offering her a hand up. She took it and was pulled easily to her feet, up from the chill of the snow-covered ground to the wave of heat still coming off the burning flat bed.

"What the hell?" she muttered, barely able to hear her own words over the ringing in her ears and the roar of the crackling fire that was enveloping not just the truck but the buildings on either side as well.

Kan-Ten was limping over to her, one hand gripping the

arm of Prya Shaw, who seemed unharmed but in shock. The Tahni gestured upward and Sandi finally looked above her, seeing the massive silver bulk of the *Acheron* descending on columns of fire a hundred meters or so down the road from them in an open lot.

"Ash." It was one word, one name, but it seemed to contain paragraphs of relief.

"This way," Fontenot put a hand on Sandi's shoulder and guided her through a small gap in the wreckage that blocked the alleyway. "Hurry."

Didn't I have a gun? Sandi wondered dully, still stunned. Then she looked down into her right hand and saw the pulse pistol still gripped there instinctively; she moved her finger farther off the trigger pad and pushed the weapon out in front of her.

The gap in the wreckage led them through the empty hulk of the devastated warehouse, pitch black until the flashlight attached to Kan-Ten's carbine lit up the wrecked hollow, glinting off the ice that frosted every flat surface. Sandi could hear Fontenot's heavy footsteps crunching through the drifts of ice-covered snow that had blown in through the gaps in the collapsed roof and solidified, and she made sure to watch where she placed her own feet.

Behind her, she heard Prya Shaw gasp and looked back to see the woman clutching at Kan-Ten's arm, barely able to keep her balance. She felt a momentary scorn until she reflected that the woman was probably scared out of her mind. Hell, Sandi had seen combat, been in several gunfights, and she was *still* scared out of her mind.

Finally, they reached one of the doorways that led out to the main road, gaping open, with the door itself collapsed inward, the metal burned black but still solid. Fontenot squeezed past Sandi, motioning for her to wait and then ducking out the door with surprising grace and speed for a woman carrying around nearly a hundred kilograms of metal. Sandi edged closer to the doorway, feeling an itching impatience to be out of the building, but it was only seconds before Fontenot reappeared, waving for the others to follow.

"Quick," she urged, motioning the others ahead, facing back behind them, carbine at the ready. "Get to the ship."

"What happened to the other truck?" Kan-Ten asked, scanning the street as he half-supported Prya. The woman's face looked positively grey, her eyes wide as she glanced furtively around.

"It's gone," Fontenot reported, her voice cutting through the whine of the *Acheron*'s turbojets. "That fucker's too smart to stick around when the odds are against him."

Sandi was having nightmare visions of Singh jumping out of every shadowed corner along the ruined, deserted stretch of industrial buildings, and the hundred-meter walk to the idling ship seemed to take hours. Ash was at the foot of the ramp, waiting for them with a pulse carbine cradled in his arms, shifting his weight nervously from one foot to another.

"Hurry," he said. "They have a lighter in orbit; I took down two of their shuttles, but they have to have at least one other around in reserve."

"Thanks for bailing us out." Sandi kissed him quickly, resting her head on his shoulder for just a moment before she had to move and make way for Kan-Ten to escort Prya up the ramp.

"Next time though," Fontenot interjected dryly, clomping up behind them, "don't blow shit up right next to us."

Ash chuckled apologetically as he hit the control to close the belly ramp, then rushed back up to the cockpit. Sandi sagged, leaning against the bulkhead for just a second, thinking that this wasn't even the hardest part. Now, somehow, they had to convince the netdiver to share privileged information with them before they got her back to the *bratva*.

"Thank God," Prya Shaw sighed, letting Kan-Ten settle her into an acceleration couch. "I can't believe they came after me... they must have figured out I was a spy." She met Sandi's eyes with a look of utter gratitude and hero-worship. "Thank you, thank you all for getting me out of there. If there's anything I can do to repay you..."

"You know," Sandi mused, grinning as the belly jets began to power up for takeoff, "there might be something after all."

CHAPTER FOUR

Jagmeet Singh reached instinctively with his left fist to knock on the hatch of the captain's cabin, used to the discipline of keeping his right hand free to draw his weapon. He hesitated before the black matte metal of the bionic hand touched the plastic; he still hadn't mastered the art of controlled, subtle motion with the prosthetic and he was just as likely to crack the door if he tried knocking with that fist. He lowered the bionic limb and rapped on the door with the measured force of his right hand.

"Come." Captain Deruda's tone was harshly abrupt, the same as it had been when he'd radioed to their shuttle on the way up from Peboan that he wanted Singh to report to his cabin immediately after Transition. Singh pushed the handle down with his artificial hand and shoved the hatch open with his shoulder.

The Captain's cabin was more than twice as large as any of the crew quarters on the lighter, nearly the size of the ones he'd seen on Fleet cruisers back in the day, which seemed like an absurd waste of space on a ship like the *Gitano*. It wasn't a cutter or a courier, but living space was still at a premium, as it was on any starship. Deruda was seated in a divan that could double as an acceleration couch at need, drinking something that smelled vaguely alcoholic from a squeezebulb. He was a round-faced, pudgy bear of a man with wiry salt-and-pepper hair that descended down the half-domes of his cheeks in absurd mutton chops.

"Close the door behind you, Singh," he ordered in his annoying, nasal voice.

Singh swiped backward with his prosthetic and the hatch crashed shut hard enough to make the shipmaster flinch.

"Jesus Christ," Deruda whined, "can you try not to break the fucking ship?"

There was another seat available, but the man didn't offer it and Singh wouldn't have taken it in any case.

"What do you want, Deruda?" He heard the slight slur of his words and felt a flare of anger. It didn't matter that he'd made the decision to keep the bionics for now instead of replacing them with cloned flesh, the weakness of it gnawed at him. That was what he'd wanted, a constant reminder of what Hollande and Carpenter had taken away from him: his arm, his face, his Freya...

"It's 'Captain Deruda' on board this ship," the man reminded him, trying to sound threatening but ruining it with his plaintive tone.

"What. Do. You. Want."

"This has been a fucking disaster," Deruda said, slamming the bulb down on the table bolted to the deck beside the chair, the effect slightly spoiled by the fact that both the drink container and the surface were cheap, yielding plastic. "We lost *two* fucking assault shuttles and ten people down there. Jordi's going to fucking kill me."

"Assault shuttles," Singh repeated, laughing at the absurdity of it. He didn't like to laugh; it hurt. "Strapping weapons pods to a cargo bird or a lander doesn't make it an assault shuttle. And you have plenty of troops on board."

"Are you fucking serious?" He gaped at Singh, eyes wide. "This mission is *over*. We're burning down the fastest Transition map to La Hondonada, and I'm filing a full report to Jordi. I just need to make sure that you take the responsibility for losing those two boats."

"We're not going back," Singh declared flatly. "We know exactly where they'll take that girl, and we're going to track them down. We're changing course for the *bratva* settlement on Thunderhead."

Deruda pushed his bulk out of the seat and squared off with Singh, one hand going to the pistol in his shoulder holster, anger flaring behind his piggish eyes.

"You listen to me, bounty hunter," he bellowed. "You may think you're hot shit on a stick because Jordi sicced you on those two shitbag drifters, but *I'm* the Captain of this ship, and *I* set our fucking course! If you think you can swing your dick around *my* ship and order my crew around, you're as fucking crazy as you look! My crew is loyal to *me* and..."

The backhand was casual, almost as if his arm had moved on its own, but the motion was a blur faster than a human eye could follow. The edge of the black, metal hand sank into Deruda's left temple with a crunch of splintering skull and a spray of blood that spattered against the dull white of the bulkhead. Deruda went slack, collapsing sideways half-on and half-off his bunk, a wet gurgling the last sound he made before he went silent forever.

Singh bent and pulled the pistol from the man's shoulder holster, dropping it into the deep pocket of his duster, then he threw the door open and stepped out into the passageway. The bridge was up a set of metal steps to the left and he took them two at a time, walking past the galley and the small medical bay. A half a dozen pairs of eyes turned his way, Deruda's bridge crew.

They were a motley lot, dressed in a mix of old military gear, colorful flash and spacer's leathers, two of them with the towering, slender build that spoke of a childhood spent in low gravity and one stocky and muscular enough that he might have hailed from a high-g world. The oldest was the First Mate, who looked as if he could have been well over a hundred and lacked the benefit of modern anti-aging treatments, while the girl at the sensor station might have been in her twenties. They stared at Singh with looks that ranged from suspicion to horror, and the bounty hunter realized that his bionic hand and the entire left sleeve of his jacket were covered in blood. It dripped fitfully onto the deck, a tip-tap sound that cut through the stunned silence.

"Captain Deruda and I had a disagreement about our course of action," he told them, his voice calm and unhurried. "I'm afraid he won't be joining us for the remainder of the voyage. Navigator," he turned one brown eye and one dull grey metallic one on the older woman with the purple bobbed hair and a leather jacket covered in holographic unicorns, "I'm going to need you to take us to Thunderhead."

He paused, looking at each of them in turn, watching for the first twinge of a move for a weapon, the first step one might make to run.

"Will that be a problem?"

The First Mate took a slow, hesitant step forward, then he gave what might have passed for a salute a century ago.

"No, sir," he said firmly.

"What's your name?"

"First Officer Kittner," the old man told him. If he was

scared, he was doing a good job of concealing it. Singh wondered if Kittner wasn't happy to be rid of Deruda.

"Well, *Captain* Kittner," Singh said, half his mouth twisting into a smile, "the ship is yours." The smile faded. "And if we aren't in Thunderhead in eighty hours, then I'll be having this conversation with the next officer in line. Clear?"

"Clear, Mr. Singh."

Singh nodded to the older man and turned on his heel, heading back for the cabin he'd been assigned; he'd leave Deruda's and its cleanup to the First Officer. He liked Kittner; the man struck him as a pragmatist. It was always pleasant dealing with people who accepted the inevitable.

——

Prya Shaw hunched under the upturned hood of her borrowed rain slicker and tried to divide her attention between oncoming pedestrians on the Freeport sidewalks and what seemed to be a constant watch for the ankle-deep puddles and mud bogs that no amount of maintenance could prevent.

I've been here a day, she fumed silently, *and I already hate this damned place.*

Thunderhead was the sort of place that you lived when you'd been kicked out of anywhere nicer. That was how the *Novya Moscva bratva* had wound up here, from what her uncle had told her. No other cartel wanted the planet; Freeport was its only real settlement and even that had been basically leaderless when they'd come in and taken over a year ago, after the Sung Brothers' mercenaries had beaten *their* mercenaries and kicked them off of Peboan.

She could see why. Peboan might have been bitterly cold in the winter, but at least there the sun shined *sometimes*. She glanced upward, blinking at the raindrops that splashed on her, searching for any hint of a break in the gloom. It was technically daytime, but the clouds were so thick that she couldn't honestly tell, and it had been raining nonstop since she'd stepped off the *Acheron.*

I should be grateful, she chided herself. At least here, she wouldn't be constantly paranoid, looking over her shoulder, deathly afraid that she'd be found out. *No, here I just have to worry about mudslides, floods, lightning strikes and the background radiation giving me cancer.*

She looked up instead of down at the wrong time and her foot plunged up to the calf in a puddle, the water flooding over the top of her water-proof boots and soaking her right leg.

"Goddammit!" she yelled, yanking her foot out of the washed-out hole in the sidewalk and trying to shake off the excess water.

A couple passers-by glanced at her outburst, one of them chuckling at her discomfort. She scowled at the man, a spacer by the look of his clothes, and far too handsome and healthy-looking to be from this miserable planet. Easy for him to laugh; he could fly out of here in a day or two and never have to come back.

Oh well, at least half this city isn't burned down.

The buildings here were nicer than back on Peboan, she had to admit. There was a style to them, something more aesthetic than the starkly practical designs in Shakak. Her aunt and uncle had a very nice two-story townhouse not far from Alexi's business offices, and they'd secured her an apartment only a kilometer away in "gratitude for her service." She hadn't thought of asking for a car, but maybe tomorrow. Might as well take advantage of the gratitude while it was fresh.

Freeport's main street ended in a T-intersection and she followed it to the left, out past the edges of the entertainment district, well past the luxurious townhouses of business owners and cartel executives and into the rowhouses where the tech workers and managers lived. The neighborhood was still nice, but the accommodations were smaller and more basic. She tapped an alphanumeric code into the access pad on the outside security door for her building, feeling a surge of irritation that she couldn't use a wireless ID key like she had back on Peboan; the background radiation on Thunderhead made any sort of wireless communication problematic.

The interior stairwell was empty, most of the tenants still at work and the lights still dim since it was technically daytime. She threw back her hood and reveled in the dryness of the air, shaking water off on the floor and not caring. She was only one story up and as she stepped slowly and carefully up the stairs, she began to muse whether she might have the place redecorated once she'd settled in; after all, she'd be living here for a long time, perhaps years.

She was so lost in thought, she almost didn't notice the broad-shouldered, rough-looking older man coming into the entrance hall at the foot of the stairs. She frowned as she looked over her shoulder at him; he didn't look like the sort that would live in this building. He wore a shaggy beard and spacer's clothes and she could see a pistol holstered at his waist, not strange for drifters and smugglers but not typical for residents. But how would he get in if he didn't live here?

She quickened her pace up the stairs, hearing the impact of his boots on the bottom steps even as she reached her floor and walked quickly to her apartment. Her heart was thumping against her chest by the time she got the code keyed into the lockplate and saw the indicator light up green. She yanked the door open and rushed inside, pushing it shut behind her and throwing the security bolt. She stared at the blank, white surface of the inside of the door and tried to slow her breathing.

She was probably being paranoid, a holdover from the last year she'd spent on Peboan.

"Good afternoon, Ms. Shaw."

She screamed reflexively, spinning around. Stepping out of the shadows of her apartment's small kitchen was a tall, menacing figure dressed in black, the left side of his face swathed in darkness. As he came closer, she could see that the darkness wasn't shadow but matte black metal.

She felt panic surging through her and she jerked back the bolt, pulling the door open desperately, thinking maybe she could get back down the stairs before him, could get back to the crowds of people and safety. The bearded man stood just outside, his broad chest blocking her way, an impassive, neutral look on his lined, craggy face and his pistol hanging by his side, held casually in his left hand.

"You don't wanna' be doin' that, ma'am," he drawled, nodding back into the apartment.

She backed up carefully, looking between the two men, the fires of panic burning cold in her gut. The half-faced man pushed back his leather duster and hooked his right thumb on his gunbelt, the impersonal regard of his natural eye as lifeless as that of the metal one.

"What do you want from me?" she stuttered, barely able to form the words past hyperventilating breath.

"The people who brought you here," the cyborg said. "The pilots, Carpenter and Hollande. I want to know where they went, what they told you, what you heard."

"They...they didn't tell me anything." She shook her head, a sharp, jerking motion. She tried to back away from both of them, away from the front door and the kitchen, back towards her living room. "They didn't say anything about where they were going, I swear."

"That would be most unfortunate."

He stepped closer and now Prya could see that his left hand was metal as well, bare and undisguised under the sleeve of his jacket. She backed away another step and felt the back of her legs hit the edge of the couch. The man's natural hand reached out and shoved her in the center of her chest and she cried out as she fell backwards, toppling into a seat on the ratty cushions of the sofa that had come with the apartment.

She stared up at the cyborg, the metal half of his face thrown into sharp relief in the dim light filtering through the shades over the front window. She was shaking and she couldn't stop it, couldn't get her breathing or her heart rate or her fear under control. He was death, and he'd followed her here all the way from Peboan, and there was no escaping him.

His biological hand struck out as quick as a snake and grabbed her left wrist, twisting it above her painfully and she gasped and tried to kick at him. She could feel that his legs were flesh and not metal, but she might as well have been kicking at the bionics for all the reaction he gave her. He twisted her wrist further and she screamed and stopped trying to kick him.

"I don't know!" she screamed over and over. "I don't know!"

His metal hand unfolded above hers, the mechanical thumb and forefinger grasping her left pinkie and straightening it. She clenched her teeth, shaking her head, murmuring "no, please," and knowing it wouldn't do any good.

She screeched when the finger broke and neither of them seemed inclined to silence her. They'd scouted the place out, some part of her realized dimly, through a haze of pain. They knew no one was home in the apartments around hers. They could do whatever they wanted, she could scream as loud as she wanted, and no one would hear. The scream choked away into sobs and she clenched her eyes shut and looked away from her finger, bent backwards at an unnatural angle.

"You have nine more," the man declared in a cold, businesslike voice. "And after that, I'll be forced to get serious."

"There..." She trailed off, hating herself, but knowing she'd reveal it eventually. She wasn't a hero, wasn't like Sandi or Ash or Korri or even the Tahni. She was a technician, a computer netdiver, not a soldier. "There was one thing...," she panted, barely able to see through the tears welled up in her eyes. "There was a system in the Sung Brothers' files, out near the edge of the Cluster...one of their mineral scouts had surveyed it a few months ago."

"They wanted to know about it," he surmised. "What was there?"

"The files...the scout said he found a ship there, a Fleet cruiser, he thought."

"In a system that far out?" He frowned, seeming less than self-assured and in control for the first time since she'd entered the apartment. "Why?"

"He didn't know," she insisted quickly. "Once he saw it, he got the hell out; he didn't want to tangle with a military ship." She shook her head. "That's it, that's all they wanted to know about, I swear to God."

Those mechanical digits hovered over her left ring finger and she whimpered helplessly, shaking her head.

"Tell me," he intoned with the threat left unspoken, "where."

She wished she didn't remember, but she'd recited the coordinates for Sandi and Ash and her memory had been nearly eidetic even before the modifications she'd been given. She had to repeat them twice while the bearded man copied them down on his 'link, but once she'd finished, the cyborg let loose of her arm and she cradled her hand against her, hissing in an agonized breath.

The bearded man went to the door, and the cyborg followed and she stared at them wide-eyed.

"You...," she stammered, knowing she was tempting fate but unable to stop herself. "You're not going to kill me?"

The metal man turned back just inside the doorway, eyeing her with what might have been amusement.

"You," he told her, "are not the one I want to kill."

The door slammed shut and both of them were gone.

CHAPTER FIVE

"THIS REALLY IS THE ASS-END OF NOWHERE," KORRI Fontenot mused.

Looking at a computer-enhanced map of the system on the main screens, Ash couldn't argue with the assessment. The red dwarf star was attended by only two planets, an ice giant so far out that its orbit took well over 300 standard days and a gas giant about three quarters the size of Saturn circling much closer in, about where Venus would be back in the Solar System, with a half a dozen moons to call its own. A few million asteroids, a cometary halo and that was it. The system was unremarkable...except in its isolation.

"We're as far as you can go in the Cluster in this direction," Sandi agreed. "Feels..." She shrugged, her whole body moving against her restraint harness in the microgravity. "Feels weird out here. Lonely."

Ash saw what could have been a shiver running through her shoulders and he reached over to grip her hand, an instinctive reminder that she wasn't alone. Or maybe it was a reminder that *he* wasn't alone. He hadn't decided yet.

"You have used this term before," Kan-Ten spoke up,

strapped down at the navigator's station beside Fontenot. "This term 'Cluster.' What are you referring to?"

Ash looked at Sandi and Fontenot, a bit surprised. He figured everyone knew what the Cluster was. Then again, maybe his concept of "everyone" didn't really include a Tahni exile who'd learned English out in the Pirate Worlds.

"You know what the Transition Lines are, right?" he asked the alien, suddenly wondering what sort of education the average Tahni received in physics. "The gravito-inertial lines of force between stars that we travel on when we go to Transition Space?"

"I have heard of how the Transition drive works," Kan-Ten confirmed. Ash was still not quite to the point where he could read the alien's expressions, not even after six months travelling and working with him, but he thought the Tahni might have been annoyed. "But what is the Cluster?"

"Those lines," Sandi interjected, "they connect thousands of stars in a globular formation we call the Cluster. It's kind of like a road system, except you can't stop anywhere but where one of the lines ends, inside the gravitational influence of a star system. But the Cluster is, as far as anyone can tell, a closed formation, with no way out."

"Some people *think* there's a way out," Ash said. "They call it the Northwest Passage, but no one's ever found it. So, this," he waved a hand at the star system on the screen, "is as far as you can go on the inner hemisphere of the Cluster...that is, the side of the Cluster that's closest to the galactic center, rather than the edge."

"Which is why it took three interminable weeks to get here," Fontenot cut in, scowling. "No offense to you, Ash, but I'm ready to get off this fucking boat."

"There's your chance," Ash told her, pointing at a sensor reading highlighted in red by the computer. It was still hundreds of thousands of kilometers away, much too far for the optical cameras to pick up as anything but a glint of reflected light, but the computer had already assigned it the shape of a Fleet cruiser. "Going to have to go in suited up, though. We're not getting anything off her reactor, and she's an ice cube. Life support has been off for a long while."

"You think it's been orbiting that moon this whole time?" Sandi wondered. "Ever since the war?"

"From the readings, it looks like parts of the moon might be habitable," Ash told her, scrolling through the sensor display with a flick of his fingertips. "Cold as shit," he equivocated, shrugging, "but habitable. Maybe they went down to the surface? If any of them survived, that is."

"There's only one way to find out." Sandi nodded at the representation of the ship.

"It's your turn to drive," he reminded her, grinning crookedly.

She laughed, raising her hands palms-up in surrender.

"Hey, if you think cramming yourself into a suit and floating around a frozen ghost ship is a fun adventure, more power to you."

"I'll go," Fontenot declared. "At least it's something different." She twisted around and cocked her natural eyebrow at Kan-Ten. "Unless you wanted to go?"

The Tahni made a gesture with his hands that Ash had learned signaled negation.

"I don't care for your vacuum suits," he explained. "They fit me poorly. And I don't know that I care for your concept of 'adventure' either."

"You were a soldier," Ash said. "And after the war, you left home and went out to the Pirate Worlds to live with human criminals. Why would you do any of that if you didn't want adventure?"

"I was a soldier to serve my Emperor. Once he proved that he was not worthy of the name or of my service, I did not care to stay..." He paused. "What's the human term? Under the heel, I think. Under the heel of our conquerors. I read much of your literature when I was trying to learn your language, and there was a writer who said it was better to rule in Hell than serve in Heaven. If I understand that phrase correctly, I have chosen Hell."

Fontenot snorted laughter.

"I don't know about you two," she said to Ash and Sandi, "but I feel insulted."

"Hold that thought," Ash said, spooling out the interface cables and re-entering the meld with the ship. "We're heading in."

———

"I don't like hanging your ass out in the wind like this."

Sandi's voice sounded tinny coming out of his helmet speakers, further emphasizing the feeling of isolation that sank into him every time he went out in a vacuum suit. The *Acheron*'s utility airlock was small, smaller still with someone as large as Fontenot sharing it with him and both of them wearing External Maneuvering Units, but the suit separated him from even that enclosed space, enveloped him in a bubble of unreality. He'd been surprised to find the feeling comforting.

"Ain't no wind out here, shor'," he murmured, unconsciously slipping into the slurred patois of the Trans-Angeles housing projects where he'd grown up. He'd made a concerted effort to abandon that accent for a generic-North-American English one when he'd left for the Commonwealth Military Academy, but sometimes it slipped out when he wasn't paying attention. "I'd rather keep the ship clear, just in case," he said, louder and in his normal voice. "We'll be fine. Just get us as close as you can without scuffing the paint."

"She doesn't show any exterior damage," Fontenot mused, staring out the thick, transplas port in the outer airlock hatch.

Ash crowded in over her shoulder, feeling a bit of awe at the size of the ship. The *Metaurus*, if that was indeed what she was, loomed beside them, glowing in the reflected light of the star. She was a floating mountain of nickel iron and BiPhase Carbide, over a kilometer long and half that wide, a monolithic mass of constrained power and death. He could feel the maneuvering thrusters kicking the cutter gradually closer to the huge vessel, and he gnawed at his lip to silence the protest he wanted to make that they were going to collide with her. Sandi was a hell of a pilot, and he trusted her in the left seat.

Out the portal, he saw the barely-perceptible lines of the rounded service airlock at the edge of the ship's docking bay and another burst of maneuvering jets matched their relative motion with that of the cruiser, just over the entrance and perhaps a half a kilometer away.

"This is as close as I want to get," Sandi confessed.

"Close enough," he assured her. He reached past Fontenot's shoulder and touched the control to open the exterior lock.

There was no sound; the lock had been drained of air minutes ago. Just the slow slide of white metal and plastic into the gap in the hull and then there was nothing between them and the *Metaurus* but the almost nonexistent atmosphere of high orbit. Fontenot pushed herself out of the lock, gaining about six meters of clearance before she hit the controls of her EMU and began slowly accelerating across the gap between the *Acheron* and the cruiser.

Ash waited until she was maybe fifty meters away before he grabbed the edge of the outer lock and pulled hard. Emptiness swallowed him up, and around the silver wedge of the cutter behind him and the mountain of metal ahead, he could see the brilliant field of stars that stretched out into infinity. They called to him, as they always did, distracting with their siren song, promising new worlds and alien horizons and everything that wasn't the Kibera slums of Trans Angeles, everything that was bigger than his family and their obsession with territory and face and respect.

Those stars, they were why he'd left, why he'd risked everything to leave. He'd found other reasons since, of course: honor, and duty, and love. But the stars had been first, and weren't last even now. With Sandi and the stars to keep him company, even life on the run didn't seem so bad.

He shook his head, clearing away everything but the present, and squeezed at the control butting up against his left hand. Maneuvering jets kicked him in the pants and the gleaming hull of the cruiser began to race towards him until he twisted the control a different direction and the braking jets squeezed the mounting straps against the front of his shoulders and his waist. His approach slowed and he could see Fontenot ahead of him, tethered to a ring affixed to the hull, working at a control panel next to the service lock.

They lacked the RFID chips that the crew of the cruiser would have had, but they did have the emergency codes that Fox had given them on that crystal spike, and that proved to be enough. The outer airlock slid aside even before Ash touched lightly against the hull, activating the magnets in his boots to stick there. Using those and the ones in the fingers of his gloves, he scooted across the surface of the hull, feeling like a bug on a plate. He pulled himself over into the recess of the lock, grabbing Fontenot's outstretched hand and moving into the shadow of an overhanging ridge of BiPhase Carbide armor. Beside the lock and stretching out for dozens of meters on either side, he could see the rows of circular hatches that marked the ejection ports for the ship's main complement of life pods. They all seemed to be intact; no one had ejected during whatever had happened.

"At least the airlock is working," Ash said, hitting the control to close the outer door. The lights inside the lock were harsh and omnidirectional, leaving no gaps for shadows.

"Emergency backup batteries," Fontenot guessed. She started the lock cycling with a punch of a button affixed to the bulkhead, but rather than the usual inflow of air to match pressures to the interior of the ship, the inner door simply slid into its recessed niche with a flashing red warning that the other side was still in a vacuum.

The service bay was dark and cold and airless and suddenly, Ash wasn't so eager to leave the airlock. He stalled, unlatching the straps of the EMU and leaving it floating behind him, gesturing for Fontenot to do the same. It might have been handier to have the jetpacks strapped on aboard the cruiser in microgravity than to have to rely on their suit magnets, but the EMU's woud be bulky and awkward inside compartments or in narrower passageways.

With the framework of the maneuvering unit shed, he reached back and freed his pulse carbine from where it was strapped to the environmental pack that heated his suit and generated its air. The carbine had a tactical light affixed to the forearm, and he'd need it in here. His helmet's optics had infrared filters and light-intensifying software, but he couldn't count on having any light, infrared or visible, if the power was down. Main passageways and vital compartments such as the bridge or medical bay would have chemical ghostlights, but much of the ship would be pitch black.

He touched the rubberized button on the stock and the light snapped on, turning hulking, shadowy monsters into industrial exoskeletons, remotely operated zero-g cargo jacks and polymer crates stacked from deck to overhead in metal locking frames. And a desiccated, floating corpse surrounded by an orbiting halo of frozen blood.

"Fuck!" he blurted, barely restraining himself from shooting.

The body was dressed in Fleet blue utility fatigues where they weren't ripped apart, and his short, dark hair seemed incongruously fresh and lifelike against the mummified, grey skin. The eyes stared out blindly, milky and mesmerizingly wide open.

"Cover the door," Fontenot snapped, her carbine going to her shoulder.

Ash had to force himself to look away from the body, training his weapon and its attached light on the closed hatch while Fontenot clomped across the floor on magnetic soles to check out the dead man. His eyes kept flickering back towards it, seeing on the darkened edge of his own helmet's faceplate; he felt an irrational paranoia that the corpse would suddenly reanimate and come after them with undead fury.

"Something tore this poor son of a bitch apart," Fontenot muttered, sounding thoughtful but otherwise unaffected. That wasn't surprising, given that she'd been working in one violent profession or another nearly all of a life that stretched over 150 years. How many dead bodies had she seen in a century and a half? "It doesn't look like a projectile weapon...but the fatigues aren't burned, either, like they would be from a laser. It looks like it was *sliced* open."

"A knife?" he grunted, trying to sound as if his stomach wasn't churning. "Easy to conceal, I guess."

"It'd have to be a monomolecular edge to cut this deep. It's down to the bone...shit, it's *through* the bone in some places."

Ash swallowed hard, suddenly glad he was watching the door.

"But that doesn't make sense," Fontenot went on, and he could almost hear her shaking her head in confusion. "The clothes...the cuts through them aren't clean, surgical. They're rough, like whatever ripped them up wasn't that sharp."

There was a long pause and then, "His name was Raymond Castro, and he was a Technician Fourth Class, worked here in supply. No weapons, no 'link, nothing useful on him."

"I need to take a look," Ash decided. He didn't really *want* to, but if he was going to be a leader, he needed to act like one. "Watch the door for me."

Fontenot moved over to replace him without a word. He couldn't see her face, but he felt like if he could, she'd be wearing a wry smile. She was smart and experienced enough to know why he was doing it, and it undoubtedly amused her.

He clenched his jaws shut at the sight of the mummified corpse, pale and wizened and drained of blood. The frozen, crimson globules orbited him like the rings of a gas giant, twisting and spinning hypnotically, making it harder to concentrate on the details of the body. He forced himself, made himself look past the bloody kaleidoscope and into the wounds.

They were horrific, large and gaping and, as Fontenot had said, right through skin and muscle and scoring the bone. Castro's left ulna was exposed, the flesh ripped away, and he could see that it had been splintered with the force of the blow. His chest had been split open, the ribs cracked, and he was reluctant to shine the weapons' light into that wound, not wanting to see what had happened to the organs inside.

Whatever had killed this man had been incredibly, inhumanly strong, like the exoskeletal load-lifter in the corner, and he could almost believe this had been a work accident, maybe caused by the loss of power. Yet Castro's 'link was missing, gone from its mount on his fatigue sleeve. It had been taken by whoever had killed him.

He shook his head. Fontenot was right; they weren't going to learn anything else here.

"Let's get to engineering," Ash told her, pausing to take a sip from the helmet's water reservoir; his mouth was dry, for some reason. "We need to get the power back on."

CHAPTER SIX

"THIS IS JUST ALL KINDS OF FUCKED UP," ASH SAID, standing stiffly behind the Captain's station on the bridge, trying to avoid the blood.

He hadn't thought about the blood when he'd turned life support back on after powering up the ship's reactor, but by the time he'd made it to the bridge from engineering, the atmosphere had begun to thicken and everything was warming up. The red crystal tears were melting, and the air currents from the vents were pushing them out of their stable orbits, making them splash wildly against any surface they impacted.

He'd sent Fontenot to check the docking bay, and they'd both been trying to shove any loose bodies they came across into closed compartments, but there wasn't much they could do about the blood. There'd been a steady trickle of the dead, here and there, maybe a half a dozen that he'd found and another few Fontenot had reported. The bridge though...

Whatever had happened, it had culminated on the bridge. The emergency seal had been about three fourths of the way down when he'd reached it; he'd had to crawl under it before he could find the control to raise it back up. Something had interrupted its descent, something sturdy enough to stop the massive BiPhase Carbide hatch without being crushed. There were laser burns all over the bulkheads, and exploded plastic where the pulses had struck the viewscreen display projectors, and then there were the bodies.

Seven of them in here, six of them ship's security, armored and toting pulse carbines much like his own, not that either the armor or the weapons had done them any good. Something had torn right through their armor, peeled them like bananas and then torn apart the soft, chewy insides. The last corpse was the ship's Captain, a man named Cornelius Schofield according to the records that Fox had given them. His face was intact, as well as the name tape on the shoulder of his fatigues. He'd been armed with a pulse pistol...at least Ash *assumed* that was his arm, spinning sedately with the gun still in its hand. Since Schofield was short one, it seemed logical.

"Jesus Christ, Ash," Sandi said over his helmet radio, her tone sounding reverent rather than blasphemous. "What the hell have we walked into here?"

She and Kan-Ten had seen it all through the video pickup in his helmet, just as he could monitor what Fontenot was seeing in the docking bay.

"We got one shuttle gone in here," she reported, redundantly he thought since he could see the image of the empty niche where the lander had once nestled, a transplas tube that led through the hull and into vacuum. "And the other..."

Her helmet swung around, and with it the view, and he could see what remained of the other shuttle. It still sat snugly in its launch enclosure, the airlock and docking umbilical still intact...but the engine bell was cracked and blackened, hanging off the rear of the bird loosely, as if the lack of gravity was the only thing keeping it from smashing to the deck. There'd been an internal explosion somewhere near the fuel feed, and Ash couldn't help but think it had to have been intentional. Someone wanted to make sure no one else got off the ship.

"Several bodies down here, too," she added, panning to where the corpses floated, spinning slowly in the air currents. They were dressed like Marines---not the battle-suited behemoths that were dropped from troop carriers, but Recon Marines like the ones you might find stationed as the Reaction Force on a ship like the *Metaurus*. "I think whatever did this was either trying to get out on a shuttle or trying to stop the ones who did."

"That tracks with what the engineering board is telling me," Ash confirmed grimly. "The Transition Drive isn't just shut down, someone physically severed the power trunk to the Teller-Fox warp unit. Someone didn't want this ship leaving this system and they didn't want that shuttle leaving the ship, either."

"Shit," Fontenot muttered. She sounded worried, and Ash couldn't remember the last time she'd sounded that way. "That either means someone was so suicidal that they wanted to take everyone on this ship with them, or else there was something the officers on the *Metaurus* were so afraid of that they couldn't let it get away."

"Ash," Sandi said, some of that same trepidation creeping into her voice, "you guys need to get off that ship."

"Yeah, I think you're right," he acknowledged. There was a cold feeling in his gut, and he tried not to let it freeze into a full panic. He pulled the dataspike Fox had given them out of a utility pouch on his pistol belt. "I have the computer systems back up; it shouldn't take me more than ten minutes to download the log. Korri, I'll meet you at the lock in a half an hour and we'll head back to the *Acheron*."

"I'll have the ship in position," Sandi promised.

Ash nodded and signed off, then quickly got to work manipulating the data systems...and keeping one eye on the blood.

———

The first sensation she'd experienced in six years was warmth.

Through that hazy borderland between sleep and wakefulness, she realized it had also been that long since she'd felt warmth at all. Her last memory was the creeping cold, the lethargy that had come with it as systems beyond her control had buried her in protective sleep. But now the temperatures were rising slowly, passing the freezing point of water as the air around her thickened.

She was in a tight space, a place she'd crawled into from instinct, the last warmth and energy she'd sensed before things had gone dark. With the warmth, feeling came back to her body, and with feeling came the pain. She'd almost forgotten the pain. It had been a constant before, a background noise she'd almost learned to ignore, but now it seemed new again and freshly intolerable. It was impossible to localize it, impossible to even categorize it as an ache or a sharp pain or a feeling of sickness. Instead, the pain was a part of her being, a field that bound together her molecules and existed in every atom of her every element.

The pain was almost enough to make her hate the warmth, to blame it for her suffering, but as the warmth and the pain returned, the memories also returned. And she remembered who was to blame for her pain. It was the man. The man had caused her pain, and he was somewhere else, somewhere far from her. Part of her wanted to get to him, but instincts were pulling her in different directions. She felt confusion, the same confusion she remembered from before she'd slept, because two overwhelming urges tugged at her, leading her down disparate paths.

Part of her wanted more than anything to go home. She could see home in her mind's eye, green and warm and welcoming, and she thought she knew how to get there, but when she'd tried, things had gone badly. The others had tried to stop her, and when she couldn't go home, she did what the other voices were yelling at her to do: she killed. The other voices, the ones that didn't care about her home or her pain, wanted her to kill and they wanted her to find the womb and reproduce others like her.

The womb, that was what she thought of when they put the feeling in her head, but that wasn't the word the voices were saying. They were calling it something else, something she couldn't visualize except perhaps as a seed pod. Maybe seed pod was a better word, but she would keep thinking of it as the womb, because it felt right.

If she couldn't get home, maybe there was a way she could get to the womb...and the man was there, too, she remembered. The man had caused her pain, and killing him would feel just and satisfying. She had to move.

She uncurled from her darkened nook beside the air vent, stretching out to her full length. Someone, one of the others, they had to have turned the warmth and the air back on. They were here, on this ship, and they had to have come in one of their own. She would kill them and take it. Killing felt right. Killing would quiet the voices nagging at her, would quiet the pain. She reached out with senses that she couldn't understand and wouldn't have been able to describe, and she found them.

She skittered away, hugging the darkness, embracing the shadows as she embraced her purpose.

———

Fox had told them to download the log; he hadn't said to listen to it. Ash's hand hovered over the control, finger tracing the line between the "Download" indicator and the "Download and play" selection, wondering if there was any way the Intelligence officer would know.

"What the hell?" he murmured to himself, and hit "play."

The holographic image showed just the head and shoulders of the ship's commander, projected above the communications console at about one third life size. Captain Schofield was a handsome man when he wasn't dead and mummified, Ash decided. He had one of those faces that you saw on advertising videos, ruggedly good looking but also sympathetic and understanding, a cross between a movie star and the idealized version of a dad he'd seen on ViRdramas and nowhere else in his life.

"Mission log 10469-A," Schofield intoned, his voice as stern and serious as his demeanor but with an edge of exasperation, like this was just another routine he'd grown tired of performing. "Commonwealth Space Fleet cruiser *Metaurus*, Captain Cornelius Schofield commanding. The ship was refueling and resupplying at Andalusia when we received a coded message on the Instell ComSat addressed to the first Fleet starship to make it insystem. It was a priority mission with an authorization that came straight from President Jameson, tasking us to travel immediately to a system out way past anywhere I've ever been before to provide transportation for items vital to the war effort."

Schofield couldn't keep the skepticism off his face. "We're 160 hours into the trip and the orders don't make any more sense now than they did then." He shrugged, abandoning the thread. "The latest engineering tests show that..."

Ash paused the playback and scrolled past what he estimated the travel time between Andalusia and this system would be, then restarted it. He blinked when the image of Schofield reappeared. It looked like a completely different man, his eyes haunted, his formerly ruddy cheeks now ashen and hollow; he looked like a man who'd stared death in the face.

"We've thrown everything we had at it," he intoned, his powerful voice now a dry rasp. He was in microgravity, you could tell by the way he moved, yet he still seemed as if something stronger than the mass of a world was weighing him down. "Everything we could do short of destroying the ship, and now it may come to that. I've sent teams to sabotage the Teller-Fox unit, to keep it from using this ship to get elsewhere. I wouldn't have thought it had the intelligence for that, but from what Dr. Nagle tells me, it most assuredly does."

He sucked in a breath of air, coughing at the end of it, wiping at his mouth with the back of his hand. "I've..." He trailed off, staring past the video pickup for a moment, mind trapped into recalling images he was trying to forget. "I've lost most of the crew. We're trying to lure it to the bridge to give Commander Busick a chance to get everyone else who's left into one of the landers and take them down to Nagle's research base. It's nasty down there, barely habitable, but inside the tunnels, they should be able to make it."

His expression firmed with resolve. "Several members of what remains of the ship's security complement have volunteered to try to keep the thing occupied while the others escape. If we can't kill it, then I'm prepared to shut down the reactor, shut down all life support. If that doesn't kill it, well...at least it'll be trapped in here, with us dead, and it won't be able to hurt anyone else."

Someone called his name off-projection and he turned. His eyes closed for just a moment, then opened again with a look that might have been acceptance.

"It's coming." He paused. "Tell my wife and daughter that I love them."

The recording ended and the image faded into the projector

with a snap.

"Shit," Ash hissed. "What the hell is 'it?'"

He started to run the message back before that segment, but the notification pinged to let him know that the log file had been backed up. He cursed and yanked the dataspike out of the socket, tucking it safely away into his belt and moving over to the Tactical station. He activated the console and started running sensor scans of the moon below them.

There was a base down there, Schofield had said. It had been six years, but maybe...

There.

The clear thermal signature of a small fusion reactor, barely the size of the one on the *Acheron* but big enough for a small outpost. He couldn't tell much else about the place, and he imagined most of it was probably underground, but he had a location.

"Sandi," he called into his helmet pickup. He hadn't taken his suit or even his helmet off despite the life support returning, because he hadn't been sure if there might have been any problems with atmospheric production in the last six years the ship had been floating here. "Sandi, you paying attention? Kan-Ten?"

"I'm here, Ash," Sandi responded. "What's up? You done in there yet?"

"I got the files," he told her, "but there's a base down there on that moon, one with an active fusion reactor. I think there are survivors down there."

"Damn," she said, sounding awed and slightly annoyed. "This is getting a lot more complicated than it sounded when Fox handed it to us."

"Yeah," Fontenot piped up. "A lost Fleet ship on a secret mission out in the ass-end of nowhere, that sounded simple as hell. Who could have predicted it would get this complicated?"

"Maybe I liked you better when you were aloof and stand-offish," Sandi shot back, but he could hear the grin in her voice. "What are you thinking, Ash? Should we head down there and check it out?"

"Let me see if I can raise them," Ash decided, scraping across the floor with the magnetic soles of his boots, moving toward the Communications console. "If there's anyone down there, we probably don't want to surprise them."

He hadn't made it more than two steps before he heard the beeping of the alarm from the Tactical display. His head snapped around automatically, and he cursed as he remembered to turn his whole body so he could see anything besides the interior of his own helmet. There was a new icon on the threat display, glowing red as it accelerated at six gravities, the rainbow halo behind it representing a warp corona.

"We got a ship Transitioning!" he shouted it into the helmet pickup, heedless of the feedback it caused in his own speakers. "What the hell?"

"Who the fuck else would be out here?" Fontenot demanded. "Especially now? Did Fox put someone else on this? Is it military?"

"Ash, get the fuck out of there!" Sandi exclaimed. "Get out now!"

"What? What is it?" He peered at the icon, at what seemed to be a normal-looking cargo ship. "Do you recognize it?"

"He followed us out here," she said, sounding desperate and scared. "Jesus Christ, he followed us..."

"Who followed us?" Ash wanted to know. "How could anyone follow us in T-space?"

"It's the *Gitano*," Sandi told him, and on the screen, he saw the cargo ship heading on an intercept course towards her, saw a flight of missiles separating from the *Gitano* and streaking out away from her weapons pods. Heading for Sandi.

"It's Singh!"

CHAPTER SEVEN

"Strap in!" Sandi yelled back to Kan-Ten.

She didn't wait to make sure the Tahni had heeded her warning; she was already jacked into the pilot's control station, and with an act of will she dove into the interface and ignited the *Acheron*'s drive. From zero to seven g's just as fast as the ship would accelerate, the raging flare of plasma from the ship's drive smashed her into the liquid cushion of the acceleration couch with bruising force, and it still wouldn't be enough against missiles that could boost at over twice that.

Another few hundred thousand kilometers farther away from the moon, farther out of the gravity well of the gas giant, and she could have Transitioned, just a micro-jump out an Astronomical Unit or so. She could have run rings around that old piece of shit converted freighter that Jordi Abdullah called a warship. But gravity constrained her, enslaved her, and those damned missiles were going to fly right up her ass if she didn't shake them.

The moon. If she could get down into its atmosphere, she could lose the missiles; they were space-to-space, she could tell by their sensor signature, not designed for flying in the soup.

Using the ship's belly jets and maneuvering thrusters, she banked away from the bulk of the *Metaurus* and burned downward, surrendering to the gravity well. Re-entry at this speed was dangerous as hell; the thickening air buffeted the ship and the view from the exterior cameras burned white with friction flame. Only the ship's electromagnetic deflectors kept the star-hot plasma away from her skin and kept the interior temperature anything near survivable.

Sandi could still feel the wash of nearly unbearable heat baking the inside of the *Acheron*, distracting enough that it nearly drew her out of the interface at a moment when the slightest inattention could leave little bits of them descending like fairy dust all over the planet. There was a narrow corridor she had to follow, and deviating from it would put them on a steep enough trajectory that not even the interface could keep her conscious against those sorts of g-forces, and not even the deflectors could save them from the fury of the fire.

She felt the inferno of their reckless descent against the hull, more real than the sweltering air inside the ship, felt the air passing over her own skin, her arms and legs the control surfaces, as close to skydiving as she ever wanted to get. And nagging at the back of her mind, never quite forgotten, were the missiles. They were catching up to her despite the best speeds she could manage without losing control, still boosting, not quite out of fuel yet. But there was that heat, heat so great the chemical bonds of the diatomic molecules of air were broken, heat so intense that the air was ionized into plasma...and the missiles didn't have deflectors.

Sandi nearly cheered when she saw the first of them fall away, pin-wheeling in a spray of fire and then disintegrating, scattering itself across a continent; but the others kept going. She gritted her teeth and made the decision to go lower, knowing that meant she was going to have to decelerate, knowing how much velocity she'd lose when she switched over from the fusion drive to the turbojets. But she needed the thicker air to shake the other missiles and she didn't have much time left.

The flames engulfing the skin of the cutter began to die down as she levelled the ship off and throttled back the drive, sinking through the upper layers of the atmosphere, through sheaths of grey clouds a kilometer deep. There was a heart-skipping moment between the second the fusion drive cut off and the turbojets kicked in, just an angstrom of doubt as the pressing fist of acceleration ceased and breath rushed back into her lungs. But the jets roared to life and she was pressed back again into her seat with their comforting power.

Dropping out of the clouds, she could see that the missiles had gained on her, but at a price; another was down, spinning wildly out of control and heading for the depths of a frozen sea. The remaining two were ten kilometers away, and just *had* to be nearly bingo fuel by now. There was no way they couldn't be. She kept telling herself that, praying it, wishing it, projecting it like a weapon at them.

Eight kilometers...

There. There it was, and she nearly jumped out of her seat when she saw it, saw both of the weapons sputtering, slowing, beginning to nose in.

And detonating.

The *Acheron* had drawn away by a few more kilometers when the missiles' drives had died, and the added distance was the only thing that saved them from being incinerated in the fireball of fusion energy spreading like an exploding star expanding to paint the roiling clouds with the fires of creation. Sandi screamed at the wave of static that pushed her out of the interface and the wall of superheated air that slammed into the cutter and sent her tumbling across the sky, spinning over the sea and half an ice-bound continent before she began the long fall.

The interface was rebooting, blocking her every attempt to reenter it, and there just wasn't time to wait for it. G-forces were trying their best to pin her back into her seat and the spin was about a half a second from forcing her to black out. Summoning all the strength she could pull out of the deepest places in herself, she forced her hands back to the flight station and grabbed at the physical control stick, latching onto it like it was her last lifeline.

It was hard to think, hard to stay conscious, and she acted on instincts honed from years of training and experience and tried to power out of the spin. If she'd had more altitude, she might have done it; the cutter was about as aerodynamic as a brick, but even a brick can fly with a fusion reactor powering it. But she'd tumbled out of the sky in the seconds it had taken her to reach the controls, and the ice pack of the massive glacier covering most of the moon's northern hemisphere was rushing up at her; she couldn't see it, could barely focus her eyes enough to work the controls, but she knew it was coming.

Desperate with a sense that she had seconds to live, Sandi shifted power to the belly jets and felt herself crushed into the bottom of the acceleration couch and praying to a God she'd never been sure she actually believed in that the *Acheron* wouldn't break in half...

Something slammed into her with the weight of a world and blackness swallowed her up.

"It's Singh!"

Sandi's warning was still echoing around in his helmet but Ash was already in motion, cutting loose the magnets in his boots and pushing off toward the Tactical Officer's station, punching desperately at the controls even as he arrested his motion. He had to bring the ship's proton cannons online, had to target those missiles, and then he could take out the *Gitano*.

He cursed, and slammed a fist into the console. There was a fault, a short in the power trunk where it split between the weapons and the Teller Fox warp unit, and he knew exactly what it was: when the crew of the *Metaurus* had sabotaged the Transition Drive, they'd damaged the power trunk. He could bypass it, but not from here...

"Korri!" he yelled. "Get to engineering fast! I need you to do a manual bypass on the main power trunk to the ship's weapons control systems and I need it done five minutes ago!"

"On it," Fontenot assured him, refreshingly not questioning his orders for once. Then she added, "The engines still work, don't they?"

He grinned savagely. "You're damn right they do. Prepare for one gee acceleration."

Maybe they couldn't take out the missiles yet, but they could keep the lighter busy. He pushed back over to the Helm control station and jammed a thumb down on the control to ignite the plasma drive, then traced the power level up to one gravity. The metal mountain of a ship rumbled up and down the length of her, a volcano erupting into space, and he felt the faux gravity of acceleration begin to push him back down to the deck as the *Metaurus* moved under her own power for the first time in six years. Around him, blood that had been floating since before the war with the Tahni had ended began splattering across the deck and the control stations and the acceleration couches, and bodies suspended for just as long hit the metal grating of the deckplates with the unforgettable sound of dried bones snapping.

A course. He needed to set a course; right now, they were

just accelerating into a higher orbit. He needed to know where the lighter was, which way she was going. He trotted back to the Tactical station, cursing, wishing he'd brought Kan-Ten along; it was impossible to run a ship this size with just one person, even if he'd been jacked in, which he couldn't in a suit not built to accommodate the interface cables. And the damned vacc suit must have weighed twenty-five kilograms; it felt like a lead weight between his shoulder blades.

He spotted the *Gitano* immediately, boosting away from the path of the cruiser, trying to get to a lower orbit that would give them some separation from the *Metaurus* and her weapons. And he also spotted something else on the threat monitor: a shuttle had forced a docking with the service airlock, latched on with a universal umbilical that melded itself to the hull magnetically. That wouldn't get them through the lock, but it would hold them in place while they cut through the hatch, and there wasn't a damned thing he could do about it from the bridge.

"Korri," he called to Fontenot. "We have company. Singh's crew has a shuttle docked at the lock we used, and it won't take them more than a few minutes to break through."

"I got it." She sounded way too calm. "One emergency at a time, Ash."

He grunted a humorless laugh, then stepped back to the Helm control and began swinging the ship's course around gradually, trying to get closer to the *Gitano*. He shifted his carbine off his back and held it against his right hip, waiting, wondering which weapon he'd get to fire first.

Korri Fontenot ran down the passageways of the *Metaurus*, dodging the desiccated lumps of what had once been humans and wondering just how the hell she'd wound up here. When she'd volunteered for the Commonwealth Marine Corps over a century ago, she'd fully expected to die fighting the Tahni...and she very nearly had. Most of her had. After that, after the cease-fire to a war that never ended, she'd gone just as far away from anyone she'd ever known as she possibly could. She'd worked hard to not stay in any one place long enough to make friends or put down roots, trying to find a meaningful way to finish what the Tahni had started.

And then, just like that, she'd let these people pull her into their circle and into their lives and, at the time, she'd finally just decided hell, why not?

No, be honest, she adjured herself. She'd done it because Sandi had reminded her of herself, her younger self. And if she hadn't been able to save that girl, back when death seemed like the better alternative, then maybe she could save this one. And somehow, that idiotic impulse had led to her running through the corpse-littered hulk of a ghost ship, fighting pirates and wondering if some mysterious killing machine wasn't going to get her first.

Fucking serves me right, she mused.

There was Engineering, right where they'd left it, except the bodies were on the deck instead of floating at eye level and she decided she liked them better that way. She sprinted to the power trunk that grew like a tree out of the center of the deck, extending upward from the shielding over the fusion reactor and stretching above into the overhead, disappearing into a maintenance tunnel just wide enough to allow the one-person sled up to service it. And that was just where she needed to go. She twisted her helmet off, knowing she wouldn't be able to look up while she was wearing it, and set it on the deck beside the lift before she boarded. The air was cold, and clammy, and smelled like dust, and she hoped there wasn't some biohazard floating around in it, but there wasn't time to worry about it.

The controls were simple, just a lever that you pushed up or down, which she thought was awfully thoughtful of the Fleet design techs; they usually made even a toilet so complicated that you needed a manual and a two-week course to qualify with it. She pushed upward, and felt the sled lurch into motion, taking her up into the dimly-lit recesses of the access tunnel. The next section up from Engineering was the warp unit, and it was sealed off, far too complicated to repair en route with the tools you could carry on a cruiser.

Not too sealed off to blow the shit out of it, though.

They'd used HyperExplosives, most likely, and you could see the damage it had done even down at the base of the thing. It had done more than take out the Transition Drive, though; it had damaged the port side of the power trunk. She saw the connection for the weapons pods glowing red in the computer-enhanced image projected on her Heads-Up Display; it was a sealed superconductive cable as thick as her arm, plugged into an armored socket set in the side of the trunk.

The socket hung loose, its housing charred and cracked from the explosion; and when she tried to twist the cable's plug to disconnect it the way it was designed, the socket broke off the trunk completely. She muttered a curse and took the cable's plug in one hand and what was left of the socket in the other, squeezed down with as much force as her bionics allowed, and twisted. The plug popped out and the socket shattered and she blurted the curse out loud this time, realizing that the jagged metal shards had sliced through her suit's glove. Not that it mattered here with the life support running, but it was the principle of the thing; you took care of your equipment.

Trying to ignore the ragged hole in the palm of her glove, she yanked the power cable around to the other side of the trunk, the one unaffected by the blast, and found an open socket. She jammed the plug into it, twisting it to the right and hoping it wasn't too damaged to lock in place. It gave a satisfying click, and the indicator above the socket lit up green.

"You're good," she called to Ash over her 'link's ear bud. "You should have power!"

"You're the best, Korri," his response was tight, distracted, as if he were already targeting the weapons. "Get out of there and hold up somewhere safe until I contact you again."

She was already bringing the maintenance sled downward, the metal half-cage rattling and grinding its way down the track, out of the half-lit dusk of the service tunnel and back into the harsh, clinical brightness of the Engineering compartment.

Hope I got it done in time, she fretted, tapping a gloved finger against the control lever, willing the sled to move faster. *Where the hell does he think is safe on this ship? I need to be out hunting down those assholes instead of hiding...*

She had to let her carbine hang at her side to fit into the cage, which was the only reason she didn't open fire reflexively the second the sled stopped. There were seven of them, dressed in the khaki fatigues and body armor of *La Sombra*, Jordi Abdullah's soldiers, all of them armed with identical mini-rocket carbines, all of them levelled at her chest. Standing in the midst of them, a snarl twisting his mouth, was Jagmeet Singh.

"Hello, Ms. Fontenot," he said, gesturing with his Gauss machine pistol for her to toss down her carbine. "I love what you've done with your face."

———

Power surged into the *Metaurus'* weapons systems with a cheerful line of green indicators, and Ash hunted desperately in the tracking screen for the flight of missiles that had been on Sandi's tail. He found them, faint pinpricks of red tracing a reentry path through the atmosphere...and then disappearing from the scope as they rounded the terminator of the moon toward the day side.

He wanted to rage, wanted to pound at the console in futility, but he forced himself to be calm, to trust Sandi's ability to fly her way out of the jam the way she had so many times before. And in the meantime, there was still one other target he could take out his frustrations on. The *Gitano* was trying to run, trying to chase down the *Acheron* and get clear of the cruiser's firing arc, but Ash wasn't going to let that happen. The targeting lock he'd put over the cartel lighter flashed red in the Tactical display and his thumb hovered over the firing control.

"Carpenter." The voice was familiar by now, like a stray piece of food caught in your teeth that your tongue kept seeking out until it was raw and sore. "I know you're probably getting ready to do something stupid, so let me show you why it's a bad idea."

A 2-D visual transmission popped up on his helmet's HUD, and through the video pickup of a hand-held 'link, he could see Korri Fontenot, her helmet off, her weapons taken, standing under the guns of two of Singh's troops. Her gaze was narrow and her expression annoyed; if he had come to know her at all as well as he thought, the scowl was probably because she'd let them get the drop on her.

The video's field of view changed as the 'link swung around to show Singh's bifurcated face.

"Give yourself up and meet us in Engineering within the next ten minutes, or she's dead."

Ash glanced back at the *Gitano* beginning to pass clear of the targeting reticle on the tactical screen, and he scowled.

"Sure," he replied easily. "No problem, be right there."

He jammed his thumb into the firing control almost spitefully, just before the cartel ship slipped out of the firing arc of the proton cannon. The weapon had no signature in the near-vacuum, but the computer simulated its passage with a glowing white line of energy not very dissimilar to how it would have appeared in the atmosphere, and that streak of fusion-fed charged particles sliced through the cartel ship's portside weapons pod.

Another second, another dozen meters, and it would have missed entirely; instead, the whole portside of the lighter was swallowed in a globular flare of burning gas from igniting missile propellant and onboard oxygen stores and vaporized metal. The ship began to spin with a quarter of its mass converted to an uncontrollable maneuvering rocket, but Ash was already lunging away from the Tactical station and back over to Helm.

The picture from the cartel was still being broadcast to a corner of his HUD, and he could see Singh's expression change, his eye clouding over with the look of concentration that people got when they were hearing a transmission in their ear bud or an implant mastoid communicator. A snarl began to form on the natural side of his face, but Ash was at the Helm control and he grabbed hold of the restraint harness of the acceleration couch there before he fired the aft starboard maneuvering thrusters at full power.

Lateral g's tried to throw him towards the right bridge bulkhead and he felt his arm nearly yank from its socket as he stopped himself with the seat restraints. The view from the 'link pinwheeled as the device flew out of the hand of whoever had been holding it and tumbled across the compartment. He gritted his teeth and pulled himself back to the control board and cut the lateral thrust, his feet coming back down to the deck.

He fought an urge to run to the lift station and help Fontenot, knowing it would take him at least five minutes to make it down to that level and that things would be over by then. Instead, he sprinted over to the Security station, calling up the holographic video feeds from the different compartments and scrolling through them until he found Engineering, then enlarging it with an expansive motion of his fingers until he could see the details.

The *La Sombra* soldiers were sprawled out on the deck, some trying to get to their feet, some still flat on their backs; the only people standing were Fontenot and Singh. Fontenot was moving, moving *fast*; it was easy to forget how quickly she could move at full power. She swept her carbine and pistol off the floor where she'd discarded them, and kept running, putting the main power trunk and the control consoles around it between her and the cartel troops.

Singh was fast, too, faster than Ash would have imagined, though not quite as fast as Fontenot because she had decades of experience on him. He was shooting, his Gauss machine pistol held stiff-armed in line with his body like an old duelist, but the rounds were spalling off the power trunk in showers of sparks, keeping Fontenot's head down but not coming anywhere near her.

Unfortunately, that might be enough, Ash worried. If the others recovered while she was suppressed, they could outgun her, outflank her, and end her in short order.

"Shit," he murmured.

Security had to have some sort of systems to take down boarders or mutineers or some such crap. He looked at the control station helplessly, realizing he had no idea. He'd been a pilot on a cutter for nearly his whole career and never once served on a cruiser. Some controls were universal, like the warp unit or the reactor or the drive, but they didn't put stun-field generators or sonic disruptors on a ship built for a crew of two.

Maybe he could use the drives and thrusters again to distract them? The thought was still bouncing from one side of his head to the other when he saw it...or rather didn't quite see it.

It was big, he could tell that by seeing how it towered over the cartel soldiers, and it was dark and it was fast and it was...*fuzzy*? It seemed as if the optical pickups didn't want to focus on it, like they didn't believe it was there. What he could see of it was a blur, and that blur slammed into the *La Sombra* gunman closest to the door; and when it did, the man disappeared in a spray of blood that seemed to explode out of him.

Before the first body had hit the ground in a tangle of exposed bone and ripped flesh, the next had already died, and then the gunfire erupted in a panicked paroxysm that filled the whole compartment with the angry fireflies of minirockets, streaking everywhere and hitting nothing. Except the power trunk and the engineering controls.

Something exploded in an electrical arc that whited out the camera pickup, and then the holograph faded with a snap and every control panel went suddenly and irrevocably dark. Ash was left staring at nothing, eyes wide, mouth agape.

"What the fuck was that?" he muttered reflexively. But he knew what it was before he asked the question. It was what had killed the crew. It had survived the cold and the vacuum and six years on this ship.

And it was in here with them.

CHAPTER EIGHT

Korri Fontenot couldn't remember the last time she'd been scared. Momentarily alarmed, sure. Startled, of course. But not bone-deep, hind-brain, gut-level scared. She'd been close to death so many times, seen so many people die around her, some horribly, that the fear of death didn't hold sway over her.

This thing scared the shit out of her. She could barely see it with her natural eye, and what was even scarier was that she *couldn't* see it with her bionic ocular. It was a blur, a fuzziness in space that wasn't quite there. It threatened to freeze her in place with panic, and when the gunfire began she nearly joined it. But she'd been around a long time, and it had taught her that there were some fights she couldn't win.

She ran.

She wasn't sure if the thing would catch her, if it would ignore Singh and the cartel soldiers and chase after her, if she'd take a mini-rocket in the head the second she stepped out into the open; but she knew for certain that if she stayed where she was, she was worse than dead. She was a lot harder to rip apart than a Norm, and it would hurt so much more...

So, she gave into the terror and ran, ran so fast that everything around her was a blur, ran so fast that she could feel her cybernetics abrading the flesh that had grown around them over the decades, so fast that the servomotors in the joints began to heat up. Time slowed, the thirty meters across from the power trunk to the Engineering hatchway stretching out to a dozen kilometers, twenty, a freaking marathon. Each mini-rocket munition from the cartel carbines seemed to crawl by at a pace sedate enough that she could count the stabilizing fins, the sound of their engines lost in the audio exclusion of tachypsychia.

And the thing was *still* moving too fast to get a good look at it, just a vague sense of a bipedal, bilaterally symmetrical humanoid shape. She thought it was looking at her, thought she had the impression of black, shark-like eyes staring through her, but then a mini-rocket actually struck it and it turned toward the shooter and she was through the Engineering hatchway. Time caught up with her in a cacophony of sound and a blinding flash of light so bright it threw shadows a hundred meters up and down the central passageway, and she could smell the smoke though she didn't dare look back to see it.

"Ash," she gasped into her 'link pickup, out of breath for the first time in nearly as long as she could remember. "Ash, are you there?"

"Korri, thank God! Are you out of there? Are you okay? I lost visual..."

"That thing," she said, "it's got to be what killed the *Metaurus'* crew...it's still alive. And there was some kind of explosion..."

"I know," he interrupted. "I was watching. And whatever blew up, it's fried the bridge controls. The ship is locked into our current course and acceleration and I can't control her. We're going to de-orbit in less than thirty minutes."

He sounded amazingly calm about it, she thought; but of course, he *was* a pilot and they always tried to sound calm.

"Can you contact Sandi?" She hoped she didn't sound desperate. She would have been damned embarrassed if the pretty-boy pilot was calmer than she was.

She'd reached the lift station, but she ignored the lift cars; there was no way in hell she was getting into one of those when the ship was out of control and the power trunk was damaged. Next to the cars, though, was the Central Access Tube, a padded, vertical passageway used when the ship was in micro-gravity...with ladder rungs down one side, in case of power failure. She'd used it to reach Engineering in the first place, but it wouldn't be so easy with her full one hundred and twenty kilograms weighing her down.

"She went into the atmosphere to try to lose the missiles. There's no way she could get here in time even if I could contact her." He paused and she slung her carbine over her shoulder and grabbed the safety rail, swinging her legs out onto the ladder rungs.

"We need to get to the life pods in the docking bay," she said, grunting more from the feeling of her considerable mass hanging over the stories-tall drop than from any physical effort.

"There'll be more *La Sombra* troops down there," he warned, and she could tell from the effort in his voice that he was running. "Their shuttle's docked at the service lock."

"You got any better ideas, I'm all ears."

"I'll be there as quick as I can," he told her. She was sure if she could afford to look up, she'd see him somewhere far above her, getting ready to climb down from the bridge level.

"Take your time," she muttered, concentrating on descending the narrow rungs. "You got the rest of your life to get there."

———

About ten meters down the Access Tube, Ash was wishing he'd taken off his suit's helmet. It wasn't just the sweat that was pouring down his face and his inability to wipe it off, and it wasn't just the increasingly intolerable sound of his own, labored breath loud in his ears. It was that it was damn near impossible to look down at his own feet, and when you were climbing down a ladder hundreds of meters long, you really wanted to be able to see your feet once in a while. He blinked, thinking his helmet filters were going out until he realized that it was the Access Tube lighting flickering as the power fluctuated from the shorts in the main trunk.

After another fifty meters, he fell into a rhythm, hitting every other rung; that seemed to work well until his forearms and fingers started to cramp. He was in fairly good shape, at least as good as he could be when he spent half the time on a small starship, but the vacuum suit was really designed for microgravity and it was way too heavy to be crawling down an Access Tube with the full weight of Earth pulling down on him. He kept going, knowing time was running out, but every step downward was torture and he knew it was only a matter of time before his grip gave out, and at one gravity acceleration, he'd wind up at the bottom of the vertical tunnel with a shattered spine.

Maybe it hadn't been the smartest thing to try to maneuver this ship when the biggest thing he'd ever flown was a hundred-meter-long cutter.

Now you tell me, he griped at himself.

"Korri," he called, his voice a dry rasp. He took a second to suck water from the nipple inside the helmet and tried again. "Korri, are you still in the Tube?"

Nothing. He was hoping Fontenot might be able to tell him how much farther he had to go, since he couldn't look down. He saw that he was passing the purple markings of the main crew quarters, but he couldn't for the life of him remember what level they were on or how far past the docking bay they were located. Was it level three? Four? There were markings there, and maybe they gave the distance, but the lights were dim and even though his helmet had IR capability, the lettering seemed blurry and indistinct.

Shit, he thought. *I should have paid more attention in those Academy familiarization classes.*

But he'd wanted to be an assault shuttle pilot, and after that a missile cutter pilot, and serving on one of the massive cruisers had seemed to be just about the most boring thing in the galaxy.

Not as boring as I'd hoped for.

His forearms were screaming at him by the time he made it past Engineering. He told himself that this was it, that the docking bay was the next level, but unfortunately it wasn't a straight-line difference; there was a big gap between the two, a gap filled by the Teller-Fox warp unit.

How big was one of those things on a cruiser? He couldn't even come close to remembering. Maybe the size of his whole starship? Bigger?

"Korri," he called again, this time louder. *Damn it, answer me!*

"Shut up," she hissed so softly he barely heard her. "There's ten of them down here patrolling."

And she wasn't wearing a helmet, which meant there was a chance they could hear his transmission over her ear bud if he was loud enough.

A spasm went through his right arm and he had to let off the ladder rung, putting all his weight on his feet and swinging to the side with just his left hand holding on. He swayed back and for just a moment, he was able to look up, back to the Engineering entrance maybe twenty meters above him.

Something crouched curled up above him, hanging off the side of that entrance, something big and vaguely humanoid, something so black that it seemed to absorb all the light around it and change shadows to gloomy midnight. Black eyes glinted and blood dripped fitfully off of flat black claws, spattering off Ash's chest.

He screamed and let go, dropping off the ladder, surrendering himself to the fall, to broken bones and certain death just to get away from the thing...and hit the bottom of the Tube one second later, his feet going out from under him and his butt slapping into the padded surface there, jarring him painfully up and down his spine, but far from fatal. He had, he realized dully, been less than two meters from the end.

The thing, the creature, the whatever-the-hell-it-was began to uncoil on its perch and Ash moved. Gathering his legs beneath him, he bolted out the hatchway into the corridor by the docking bay lift station, forgetting his carbine, forgetting his sidearm, forgetting Fontenot...and forgetting the ten *La Sombra* soldiers she'd told him about.

He saw them the second he sprinted into the docking bay; they were scattered around with the look of restless boredom troops anywhere had when they were left to guard the rear while someone else gets to head into combat. There was no decision to be made, he never even considered stopping; what was behind him was inhuman terror and these were just some guys with guns. The only concession he made to their presence was to adjust his split-second search for a hiding place to include good cover from gunfire.

That narrowed things down and he headed straight across

the docking bay to the heavy gantry of a cargo crane. Designed to unload heavy cargo shuttles, the gantry of the crane was anchored to a gearbox of solid metal molecularly sealed to the surface of the deck and it was the most bulletproof thing he could find on short notice, with the only downside being that it was twenty meters away and they were shooting at him.

Ash ignored the hail of wild gunfire, ignored the flare of vaporized metal splashing off the deck around him and spalling off the far bulkhead, but he couldn't ignore the round that hit him high in the right side of his back. There was a spear of white-hot pain that knocked him forward off balance, tumbling off his feet and hitting hard, face-first. His forehead bounced off the inside of his helmet, and even with the padding there, he still hit hard enough to see stars swimming across his vision.

There was no way he was going to be able to get up before they finished him off, but then he was moving, sliding across the deck on his side, and it took his fogged brain a moment to realize he was being dragged. He pushed himself up, crying out as the motion caused intense pain in his back, and followed the pull forward to cover, behind the body of the crane motor.

His vision cleared enough to see that it was Fontenot, and she was leaning out, returning fire with her laser carbine. He felt a rush of fear and grabbed at her shoulder.

"No, stop!" he yelled, and was dimly aware that she wouldn't be able to hear him through his helmet. Impatient, he reached up and yanked the yoke seal levers on either side and twisted the helmet off of him, feeling a cold rush of air against his sweat-soaked face. "Stop!" he shouted over the crackle-snap of the laser weapon. "Don't shoot!"

"Why the fuck not?" she snapped, glaring at him with her natural eye.

"Because it's coming!" he insisted, and he realized with a

start just how desperate and panicked he sounded. "It was in the Tube!"

He actually thought he could see her face pale and she pulled back around, bringing the muzzle of her carbine up to a high ready. This close, he could feel the heat radiating off its cooling vanes, could see the emitter glowing red and hear the popping of the cooling metal in surreal detail. He could hear the mini-rocket warheads smacking into the metal plating on the other side of the crane motor with a ringing squeal that seemed to set his teeth on edge.

Then, abruptly, the incoming fire ceased and the screaming started. Ash squeezed his eyes shut instinctively, feeling as if the sound was reverberating through the metal and into the wound on his back, then he nearly yelled himself when he felt Fontenot grabbing him and yanking him away from the crane motor.

"Come on!" she urged him, keeping hold of his arm as she began trotting across the compartment. "We have to get to the life pods."

It seemed crazy to him, rushing out into the chaotic nightmare of the docking bay, but he knew she was right; they had minutes before the cruiser hit atmosphere and burned up quite spectacularly. He tried to run as fast as he could, tried not to look at what was going on only twenty or thirty meters away; but it drew his gaze like the wreckage of a crashed shuttle, and he couldn't turn away.

Three of the cartel troopers were dead already, ripped apart like the cattle carcasses they still processed on Periphery colonies or the Pirate Worlds. He remembered the first time he'd seen it, the meat packing shops out at Grenada and Loki and Sylvanus, how horrified he'd been; it had seemed barbarous and bloody. Later, he'd come to appreciate the honesty of it, the way it seemed closer to his roots as a human, but this...this went even further down the chain, back to when humans were prey, when night was the enemy and early man huddled around the fire in fear of creatures that would drag people out of their bedrolls.

The cartel troops were shooting again, at the creature this time, but their rocket rounds were zipping back and forth all over the compartment, and Ash wasn't sure if they were just missing or if the rounds simply had no effect; he could believe it either way. The lights in the docking bay were flickering as the power fluctuated, and it seemed with every wink of darkness, another of the *La Sombra* crew died. After the fifth of them fell, the situation seemed to reach some sort of critical mass and the others ran.

Unfortunately, they ran towards the same place that Ash and Fontenot were heading, the service bay, where their shuttle was docked, and where the life pods were located. Fontenot must have seen it, too, because she sped up and he could barely match her servo-powered pace; he stumbled but she kept him upright with a hand under his left arm, and kept him moving. He risked falling again to look to the side as they approached the hatchway to the service bay, and he could see the terror in the eyes of the two women and three men left alive, sprinting their way.

He was looking straight at the creature when it caught the last one in line, could see the glint of purpose in its black, soulless eyes and could see when the desperate hope left the woman's face and was replaced by the horrifying certainty of death.

Then he and Fontenot were through the hatchway and he was spared having to see the end. Fontenot skidded to a halt and he stumbled into her back, crying out as the impact wrenched at his wound. The airlock to the *La Sombra* shuttle was yawning open, but a young man dressed like a pilot was blocking the way, sweeping a carbine back and forth nervously, a look of uncertainty beneath his patchy, blond beard.

He was a criminal, part of a group who'd come here to capture or kill them, but at third and last, he was a human and the thing coming behind them was *the other*.

"Get inside!" Ash told him. "Get that shuttle ready to launch!" He took a step toward the airlock, but Fontenot stopped him, urging him the other direction, toward the life pod banks.

"It'll take too long," she threw tersely over her shoulder, tipping up the cover for the flashing red button located over the nearest pod, then mashing it down with her fist.

A siren filled the compartment, warbling plaintively, and the thick, metal hatch covering the pod swung outward with a pneumatic hiss. Fontenot pushed it wider, then turned toward him, one hand grabbing hold of the carry handle on the back of his suit like she was about to throw him inside. Her head snapped around as two of the cartel soldiers rounded the corner into the service bay, with the creature right on their heels.

He could see it more clearly now, could see the chitinous texture of the armor plates that seemed like natural growth more than technology, could see the flat, featureless expanse of a face that looked, by contrast, more like a helmet if not for the eyes set in it, if not for the oversized jaws filled with matte-black metallic teeth. They clacked together as he watched, almost too fast to see, an unending castanet chittering.

Ash got the distinct feeling that it could have caught them faster, could have killed them all in a moment without even being seen, but it was toying with them, drawing things out, enjoying their fear. An arm that seemed too long for its torso flashed out and a head flew clear of a body, trailing double braids that whipped around like rotor blades. The corpse fell to its knees and collapsed forward, splashing red across the deck in front of it, leaving just one of them still standing.

It was a woman, her face lean and horsey, a puckered scar running down from her forehead to her chin on the left side. Her hair was long and curled and wild, rainbow colors woven into it, and she wore a look of intense determination to live. She was only steps from the airlock when the thing grabbed her by an arm. Ash clutched at his holstered pistol, knowing he'd never be able to get his carbine unslung in time, and also knowing either was probably about as useful as spitting and harsh language.

Something smacked into the creature's head, actually causing a reaction, a flinch as if it might have hurt, and Ash's eyes went to the bay's main hatch. Standing there, backlit by the flickering overhead illumination of the docking bay, was Singh. His black body armor was shredded across the left side of his chest and his left arm, exposing the black metal of his bionics, scored white by the impact of the thing's claws. Deep cuts went across his chest just past those score-marks and blood was seeping out to soak what was left of his clothes. The natural portion of his face was as much of a mask as the cybernetic half, not afraid of this creature, not afraid of death. His Gauss machine pistol was stretched out, unwavering, laying down a spray of tantalum needles at the head and neck of the creature.

Ash hoped against hope that the weapon could penetrate its armor, but apparently Fontenot wasn't going to wait around to find out. With a massive strength anchored through spinal reinforcements into her mechanical legs, powered by servomotors in every joint and energized from an isotope reactor buried inside her thigh, she tossed a hundred and forty kilograms of Ash and his weapons and vacuum suit bodily through the elevated hatch of the life pod.

Ash felt nausea and agony course through him as the brief

flight ended with his shoulder fetching up against the bulkhead of the escape boat, but he clenched his teeth and forced himself to move clear and let Fontenot climb in beside him. There was room for six inside the capsule, and she leapt through the hatch without touching it, landing with a weighty thump on the opposite side from him, grabbing the edge of the hatch to arrest her motion.

He could see her begin to lunge forward to close the hatch behind them, but before she could, something flew past her, through the pod's hatch, to impact on the padded curve of the acceleration couch that ran the circumference of the capsule. Ash jumped, reaching for his pistol again, sure it was the creature coming in after them, but instead he saw immediately that it was Singh. Ash wasn't sure if he'd jumped through the hatch or been thrown, but he seemed unconscious and maybe dead and his weapon was somewhere back in the service bay.

The hatch slammed shut with a powerful yank of Fontenot's hand and then Ash felt a sharp jolt as the explosive bolts blew and kicked them out the side of the cruiser into space.

"Strap in," Fontenot told him, following her own orders over on the other side of the pod.

Trying to ignore the red-hot knives in his back, Ash did as he was told and slipped into one of the six sets of restraint harnesses, cinching them down tight. The pod's main rockets would be firing in seconds to take them down through the moon's atmosphere, and when they did, it wasn't going to be a pleasant ride.

"What about him?" Ash wondered, nodding at Singh's insensate, motionless form, still slumped against the far bulkhead.

"The hell with him," Fontenot snapped. "If he lives through this," she waved a hand around them demonstratively, "we'll worry about him then."

———

Del Grant was trying very hard to remind himself that he was a *La Sombra* pilot used to danger, trying very hard not to scream and piss himself, but it seemed like a losing battle. The minute he'd seen that...*Jesus, that thing, whatever the hell it is*...he'd thrown down his gun and ran for the shuttle's cockpit, forgetting even to close the airlock until he'd reached the cockpit. He'd abandoned anyone else who might have been alive on that old piece of Space Fleet junk and yanked his bird off the service lock without bothering to retract the docking umbilical.

The shuttle's utility lock was ruined but he didn't give a shit; he didn't have a ship to dock with, anyway. They'd blown up the *Gitano* and his only hope was to get down to that moon. They'd said it was habitable, or some small part of it was, barely, and hell, anything was better than staying on that ship.

He felt his breathing slowly creeping back to normal the farther he got from it, felt his heart rate coming down as he realized that he'd actually lived through it. Everyone else had died, but Del Grant was still alive, by God! Now he just had to come up with a plan to stay that way. Getting back to La Hondonada, that was going to be harder, but staying alive was the first step. He thought he'd spotted a place down there on the southern continent where there could be a settlement of some kind, and that's where he was going to head.

Taking the shuttle down through the atmosphere was a comforting routine, years of training and experience washing away the fear and panic and sheer awe-struck disbelief. He always heard George's voice when he got scared. George Klein had been flying for the cartel for decades and he'd become Jordi Abdullah's informal flight instructor for new pilots. He'd had to clean the old man's house and chauffeur him around town and basically be his servant for nearly three months before George had agreed to teach him how to fly.

The old man would drone on and on in the cockpit, sitting beside you in the trainer's seat, his voice low and monotone, and you had to strain to hear what he was saying. But being still and quiet made you calm, made you focus on his words and on what you were doing, like hypnosis.

"Don't worry about the ship getting blown up," he imagined George intoning, "don't worry about the monster killing everyone, just concentrate on flying the bird."

The swollen clouds finally parted a thousand meters or so above the icy, glacial plains and he could see the valley ahead, as green as anything got on this world, glowing gently in the morning light. At the foot of a mountain pass, it was free of the pack ice that covered so much of the moon, and he'd bet from what he'd seen on other planets that it was fed by underground hot springs or maybe even an underground river. He'd noticed it while they were orbiting the moon, noticed the anomalous thermal readings and thought for sure there had to be a human settlement down there.

The landing was textbook, even though he'd never read one; George would have been proud. He cut the belly jets the second the treads kissed the ground and the landing gear settled in without a single bounce. George hated pilots that bounced the gear.

Del had heard that corporate types back in the Core colonies let their computers land the birds for them, let them fly them too, most of the time. He didn't know how they could even call themselves pilots; they were just along for the ride. He flew with his hands and his eyes, not even using implant jacks. He was a real pilot.

He powered back his acceleration couch and unstrapped, flexing his knees experimentally as he stood; the gravity here was on the light side, maybe half standard. Now that he was down, he had decisions to make. Should he go to the settlement and ask for help, hat in hand, or should he try bluffing them? The shuttle had a Gatling laser turret and not much else in the way of armament, but maybe he could get them to believe he had air-to-ground nukes? Then he could see if they had a way to get a message out of the system and see if there was any way at all he could get home.

Del was still turning the idea over in his mind when he stepped out of the cockpit and jerked to a halt like a column of stone, Lot's wife regarding Sodom. Black eyes froze him in place, set in a mask of featureless black, still as a statue. Then the mask split in two amid rows of black, sickled-shaped teeth and a rush of hot, rancid breath and he couldn't think, couldn't move, couldn't even control the whimper that escaped his throat involuntarily.

He didn't see the thing's arm move, just felt the sledgehammer-blow across his chest and then he was flying across the compartment and slamming into the bulkhead. He heard the bones snapping in his shoulder and back but the pain washed over his whole body, refusing to be localized. He slid to the deck, unable to move, his head propped up by the bulkhead. His eyes swam in and out of focus and he caught a glimpse of white bone protruding from his chest. He should have felt afraid, should have felt sick, but before he could process the data, that image blurred away and he saw the creature again.

It was by the utility lock, clawing at something on the bulkhead. Through the fog of agony and confusion that had settled over him, Del could only stare at the thing, uncomprehending. Then he heard a grinding hiss and felt a rush of chill wind, and some small part of his mind that was still capable of rational thought realized that the creature had managed to open the utility airlock. It paused and looked back at him, tilting that featureless face to the side, and there was something so very familiar about the motion, something not at all inhuman.

The last thing that Del Grant saw before blood loss and shock claimed him was the creature stepping out of the airlock and into the light of day.

CHAPTER NINE

"Huh," Sandi grunted, her voice muffled by the heavy scarf over her face. She leaned close to Kan-Ten and shouted over the thunderous wind gusts playing across the snow-covered hills. "Doesn't look as bad as I thought."

"Is it flyable, then?" The Tahni was almost unrecognizable under layers of cold-weather gear and poorly-fitting goggles; his people preferred a warmer climate.

Well, so do I, usually.

She had been able to manage with goggles, a scarf and a hooded jacket with internal heating circuits, but each gust of wind seemed to blast right through any gap in her clothing and pierce to her core. She'd thought about putting on a vacuum suit, but it would have been hard to get a good look at the underside of the ship with a helmet on.

"In space, sure," she answered Kan-Ten's question. "In the atmosphere..." She sighed heavily. "Not so much. The vectored thrust nozzles are pretty much fucked."

You could see it with the naked eye, the charred, cracked metal, pieces broken and lost to the storm on their way down. It was her fault, but it wasn't as if they'd had a choice. She'd overheated the belly jets on their wild descent and between the frigid cold and the overload of pressure, all four had ruptured. They'd been damn lucky that the jets had lasted long enough to get the *Acheron* most of the way to the ground first.

Most of the way. The cutter had dropped like a stone from a distance of three or four meters, and one of the landing treads was buried in its suspension. It probably wouldn't retract even if they could have taken off. If she was being honest with herself, when she'd been stunned into brief unconsciousness by the impact, she hadn't expected to wake up again.

"Can we fix it?" It was a reasonable question, and she knew that she was not the best at reading Tahni intonations, but she could have sworn she heard an almost-human skepticism in Kan-Ten's voice.

Packed snow crunched under her boots as she walked around, getting another view of the portside jets. The ship was in a meter-deep crater that the landing thrusters had burned through the snow, but the pack beneath that was still just as solid and still not down to the soil below.

"Theoretically. We have a small fabricator in the hold, and enough raw material to turn out new nozzles." It was one of the things they'd wasted Captain Fox's money on, and she would have probably forgotten it was there if she hadn't spent most of an otherwise-boring day in T-space arguing with Ash about whether it was worth the space it took up.

She ran a quick calculation in her head, staring at the ruined vectored thrust jets.

"It's going to take days. Maybe two or three. At least five or six production runs for each assembly, times four. And that's not counting sleep, which I'll need eventually."

"Could I not help?" Kan-Ten wondered.

"Sure," she said easily. "You start studying up on avionics

and stress tolerances and get back to me when you're done. Shouldn't take more than a month or so."

"I sense you're not being serious."

"Then you're better at reading humans than I am at reading Tahni." She felt a gust of frigid air find a new and even more uncomfortable gap in her jacket and she clutched her arms to herself, shivering. The hills around them were uninterrupted rolling mounds of pure-white snow gleaming in the morning light, and the sky was a brilliant blue. She hoped to hell no major storms rolled in, because that would make this whole procedure a million times harder.

"I'm going to go get started programming the fabricator," she told Kan-Ten, turning and stepping back onto the belly ramp. "You keep trying to contact Ash and Korri."

"There is no sign of the cruiser in orbit," Kan-Ten pointed out. "Do you believe they made it off?"

"Yes," she said without hesitation, almost stepping on his last words. She stopped on the ramp and turned back to face him as he was stepping up behind her. She yanked off her goggles despite the bitter cold and fixed him with a hard glare. "Yes, I do believe it, and until I find out different, I'm going to go on the assumption that they did. And so are you."

She stamped back up the ramp, barely hearing his reply.

"Aye, ma'am."

———

Light streamed through the single porthole in the life pod's hatch; Ash tried to raise his head up from the padded acceleration couch to get a look outside, but he tasted blood in his mouth and reconsidered. Every square centimeter of his body hurt, starting with the wound in his back and spreading out from there, and movement seemed like a bad idea.

He decided that the escape capsule had landed askew, tilted maybe thirty or forty degrees to starboard and tilting him backwards at that same angle, which made raising himself up even harder and staying in place an even more comfortable proposition. Fontenot was hanging canted off to her left in her harness, looking decidedly less comfortable and not very happy about it, while Singh was bruised and bleeding and slumped against the hatch, but at least he was unconscious so he wasn't complaining about it.

"Are you okay?" Fontenot asked him.

Without waiting for his reply, she yanked at the quick release of her restraints and grabbed at the straps to keep herself from falling off to the side when they cut her loose. The harness brought her up short and she lowered herself to the seat next to Ash. He felt the life pod shift with her movement and he had a moment's panic that they were about to tumble off a cliff, but it settled back down into a slowly diminishing rocking motion.

"I'm great," Ash sighed. "Let's go on that ride again, Mommy."

Fontenot snorted with amusement, pulling his restraints free. He tried not to cry out as she maneuvered his arms out of the harness, then leaned him forward against her, checking his injury. He felt her yanking at something on his shoulder, jerking him painfully backward, and this time he grunted as agony shot through his back.

"Jesus, Korri," he said, trying to yell it but only managing a gasp.

He was about to demand what she was doing, but then he saw her lowering the life support pack from his vacuum suit to the floor of the capsule, having disconnected it from his back. There was a hole the width of a stylus burned through it where it had covered his right shoulder, probably from the warhead of a rocket carbine.

"You got lucky, Carpenter," she told him, probing at the wound and eliciting another gasp. "The backpack took most of the hit. You've got a nasty burn where the plasma penetrated it, but it's not deep, just painful."

"Yeah," he moaned as she set him back against the seat. "I noticed." Knowing the wound wasn't serious, he began working his shoulder to loosen it up, gritting his teeth against the movement of the burned flesh.

"Where the hell did we land, anyway?" he wanted to know. "How far are we from the thermal signature I saw?"

"I *tried* to steer us close to it," Fontenot said, gesturing contemptuously at the center console and the rudimentary joystick mounted there that was the only attitude control the pod had. "This thing ain't exactly an assault shuttle, though. I *think* we're somewhere within a few kilometers." She shrugged. "We can get out, take a look around, see if we can see any sign of habitation."

"Yeah," Ash agreed, forcing himself up and getting his feet underneath him, then pausing to get his breath back and compartmentalize the pain. "I'll get right on that." He motioned down at Singh. "Is he alive?"

Fontenot lowered herself down beside the bounty hunter, rolling him over on his back and frisking him thoroughly before she bothered to check his vitals. She found a backup gun tucked into a pocket of his chest armor and tossed it up to Ash, who examined it carefully. It was a slugshooter, primitive and long-obsolete but no less deadly for that. He tucked it in a thigh pocket, then watched as she also produced a monomolecular-edged knife, a vibroshiv and a monowire whip, jamming the weapons into pockets of her own vacc suit.

Finally satisfied that Singh was disarmed, she touched a control on her suit's sleeve display and held her left hand over the bounty hunter's neck, letting the medical diagnostics read his heart rate, respiration and body temperature. When the sleeve display blinked, she withdrew her hand and held the device up so she could read it.

"He's alive." She sounded disappointed. "Pulse is strong, breathing is regular if a bit shallow. He probably has a serious concussion, so maybe there's a brain bleed that'll kill him." She sniffed disdainfully. "If we wait that long."

Her right hand balled into a fist, and Ash lunged forward, extending a hand.

"No, wait."

She scowled at him.

"What, you suddenly have warm feelings for this piece of shit? He's been trying to kill us for months now, in case the hard landing scrambled your brains."

"I know," he insisted, tripping over his own thoughts as he tried to sort them out and put them into words. "It just..." He shook his head. "It feels wrong."

"And you're all of a sudden Saint Ashton?" she demanded, her voice and expression incredulous. "You decide in the last month that you're a pacifist or something? Hell, you killed the guy's wife; finish off the family and put him out of his misery!"

He winced at the words, knowing it was brutal truth. So why didn't he want her to finish off Singh? They'd have to kill him eventually, or let him kill them. The bounty hunter wasn't going to give up, not after his wife had died in the ship-to-ship fight with Ash; it had driven him over the edge, and the edge hadn't been that far away to begin with.

"I can't explain it, Korri," he admitted. "Maybe it feels like..." He shook his head helplessly, not liking the phrase but lacking anything more appropriate. "...bad karma."

Fontenot rolled her eyes, the bionic one following the motion of the natural one.

"All right, all right." She raised her hands in surrender. "But

I'm not dragging him over the fucking snow while we look for this mythical settlement of yours. If he freezes to death, it wasn't me."

She stood from the motionless form of the bounty hunter, spitting on the man's back as she slapped the hatch control. The round mass of metal popped its seal with a hiss of escaping air and it wasn't open a centimeter before Ash felt the knife-edged cold of the wind sweeping into the pod, making him wish he still had his helmet. It had burned up along with the *Metaurus*, and he felt a horrifying hangover fear from a career as a Fleet officer that someone was going to try to make him pay the government back for their billion-dollar cruiser.

They'll have to catch me first.

Light flooded the inside of the pod through the open hatchway and he could see patches of deep blue sky above them, crowded on all sides by grey, dismal clouds. He grabbed the back of the acceleration couch and steadied himself against the rocking Fontenot had caused when she climbed out of the hatch. With the pendulum swing of the capsule, the blue skies and grey clouds wobbled downward with tantalizing hints of rugged, snow-capped peaks in the distance before hiding them again behind the edges of the hatchway.

He had to wait until the motion died down again before he threw a leg over the side and followed her, hunting blindly for the footholds set in the side of the hull as he held on to the edge of the hatchway. Even with the lighter gravity here, he didn't want to put his wounded back through an unassisted drop to the ground. He found the indentations in the hull and lowered himself carefully, ignoring the persistent, annoying flapping sound that was drowning out even the roaring of the wind, and concentrating on his hand and foot placement until he stepped down and his boots sank a couple centimeters into soft, muddy ground.

Past the scorched, blackened metal of the lifepod's hull, past the furrow its impact had made in the soft, loamy ground, he could see the source of the racket: the obscenely cheerful red and white parachute that had cushioned their descent was stretched out in the direction of the gusting wind, yanking in petulant futility against the cables that secured it to the nose of the capsule. He shuddered at the thought of their lives balanced on a few hundred square meters of nylon cloth, then turned away to look at their surroundings.

They were in the valley he'd seen, he was sure of it; the mountain pass loomed ahead of them, a cut between two jagged masses of white, and from the cut sprang the wedge of brown and green. The brown was the soil, while the green was supplied by thick matts of algal growth that spread out of steaming hot pools fed by underground springs. They dotted the landscape all around the valley, most of them surrounded by huge cones from mineral deposits, and the cones in turn covered with more of the fungus. It coated every rock, floated in every pool of water and somehow he was sure it lived even beneath the snow in the distance.

"What the hell is that stuff anyway?" he asked Fontenot. She'd been scanning their surroundings carefully and she turned back at his question. "That algae or whatever it is. I see it all around the Pirate Worlds and even on Periphery colonies, but I never recall seeing it on any of the Core worlds."

She raised an eyebrow.

"They didn't teach you about that shit in your Academy biology classes?" She sounded genuinely surprised.

"We mostly learned about Earth life," he admitted. "And some stuff about the Core worlds, and how their evolution paralleled ours."

"People out here who think about such things---and there aren't too many who have the luxury---call it Predecessor Weed.

The scientific types I've talked to say it's common to every habitable planet and moon in the Cluster except Earth and the Tahni home world." She shrugged. "It's the reason they're habitable in the first place. The Predecessors supposedly engineered the stuff and spread it out over every world that might be the right distance from a star to become even halfway habitable someday."

Ash had heard of the Predecessors, of course; everyone had. They'd been a staple of popular culture ever since the discovery of the carvings on Mars that had pointed human explorer towards the first wormhole jumpgate in the asteroid belt. That gate had led to Hermes, Proxima Centauri's only habitable planet and Earth's oldest interstellar colony, and on Hermes they'd found a map carved into the side of the Edge Mountains with the location of every jumpgate in the Cluster. And that had been the only traces that anyone had *ever* found of the Predecessors, or Ancients. Not one skeleton, not one ruin, not one piece of technology; no one knew where they'd come from, where they'd gone, or what they looked like.

"Every world?" Ash repeated, frowning. "I've lived on three different colonies and never seen the shit."

"On some of them," she explained, "it got out-competed by the stuff it evolved into. On others, we replaced it with Earth life. But it's always there." She cocked an eyebrow. "Why do you think the Predecessor Cult has so many followers?"

He nodded slowly. It was a daunting thought, the idea of some god-like, advanced aliens introducing life across the Cluster hundreds of thousands or even millions of years ago. And they were gone without a trace.

What the hell happened to them?

"We're at the far end of that valley I saw," he said, shaking off the wonder and getting his head back into the present. "I think the readings that could have been a fusion reactor are back that way." He gestured towards the mountain pass, kilometers in the distance. "We should get walking."

He started to take a step forward, but Fontenot caught his arm in an unyielding metal fist. He looked over in surprise and saw her staring at a point only forty meters away, beside a cone of green-covered calcite.

"What?" he blurted.

"Put your hands behind your head and stand very still," she advised him, eyes on the near distance, then followed her own advice, interlacing her fingers behind her neck.

It took Ash a moment to understand what was going on, and when he did, realization came with a jolt of fear also tinged with hope. He moved his hands slowly, putting them behind his head, wincing as the motion tugged at the wound on his shoulder blade. His eyes darted back and forth, wondering where whatever she'd seen was.

It took him a long moment to spot them; their camouflage was excellent, and so was their movement discipline. The closest he'd come to ground troops during the war were the Search and Rescue personnel who shared the carrier *Implacable* with his squadron of missile cutters, but he knew about Recon Marines and he recognized the chameleon camo coating on their armor. They seemed to appear out of the ground, only obvious once they actually moved and separated from the greens and yellows and browns around them.

They rose lithely, one after another like dancers in a ballet, shouldering military Gauss rifles, devastating weapons that fired a tungsten slug the size of a man's little finger at 2,500 meters per second. One round could put a hole through him the size of a basketball and he endeavored not to move a muscle. Getting shot once in a day was enough.

There were nine of them in all, a full squad if he remembered his Table of Organization and Equipment correctly, and they spread out quickly into a semicircular perimeter, ten meters between them, down on one knee. All except one, who walked up to the two of them, his rifle tucked into the crook of his arm like a big-game hunter of the 19th Century. He was tall and broad-shouldered, and when he reached up and pulled off his helmet, the face regarding them with cool curiosity was right out of a recruiting poster, all square jaw and high cheekbones and piercing dark eyes and hair buzzed down to a shadow on his scalp. The rank stenciled in subdued black chevrons on his right shoulder was that of a Gunnery Sergeant.

"Who the hell are you?" he asked them in a voice that would have sounded at home coming from a baritone opera singer. "And how in the name of God did you wind up in a lifepod from the *Metaurus*?"

He motioned back to the two men to his right as he spoke and they moved past Ash and Fontenot toward the open hatch of the escape capsule.

"I'm Ash Carpenter, Gunny. Commander Carpenter, Space Fleet," he added, "retired, kind of. This is Korri Fontenot."

"Sergeant Major, Commonwealth Marine Corps," Fontenot put in, her tone a bit pawky, "pretty fucking past retired and nearly into dead."

"We were..." Ash trailed off, hunting for a word. "We were commissioned by Fleet Intelligence to find out what happened to you and your ship."

"Why wouldn't Fleet Intelligence come out here themselves?" the Gunny demanded, not bothering to give them his name.

"Gunny!" One of the Marines the man had sent to check out the pod barked urgently. Ash resisted an urge to look back at him. "There's a man in here. He's unconscious."

"And he's an asshole," Fontenot contributed over her shoulder.

"Gunnery Sergeant..." Ash looked at the big man questioningly.

"Kamara," he supplied, sounding reluctant.

"Gunny Kamara, I know the Captain died on the ship. Who's the highest ranking survivor?"

"That would be Commander Busick," Kamara told him. "She was the XO."

"Maybe we could save some time explaining and re-explaining," Ash said, "if you could just take me to her and let me tell her the story."

Kamara regarded him appraisingly for a long moment before he slowly nodded.

"All right. Ramirez, Jansen, secure their weapons and zip-tie their hands. Giordano, Shan, carry the wounded." His lip twisted and he sniffed in amusement as he slipped his helmet back on. "Let's let the officers sort this out."

CHAPTER TEN

"No wonder I couldn't see the settlement from orbit," Ash said softly, shaking his head.

Gunny Kamara had led them on a five-kilometer hike back towards the mountain pass, a winding journey around thermal springs and geysers and ponds of meltwater and over layers and layers of algae. It hadn't been a pleasant walk, even in half normal gravity, not wearing vacuum suits and sucking in air that was too thin to be healthy and too near freezing to be comfortable. The Marines carrying Singh hadn't complained though, so he'd kept his mouth shut.

He'd expected to see buildings, or equipment or vehicles, but there'd been nothing until they'd cleared the hot springs and started walking a trail over and between rolling hills of moss-covered soil and algae-coated rock. That's when he'd spotted the opening in the hillside. He'd thought it was a cave at first, though he wasn't certain of how the local geology would have formed one there; but as they walked closer, he'd begun to see that the tunnel was man-made. It was also much larger and farther away than it had looked when he'd spotted it, and it took another five minutes of resolute trudging before they'd reached the buildfoam walls.

They had to be reinforced by some sort of high-strength framework to support the weight of all that dirt and rock over them, he thought. Maybe BiPhase Carbide? But that was expensive, usually reserved for starship hulls and military armor. Transporting heavy, expensive alloy here to some insignificant moon in an isolated system way out at the edge of the Cluster had to have been expensive as all hell and keeping it secret... automated construction equipment? Even more expensive.

"This is some serious shit," Fontenot commented next to him, voice pitched low, and he nodded by way of reply.

Kamara led them through the tunnel into the darkness, and Ash's eyes struggled to adapt to it; he felt like the slow child of the bunch, since Fontenot had thermal and infrared filters in her bionic ocular, and the Marines all had night vision lensing in their helmets' Heads-Up-Displays. He resisted an urge to put a hand to Fontenot's arm for support; his hands were bound tightly behind his back with plastic slip-cuffs. He had stumbled for the second time when one of the Marines took him by the shoulder and guided him to the far wall, where he could see the glowing digital readout of a security lock plate.

Kamara tapped in a code, then peeled off a glove and placed his palm flat against the plate. It flashed yellow for a few seconds before finally going green. Ash hadn't been able to make out the doorway in the shadowy gloom of the tunnel; but when it began to slide open, the yellow glow of interior lights outlined the breadth and height of it, nearly as wide as the tunnel itself. The door opened into what looked like a storage area, stacked high with plastic tubs with government markings.

Not Fleet markings, Ash noted. Most likely procured and supplied by the DSI. Fox had told them they'd been behind the mission, and he had to think they'd constructed the base as well.

The Department of Security and Intelligence was as notorious for the labyrinthian trails of its funding as it was for its incestuous ties to the Corporate Council.

Stacked opposite the full containers were three times as many empty ones. Ash wondered how much food they'd started out with and how much they could have left after six years. This world didn't seem like it had much in the way of raw material for the food processors, so when the soy paste and the spirulina powder was gone, they'd be trying to find some way to eat the algae...or each other.

The storage area was bright, and well-lit, and deserted. Not a soul met them, which surprised Ash. He was sure Kamara had been radioing ahead to the base, and he was just as sure that the arrival of an outsider and the prospect of rescue would be huge news to the survivors. Why wasn't there a crowd? He would have asked, but there was something intimidating about being marched in with his hands cuffed behind him, and he didn't think Kamara was the type to answer questions.

He kept sneaking glances at the open corridor that was the main and the largest exit from the storage room, expecting a crowd of people to come and rubberneck at the new guys, but no one did.

"Take the injured man to the clinic," Kamara told the Marines who'd been carrying Singh. His voice sounded tinny over the helmet's external speakers. "Make sure he's strapped down securely and one of you stay there to guard him."

They didn't carry Singh through the central corridor; instead, they took him off to the right, to what looked like a cargo elevator. Kamara watched them disappear behind the closing doors of the lift before he turned back to Ash and Fontenot.

"Follow me and keep quiet," he instructed tersely.

The broad corridor twisted around like a mountain road, curving downward through switchbacks, with doors randomly spaced on the inside walls of the curves. All were closed, none were labelled, and as they descended level after level, they had yet to encounter a soul.

"Does anyone else live here," Fontenot wondered aloud, "or have they all gone stir-crazy and you've got them locked in the basement?"

"I said keep quiet," Kamara snapped, not pausing in his long-legged stride.

"It's a damn strange way to treat guests, especially the first ones you've had in six years."

Now he did stop, rounding on her.

"Guests don't generally drop in riding one of our own escape capsules. You look a lot more like Pirate World shitbags than Fleet Intelligence agents."

Ash couldn't see the man's face through his helmet's visor, but he was fairly certain the Gunny wasn't smiling.

"Is that why you have everyone cleared out of the area?" Fontenot guessed. "You think we're bandits and you don't want to get their hopes up?"

"I follow orders." The words were biting, with the twist of a sneer to them. "I'd think someone who claims to have been a Sergeant-Major would understand that."

"It's been a while," the old woman said with a grin. "I'm out of practice."

"If you don't shut up," the Marine NCO warned her humorlessly, "I'll have you butt-stroked upside the head and thrown in the brig until the Commander decides what to do with you."

"Oh, I'd like to see you try." Fontenot's grin was cold and challenging and Ash swallowed hard, tensing himself. He knew that she could break the flex cuffs any time she wanted to, and he wondered if the Marines had figured out she was a cyborg.

"Is there a problem, Gunny?"

Ash turned at the voice, and so did the Marine NCO. The man walking up the corridor was short, and homely, and pale, and pinch-faced, and everything Kamara was not. He wore a set of patched and faded blue Space Fleet utilities with a Chief Petty Officer's rank on the shoulder.

"Negative, Chief Weaver" Kamara said after a moment's hesitation. "I was just escorting the prisoners to Commander Busick."

"I don't think it's been established that anyone's a prisoner yet, Gunny," the little man corrected him. "But I'll tell you what." He glanced between Ash and Fontenot. "You take the gentleman to the Commander's office and loan me a couple of your men, and I'll speak to the lady in the primary conference room. That sound good?"

"Yes, Chief." He didn't sound happy about it, but as he'd said before, he followed orders.

"And let's get these cuffs off, Gunny," the CPO told him, his voice gently chiding.

Kamara grunted, but slipped a combat knife out of a sheath on his armored vest and sliced through the plastic cuffs on Ash's wrists. Ash rubbed at them, trying to work feeling back into his hands. The Gunny took a step toward Fontenot but stopped at the sound of a loud snap. She held up the broken plastic binder, wiggling it demonstratively in front of the Marine's face before tossing it on the floor.

"I'm good," she assured him, fists on her hips.

Kamara slammed the knife back into its sheath.

"Ramirez and Jansen, go with Chief Weaver and keep an eye on her. The rest of you with me."

"Behave," Ash adjured Fontenot, eyeing her doubtfully as she followed the CPO down the hallway. Her reply was a disdainful sniff.

The Commander's office was another unmarked door, with

the look of having been repurposed from a storage room or a workshop. There was a hollow, plastic sound to it when Kamara knocked and when the clear contralto called, "Come," the sound penetrated as if the door wasn't there.

The Commander rose as they entered, her chair cheap and plastic and looking distinctly uncomfortable, her desk little more than a folding table with an old, physical keyboard and a work tablet. She was a tall woman who might once have seemed statuesque but now looked too thin and haggard, frayed around the edges. Her light brown hair was longer than regulation by a few centimeters, her fatigues as patched and beat up as Weaver's had been and the creases around her eyes and mouth spoke of years of stress and isolation. She reminded him of a ragged scarecrow, but her blue eyes still seemed clear and perceptive.

"Good morning," she said, coolly casual, as if he were her third appointment on a busy day. "I'm Commander Busick."

She extended a hand and he shook it, feeling Kamara's eyes watching him intently, ready for any hint of a threat to his commanding officer.

"Pleasure to meet you, ma'am," he said. "I'm..."

"Gunny Kamara told me," she interrupted. She cocked her head to the side. "I don't suppose you'd have any proof of your story, would you?"

"Our contact in Fleet Intelligence didn't exactly give us a work order," Ash explained. "But if you think about it, we had to have had the security codes for the *Metaurus* in order to board her in the first place. And where else would we have gotten her life pod?" He brightened suddenly, pulling his 'link off his belt. "But you can see my military ID on my 'link. That'll at least prove I'm telling you the truth about being Fleet."

He handed the device over and she looked at the screen, then held her issue 'link next to it, synching them up and checking his credentials. She shrugged and handed his datalink back.

"You are indeed Commander Ashton Carpenter, Attack Command." She sniffed in amusement. "And if I'm reading your service record correctly, it seems the war ended less than a year after we arrived here. I assume we won." She waved at one of the folding chairs on the other side of the cheap table. "Sit down and talk to me, Commander."

"Ash," he supplied, lowering himself cautiously, not trusting the look of the old, beat-up plastic chair to hold him and the heavy vacc suit. It creaked under him until he got his weight distributed. The woman fell into her own seat carelessly, used to its limitations, he guessed.

"Ash," she repeated, as if testing the word. "I'd very much like for you tell me where your ship is, why you came to be in one of our life pods, and what you saw up there."

"You want to know about the creature," Ash surmised, leaning back and crossing his arms over his chest. Her eyes widened just slightly and Ash felt rather than saw Kamara shifting his position behind him as if he was about to meet an attack.

"It was still alive," he told her, deciding not to bury the lede. "Six years in a vacuum hadn't killed it."

"Jesus Christ." Kamara murmured fervently, and Ash saw him rock backwards as if he'd been struck.

"Tell me," Busick ordered, her palms flat on the table, her voice neutral and tightly controlled. "Start from the beginning and tell me everything."

———

Ash tugged at the collar of his borrowed shirt. It was a size too small, and the fatigue trousers were a size too large, and even the self-fitting combat boots pinched his little toes, but it was all they'd had available and it was definitely better than walking around in the damned vacc suit, or in the burned-through T-shirt and sweat-soaked shorts that were all he was wearing underneath the thing. Kamara had even slapped a bandage over the burn on his shoulder and promised they'd take him to the medical bay to get it treated later. The Gunny had assured him it wasn't serious, and he could take that for all it was worth.

He glanced at the floor display next to the door of the lift car and saw that they were still moving downward, even after what seemed like five minutes.

"How far down does this place go?" he asked, not expecting either Kamara or Busick to respond.

Neither of them had said much since he got through telling them the story of how he and Fontenot and Singh had come to be there. Well, the carefully edited story. He knew that Chief Weaver would be busy asking the same questions of Fontenot and he hoped she would be smart enough to leave off the part where they were all technically wanted criminals.

After he'd brought the story to the present, Busick had shared a long look with Kamara and then said simply, "There's someone you need to talk to."

Then they'd thrown fresh clothes at him, sent him into a bathroom to change and rushed him to the elevator. He still hadn't seen any other crew from the ship or from the base, and he had to think that Fontenot had been right, that they were keeping this under wraps.

"Three hundred meters," Busick unexpectedly answered his question. He glanced over at the woman, but she didn't meet his eyes. Her voice was distant, thoughtful. "That's how deep the crater was."

"What crater?" he wondered. "I didn't see any crater around here when we flew over."

"It's been filled in by tectonic activity," she told him.

"That would take a long time," he mused.

"Hundreds of thousands of years," she agreed, still looking straight ahead at the elevator doors.

"Hey, you know, we should really be trying to contact my ship," he told her, hoping to take advantage of the fact she was talking to him again. "I don't know if she touched down or she's in orbit looking for us or what. If you guys want to get out off this rock, we need to get the word back to the Fleet that you're still alive."

"Not my decision to make."

He frowned at her in confusion.

"You're the ranking military officer, aren't you?"

"This isn't a military base," she pointed out.

No, he realized, it wasn't.

Oh, shit.

The elevator jolted to a sudden halt and the doors slid aside with a sibilant hiss. Ash felt Kamara's hand on his shoulder, guiding him out, and he shot the Marine a dirty look. The man had his helmet off, tucked under his arm, and that recruiting-poster face glared back at him challengingly. Since he was unarmed, and wounded, and would have gotten his ass kicked by the Gunny even if he was armed and unwounded, he moved out of the elevator.

The elevator let them out into an enclosed half-oval of volcanic rock, most of that space taken up by the passenger elevator they'd ridden down and a much larger freight lift station. The curved walls terminated in a hallway that led twenty meters or so down a corridor of unlined rock to a hatchway at least ten centimeters thick, fabricated from what looked like solid BiPhase Carbide. The security seal hung above it, a massive, motorized Sword of Damocles just as thick as the doorway and probably airtight.

"Damn," Ash muttered, looking at the size of the thing. Once it was sealed, he didn't think a nuclear warhead could breach it.

Waiting just inside that intimidating doorway was an equally intimidating woman. She wasn't tall, not more than a meter-six or so, nor was she physically imposing, skinny and slight enough that she made her rumpled and stained civilian casual clothes look baggy. But the face attached to that body had an expression severe enough that Ash wouldn't have wanted to be the first one to talk back to her. She reminded him of one of his Academy instructors, the teacher every cadet was afraid to get.

Her eyes were dark and swirling with what looked to Ash like barely suppressed fury, her stance was confrontational and her severely-bobbed brown hair only added to the whole strict-teacher image he'd built for her. He slowed his pace, forcing Kamara to push him forward as they closed with the woman.

"Commander," the woman said, her accent putting her from somewhere on Earth, probably North America if he was any judge. "Who is this man and why have you brought him to a top-secret lab?"

"Dr. Sanchez, this is Commander Carpenter." He nearly barked an involuntary laugh at how deferential Busick sounded to the civilian. Apparently, he wasn't the only one intimidated by her. "He's part of an investigation team sent here by Fleet Intelligence."

"I don't work for Fleet Intelligence," she interrupted, her voice louder and more strident as she went on. "No one assigned to this installation is under the military at all, as I'm sure you're aware. Whether or not he's from Fleet Intelligence, neither he nor you are allowed in this portion of the base."

"He saw the hybrid," Busick told her. "It was still alive."

That shut her up. Ash expected horror, fear, maybe a bit of awe…but the expression on her face was closer to excitement. He found that profoundly disturbing, along with the blasé attitude she had about the fact that someone had come to rescue them. Like she didn't care about ever leaving.

"Very well," she said after a moment. "*He* can enter. Dr. Nagle will want to question him. You two will have to wait here."

Kamara rolled his eyes, but Busick nodded assent, raising her hands palms up.

"Fine. We'll be right out here."

Sanchez looked Ash up and down skeptically, then motioned for him to follow her, turning and heading back through the hatch without waiting to see if he did. Ash had to jog a few steps to catch up to her, trying to fall into step with her deliberate strides.

Through the hatchway, the featureless volcanic rock gave way to walls lined with white, antiseptic polymer, and each door was heavy, solid and sealed with what looked like DNA-coded security plates. Ash saw a ruddy, round-faced man with curly red hair emerge from one of the rooms, glance at him curiously, then move on down an intersecting hallway to the right without saying a word.

He wanted to ask Sanchez how many people they had working in this place, but he doubted she'd tell him and he knew it would piss her off. He guessed it wouldn't be that many, not on an outpost this remote. With a minimum six-week transit time even from the Periphery and probably twice that to the Core worlds or Earth, you wouldn't want to be hauling replacements in all the time or rotating shifts. A place like this, you'd have to gather a handful of people so dedicated that they wouldn't care about going on leave or visiting family. They passed a single open area near the center of the complex of hallways, a small break room with a food processing unit, three tables and about nine chairs. He nodded to himself, the number of chairs confirming his suspicions.

Finally, the meandering fast-walk through the installation came to a terminus of the circuitous hallways, ending in yet another security hatch, just as big and solid as the first one but sealed shut. Ash's eyes went wide. Just one of the hatches would have cost a fortune to transport out here and install, but two? Sanchez went to a small communications panel set in the wall next to the hatch and pushed a button.

"Yes?" The voice was male, a bit on the squeaky side and also with an accent, possibly European.

"It's Susan. You need to come out."

"Be right there."

Thirty seconds later, the hatch exhaled a hiss of air and began climbing up into the ceiling with the hum of powerful motors. On the other side, the light seemed dimmer and of a different shade than the normal office lighting in the rest of the place, as if it were being filtered. A tall, gangly man stepped through once the hatch had risen to its full height, regarding Ash with obvious suspicion mixed with a curiosity that shone through his fevered blue eyes.

His head was depilated bald, and Ash thought it had to be a style choice. No one who ran an installation like this would be from any colony so far from the Core worlds that they hadn't genetically engineered baldness out of the population. The only hair on his head was a well-trimmed mustache, and his pale, china-white face seemed mild and oddly placid; he reminded Ash of nothing so much as a middle manager in some unimportant Corporate Council office.

"Dr. Nagle," Sanchez addressed the tall man, "this is Commander Carpenter. He works for the Fleet and came here to investigate the *Metaurus*. He was up there earlier today and saw the hybrid." Her voice intensified, that same excitement creeping back into it, her face practically glowing with it. "It was still alive, Adam."

Nagle's gaze sharpened and he took a step toward Ash, which nearly made the pilot take a step backwards instinctively.

"Was it active? Had the prolonged exposure to vacuum and freezing temperatures damaged it? Had it changed forms?"

The questions came rapid fire and Ash had to put a hand up to slow them down.

"I don't know if it's changed," he admitted. "I don't know what it looked like before, or how active it used to be."

"Of course not," Nagle realized, running a hand over his brow. "Come here, come with me."

Ash was hesitant to step through the security seal; they obviously kept it closed, and he didn't like the idea of being trapped on the other side of it. Nagle turned back to him, brow furling with obvious impatience.

"Come on, then, hurry up!"

"Adam," Sanchez said stringently, raising a hand to block Ash's way, "you can't take him back there. It's against protocol."

"To hell with protocol," Nagle snapped, eyes flaring with anger. "Do you really think I care about the DSI after all these years?" He motioned to Ash again, and this time the pilot followed him, worried that if he dawdled any more, Sanchez would grab him and drag him back out.

There was an open platform on the other side of the security seal, its floor a pattern of metal grillwork supporting an array of elaborate machinery that Ash thought might be sensors of some kind, feeding into multiple holographic displays and stacks of quantum computers. A younger man with his hair braided into dreadlocks sat at a simple, metal desk, staring at the displays, feet propped up on the railing that separated the platform from the pit beneath. Ash ignored the man, his eyes fixed on the pit.

Unlike the rest of the facility, the pit wasn't lined with volcanic rock walls; beyond the BiPhase Carbide struts that stabilized the whole structure, the edges of the pit were crumbling sedimentary rock mixed with the blackened remains of the impact which had formed the crater originally, eons ago. Sitting in the center of it all, connected to the sensors with cables, surrounded by scientific equipment Ash couldn't hope to put a name or purpose to, was something big, something broken, something...*alien.*

He didn't know how he knew, he just knew. There was something about the shape of the thing that made it obvious it was designed. No natural object would have the mind-bending curves or the purposefulness that was evident in its form. And that form, that shape...it was indescribable. It didn't seem to have any analog in anything Ash had ever seen. Something, some small part of him that whispered notions into his conscious mind from sources much further down, labelled it a "seed pod." It didn't look more like any seed pod he'd ever seen than it did anything else, but it was just the idea that the shape of the thing planted in his head.

"Breathtaking, isn't it?" Nagle asked, noticing his reaction and smiling in appreciation. "I remember well the first time we saw it..." The tall man trailed off, shaking his head to disperse the memory.

"How long ago did..." Ash trailed off, closed his mouth and then tried again. "How old is it?"

"It's difficult to date exactly, but the rock around it is from 300,000 years ago, minimum." That was the man with the dreadlocks. He didn't turn around, just kept his eyes on the display screens, tracing with a stylus on a pad and watching the motions control lines of numbers filing down from the top of the displays. "It could have drifted through space for hundreds of thousands of years before that, though."

"Dr. Mercier is our resident geologist and physicist," Nagle introduced. "Commander Carpenter is here from the Fleet, David. It seems they've found us, after all this time."

Mercier grunted, actually sparing Ash a glance.

"I hope you brought some real food," he said. "I haven't had real meat in so long, I probably don't even like it anymore, but I'd kill my mother for fresh vegetables."

"He's been aboard the *Metaurus*, David," Nagle said sternly. "He's seen the hybrid."

David's feet came down from the railing and he set his stylus and pad down on the desk, his dark eyes wide.

"You keep calling it 'the hybrid.'" Ash shook his head. "A hybrid of what? Where did it come from?"

"David, bring up the last images we have of her...it." Nagle had corrected himself quickly, but the slip didn't escape Ash's notice. "From just before we loaded the stasis pod on the shuttle."

"Yeah, okay." Mercier sounded subdued as he turned back to the displays and swiped one of the holographic projections clear of the data streams. With his stylus, he tapped one control after another until he found an archived folder filled with still images and videos; then he scrolled through those until he found the date he was searching for.

When the video coalesced on the holotank's projection, Ash nearly jumped back at the sight of it. It was the creature, the one from the ship, except much clearer, its form seemingly more delineated than he remembered. It was humanoid in shape, more human at the joints than a Tahni, he thought, with the regular two arms and two legs and a torso between them, and a head in the right place.

But the head...the face wasn't a face so much as a featureless mask, angled backwards like the front of a helmet. There were protuberances from the crown of the thing, just above the eyes, what he might have called antennae for lack of a better description. They gave the face an almost insectoid appearance, though the mouth spoiled that. The mouth spoiled all sorts of things, including his lunch. It split the thing's face nearly in half, and clacked up and down constantly with a chattering that threatened his sanity, and then there were the damned teeth. They were more like knives than the teeth of any animal that had ever lived, more like some threshing machine for flesh, built to do damage rather than to feed.

The thing's skin looked like a cross between an insect's carapace, a lizard's scales and Recon Marine body armor, again looking more designed than grown, and its color was a flat black that also seemed to shimmer somehow, something not quite visible to the human eye but oh, so close. The arms were long for its torso, longer than a human's would be by proportion, and heavily muscled, and they ended in five-fingered claws, long and razor-sharp, not made for fine manipulation, just for ripping through anything in their way. The feet were five-toed as well, and the talons extending centimeters from each toe looked just as deadly as the ones on the fingers.

In the projected video, the thing was trapped in a small enclosure, somewhere brightly-lit, with flat grey walls of BiPhase Carbide. It didn't seem to like the lights; it swiped at them repeatedly, leaping high enough and hitting hard enough that the picture shook from the impact. It didn't make any sound though, nothing but the endless chattering of its mouth opening and closing, its teeth clacking together.

Mercier touched a control and the clip froze on an image of the thing staring at the video intake, the glint of the light in its beady, black eyes.

"Did it appear any different when you saw it?" Nagle asked.

"It was harder to see," Ash told him. "On the ship's security cameras, it was blurred. Even just looking at it, it didn't seem as clear as it does in that video."

"Yes, our cameras here are adjusted to account for the interference. And no, even after all this time, we still don't know how it does that."

"Dr. Nagle," Ash asked him, slowly and carefully, trying not to sound like an idiot, "did that thing come out of there?" He pointed to the seed pod. "Is it an alien?"

Mercier looked at Nagle, almost as if he was curious how the older man would answer. Nagle rubbed thoughtfully at his chin, as if he was debating how to shape the words.

"Not...*exactly*."

CHAPTER ELEVEN

Sandi wiped sweat out of her eyes, pausing to peel off her vest before she pulled the next section of thruster nozzle out of the fabricator. She was down to a tank top and shorts now, and it was still uncomfortably hot.

You'd think, she mused, taking a drink from a squeeze bulb, *on a planet this damned cold, being too hot wouldn't be a problem.*

But the fabricator put out a lot of heat, and the hold was well-insulated. What it was *not* was well-ventilated, and she'd been down here for hours, ever since she'd managed to get the fabber programmed. Kan-Ten brought her water and food at intervals, but she hadn't yet taken a break. She knew she should, but she was trying to get all the parts for one of the nozzles done before she quit for the day.

"Sandi, do you read?" The voice was coming over the ear bud of her 'link, which was patched into the ship's communications system. It was the most beautiful sound she'd heard in years.

"Ash?" She jumped up from the stool she'd pulled up beside the fabricator, moving quickly to the short ladder leading back up to the utility bay. Cool air washed over her from the vents and she felt her sweat beginning to dry as she jogged back to the cockpit. "Ash, is that you?"

"Thank God you're all right." She could hear the sigh in his voice. "The last we saw, you had a flight of missiles on your tail and you were heading down."

"Well, we *are* down," she told him, hands spinning the pilot's acceleration couch around on its mount, "and it's going to take a couple days of repairs before we can get back up. Where the hell are you two?"

He hesitated a moment before he replied. "There's a research installation here," he told her, finally. "I'm including the exact coordinates as an attachment to this signal. The survivors of the *Metaurus* are down here; they came down in the missing shuttle. Korri and I got off the ship on an escape capsule, and they found us after we landed. The ship's XO is in charge of the crew, but the research team is all civilians and Commander Busick had to get the program chief's okay to let me call you."

"Well, what the hell are they researching all the way out here?"

There was a longer pause this time, and she heard muffled voices in the background, arguing maybe. Finally, she thought she heard a man's voice say something like "What difference does it make now?" and then Ash returned to the line.

"There's an...artifact here," he related slowly, as if the words resisted being spoken aloud. "It's some sort of weapon, they think, some kind of biotechnology and cybernetics combined into a...hive, maybe. It crashed here like hundreds of thousands of years ago, and it was damaged on impact, but from what they can tell, it was designed to use the natural resources of wherever it landed to make an army of some sort of bioengineered warrior drones."

"Shit," she hissed. "Damn good thing it was broken, then."

"Damaged, not broken. They were sent here by the DSI during the war to see if they could use the technology from this thing to combine with some sort of human control to make a weapon against the Tahni."

"Oh, sweet Jesus." She fell into the pilot's seat heavily, staring out the main screens at snow flurries twisting in the wind. "*That's* what happened on the ship. That's what killed the crew."

"The damn thing was still alive, Sandi. It lived for six years in a vacuum, with no food, no heat, no air. It tore apart Singh's crew, and we barely got out ahead of it. We *think* it was killed when the *Metaurus* burned up in the moon's atmosphere."

"You *think*?" she repeated, leaning forward against the control panel as if it could give her strength. "What do you mean you *think*?"

"Singh had a shuttle docked with the cruiser," he reminded her. "It was still there when Korri and I ejected, and their sensors here at the base say it touched down a few kilometers past where our pod landed."

"Shit." The word was an exhaled breath, like she'd been punched in the gut. "You don't think..."

"No," he assured her quickly, "but they're sending a team to check it out, anyway, just in case. The shuttle the crew took down six years ago was scavenged for parts, but if we can get hold of Singh's bird...would extra help speed up the repairs?"

"Not really," she admitted, groaning as esoteric fears gave way to the dread of all the mind-numbingly boring work ahead of her. "It's more a matter of letting the fabricator do its job. Installing the parts won't be that hard; Kan-Ten and I can handle it."

"All right, if you're sure." Ash sounded disappointed and Sandi smiled fondly.

"Don't worry about us." She glanced at the coordinates he'd sent and compared them to her own position. "We're pretty far from that installation; nothing out here but snow and rock."

"Keep me up to date on the status of the repairs," he insisted. "I'd really like to get out of here ASAP. The crew really wants to go home and the research staff could use a food resupply. And honestly, this place gives me the creeps. We're a long way from help."

"Aren't we always?" She was trying to keep things light and upbeat, but her own words sounded surprisingly bleak in her ears. "We'll be okay," she said, attempting a reassuring tone. "You and Korri watch your six and we'll be there as soon as we can."

"Right." The word was a sigh of resignation. There was dead air for a moment, and she wondered if he'd signed off. "I love you, Sandi." She wanted to be upset with him for being so mushy, but she couldn't. The words still felt warm in her chest.

"I love you, too." God, that was starting to sound natural. When had she gotten to be such a big softie? "I gotta' get back to work. Call you when I'm done."

The transmission ended, but she stayed in her seat, looking out at the snow but not seeing it. *Just yesterday,* she thought, *I would have said being stalked by a psycho bounty hunter was the worst thing I'd ever have to worry about...*

"I heard you speaking." She nearly jumped out of her skin at the unexpected voice.

It was Kan-Ten, standing in the hatchway to the cockpit, hands resting on the rims of it, still dressed in heavy cold-weather gear.

"Jeez, how about clearing your throat or something," she muttered. "You scared the shit out of me."

"Apologies," he offered---how sincerely, she wasn't sure. "I was coming inside to tell you that I have completed the tear-down of the damaged nozzles, and I heard your side of the conversation," he explained. "May I presume that Ash and Korri are safe?"

"They're alive," she corrected him, shaking her head. "I don't know if any of us are safe."

———

Ash let his hand fall from the control panel, slumping back in the chair. He could feel Nagle standing behind him, a tall, lanky shadow in the corner of the research base's small communications room. It wasn't much, just a wired connection to the radio transceiver and tight-beam laser setup on the surface. It would allow them to contact nearby patrols or ships overhead in orbit, but that was about it. This system didn't have a wormhole jump-gate to send interstellar messages and they didn't need a satellite network to talk to bases all over the moon or around the gas giant since there were none. Ash could have hooked up to it through his personal 'link, but Sanchez had flatly refused it. She'd wanted to be present for his transmission, but Nagle had volunteered instead, and Ash wasn't sure why.

"This Sandi," the scientist said softly, barely carrying over the two meters between them. "You two are together?"

Ash looked back at the man, Nagle's doughy face masked in the shadows of the dimly-lit room.

"Yeah," he answered hesitantly, a bit reluctant to share personal information with the man. "We've known each other since the Academy."

"Take the advice of an old and lonely man, Commander. Treasure the time you have together. I made the mistake of letting someone slip away, once, and..." He rubbed at the bridge of his nose, as if his head ached. "You think you will get another chance, but life makes no such guarantees."

"Is that why you're out here, away from anyone?" Ash wondered. "Trying to forget?"

Nagle emerged from the dark corner, his face twisting into an unpleasant grin.

"I am here because I'm a xenobiologist," he corrected Ash, "and since the Predecessors left nothing behind but carvings, my only other recourse, if not for this, was to study the Tahni." He scowled. "And the Tahni are boring as hell, from an evolutionary standpoint, since they were quite obviously genetically altered for sentience and tool-using."

Ash blinked, thinking for a moment that he'd heard the man wrong. "They were? How come I never heard about it, then?"

"Well, it's obviously not something that the Commonwealth government wanted spread around, before." Nagle spread his hands expressively. "Would you want to tell the public that we were engaged in a war with a race engineered for sentience by the Predecessors?"

"Wait, you're saying that the Predecessors created the Tahni?" Ash felt the room shifting beneath him as he tried to absorb another impossible thing before breakfast. "Even if you're right about them being genetically engineered, how do you know the Predecessors did it?"

"Occaam's Razor." The researcher shrugged. "We know of one race technologically advanced enough to create the wormhole jumpgates. Would you have us postulate another equally as advanced at the same time who meddled in the evolutionary biology of Tahni hominids?"

"What about whoever made the thing downstairs?" Ash shrugged. "They must have been pretty advanced."

"Undeniably so," Nagle granted. "But they weren't humanoid, and from the genetic makeup of their warrior drones, I very much doubt they evolved anywhere remotely like Earth or the Tahni homeworld. If they were to create intelligent life, it most assuredly would not be humanoid. Besides, we are fairly confident that creating life was not their purpose; their drones were programmed to kill whatever intelligent life they found, to infest and destroy any technological civilization in their way."

"How the hell do you know that?" Ash demanded, hearing anger in his tone and not quite knowing why, other than that the whole thing strained his incredulity.

"Experimentation, of course." Nagle sounded offended at the naiveté of the question. "Years and years of experimentation, long before I arrived. My job was not to determine the nature of the programming, it was to seize control of it, to make a weapon. The DSI, you see, wanted something that could be dropped onto Tahni worlds that would spread terror, would cause untold destruction with no risk of human life. I was led to believe that there was some competition with Fleet Intelligence on this matter, that they had their own project and we were behind." He waved a hand dismissively. "I wasn't interested."

"Not the patriotic type?"

"Oh, I much prefer human domination of the Cluster to Tahni," Nagle admitted. "Who wouldn't? They're the worst parts of human culture through history crystallized with a unifying religion and given star travel. But we were going to win that war regardless, and I knew the whole project was just a DSI dick-measuring contest with Fleet Intelligence. But this..." He leaned against the wall, crossing his arms. "This was the culmination of my career, and I wasn't going to say no."

"Dr. Nagle," Ash felt compelled to ask, leaning forward in the chair to face the man, "why are you telling me all this? This must be some really top-secret shit, and I'm sure it wouldn't make Dr. Sanchez happy you're sharing it with me."

"Susan takes the secrecy very seriously. She takes everything very seriously. But none of that matters. If the hybrid died when the *Metaurus* went down, it's all meaningless, because they will not repeat the experiment."

"Probably not," Ash agreed. "Even in the middle of a war, combining human DNA with alien biotechnology is a pretty desperate gambit." Nagle barked a laugh so harsh that it startled Ash.

"Is *that* what you think we did, Commander?" The man's tone was bitter, scornful.

Ash was about to ask what he meant when there was a knock on the door to the commo center and Chief Weaver stuck his head through.

"Doctor," he said, nodding politely to Nagle, then turned toward Ash. "Commander Carpenter, Commander Busick wanted me to collect you. That bounty hunter, Singh, he's awake. She wanted you to be there when she talked to him."

Ash thought that Nagle might have something more to say, but the scientist was still leaning against the wall, staring down at the slate-grey floor. The pilot followed the Chief of Boat out into the corridor, circumnavigating its switchback curves downward two more levels until they reached a large, open doorway leading into a well-lit and cheerily-colored chamber that served as the installation's medical clinic. There weren't any regular shipping runs back to the Core worlds here, so everything they could possibly need was included in its equipment, all the way up to a fully-functional and elaborately outfitted auto-doc that could grow organs, given enough time.

Singh had been plunged into its nanite-filled biotic fluid for hours to let the microscopic biomechanical organisms repair the damage the hybrid and the descent in the lifepod had done to him, and now he was lying partially propped up in a recovery bed. This recovery bed had been specially outfitted with a neural restraint web that would keep even the bounty hunter's bionic parts motionless while it was activated, and he didn't look too happy about it, or about the flimsy robe that was all he was wearing. He looked even less happy to see Ash enter the room.

Fontenot was already there, arms folded, an amused look on her face as she stood beside Commander Busick and Gunny Kamara. Two other Marines stood guard over Singh while a Fleet corpsman in white utility fatigues checked the readouts on the bed's monitors.

"Are Sandi and Kan-Ten all right?" Fontenot asked him.

"Yeah, they have some repairs to make before the ship is flyable again," he told her. "Sandi said it could take a couple days." He nodded at Singh. "Where did you get the neural restraints?"

"The facility has a dozen sets," Busick answered the question, shaking her head. "I didn't ask why; I didn't want to know."

"You should be in the fucking restraints, Carpenter," Singh said in almost a growl. He fixed Busick with an angry glare, the muscles in his neck straining as he tried to move and couldn't. "You know this man and his crew are all wanted criminals? They have bounties on them from the Patrol for murder, grand theft and piracy and from the Fleet for desertion."

"And I suppose you have proof of that?" Busick asked him.

"If I had my 'link," he said, settling his head back down. "It's back on the *Metaurus*."

"Then it's burned to its component atoms by now," Busick informed him. "The ship made atmospheric entry pretty violently. And you know what, Mr. Singh? Commander Carpenter here does have proof that he's Fleet. It's not your word against his, it's your word against his evidence, and I have no reason at all to trust your word. As far as I know, you're nothing but a cartel hitman."

"Then why are you bothering to talk to me at all?" Singh demanded.

"Your shuttle," she explained. "Our sensors show that it

landed not too far from here, but we can't contact it. I need you to tell the pilot and any crew on board that we have a patrol heading in and it would be in their best interest to surrender to them. I'd rather avoid any unnecessary violence."

Singh brooded on it for several seconds, and Ash thought he was going to tell Busick where she could stick it, but then he nodded curtly.

"Get me a 'link and I'll tell you the frequency and coding."

It took all of thirty seconds to get the 'link set to the right transmission coding, and then Chief Weaver held it up to Singh's mouth...very carefully.

"Grant," he snapped, "this is Singh. Come in." Nothing but silence responded. "Grant, answer the damn transmission, this is Singh." Another empty pause and Singh mouthed a curse. "Damn it, Del, answer me! Anyone from the *Gitano*, this is Singh, please respond." They waited another minute, but no one returned the call.

"The ship landed," Weaver pointed out, pocketing the 'link. "Maybe whoever took it down was injured. They could be unconscious."

"Yeah, they could be," Busick muttered, eyes staring through the wall. She glanced over at Kamara. "How close is the patrol?"

"They should be in visual range of the shuttle in a half an hour or so," the Gunny told her, checking his 'link. Ash guessed he had a readout from their IFF transponders displayed there.

"Let me know when you hear from them."

"Don't kill them." Singh's voice was soft, almost inaudible. Ash looked at him in surprise. The bounty hunter was staring at his bionic arm for some reason, at the bare, black metal. "Don't kill them," he repeated. He looked over at Busick, his human eye softened slightly, a sharp contrast to the cold grey of its companion. "Del, the pilot...he's just a kid."

"I don't want anyone to get hurt," Busick said, and Ash

thought she was telling the truth. "As long as he doesn't do anything stupid, our Marines have orders to bring everyone they find back alive."

With that, she turned on her heel and left the room, followed closely by Weaver and Kamara. The two guards stayed at their posts, near motionless behind faceless visors, while the corpsman kept adjusting settings on monitors and medication dosages and trying to sneak curious glances at them. Ash was pretty sure the man was just trying to look busy so he could stay and find out more about who they were and whether they were going to get all of the crew back home.

"Why didn't you kill me?" Singh asked him.

The question caught Ash off-guard. He'd been about to leave the room, one hand on Fontenot's shoulder to make sure she didn't stay to taunt the bounty hunter. He turned back towards the recovery bed, hesitant to meet Singh's dark gaze.

"I was definitely in favor of the idea, for what it's worth," Fontenot commented with a casual shrug. She didn't wait, just headed out the door after Busick and the others. Singh ignored her, still staring at Ash.

"I'm not a murderer," Ash said. "I've killed people when I had to, when there was no other choice, but you were helpless and unconscious, and it would have been wrong."

He turned, suddenly ready to get out of the room and away from the bounty hunter.

"I would have." Singh's words followed him out of the room. They didn't seem threatening, he thought. More...regretful? "I would have killed you."

CHAPTER TWELVE

Corporal John Ross tried to keep his concentration focused on his surroundings, on the position of his fire team and the readout from his helmet's sensors, but it was hard not to think about home. Home was Valencia City, an overly grand name for what was basically a couple of tourist resorts and the surrounding support businesses built around the New Cumberland Lake on Hermes, humanity's oldest star colony. He hadn't seen his family in over seven years now, and he knew they all thought he was dead.

The minute he got back to the Commonwealth, he was going to cash in all the back pay he was due and fly home to Hermes and never leave Valencia again. It was *warm* in Valencia. You could just sit outside on the sand of the lake shore in nothing but shorts and bask in the sun. He didn't care if ever saw snow again.

It should be a lot of back pay, he mused. *They probably promoted me while I was dead. I wonder if Heather is still single...*

"Bear," Private Kingsford called, using his nickname. He frowned. The Gunny didn't like them getting informal, but it had been six years. What the hell did the guy expect? The war was over, they knew it now and they'd suspected it already, and most of them would have been civilians if they'd had a choice.

"Yeah, what is it, Emil?" he replied, getting a fix in his helmet's HUD on where Emil Kingsford was in their wide, spread-out V formation.

Katya Dumont was on point, just ten meters ahead of him, Wole Achebe was out on his left and Kingsford was on the far-right edge of the V. Right now, the only one he could see was Katya; they were out in the badlands to the west of the base, where the moss-covered yellow mounds of mineral deposits from long-dormant thermal springs dotted the landscape and screwed badly with their line of sight. It was already dusk outside; the days didn't last long this time of year with the planet's rotation combined with that big gas giant getting in the way.

"I have eyes on the shuttle," Emil told him, sounding as excited as Bear about the prospect of getting off this ice ball. "It's two hundred meters off to our two o'clock."

"Katya," Ross said to the Marine on point, "adjust our route fifteen degrees to the south-east. Emil, Wole, fall in on the new formation."

They didn't respond; they didn't have to. He could see them changing course in his HUD, their Identification Friend or Foe transponders showing up as green triangles over the map of the badlands. There was an open plain out a couple hundred meters away, he could see it on the map; it made sense the shuttle had landed there.

He followed Katya's lead around a large, rainbow-hued mound of calcite and minerals and persistent fungal matts and then he could see it. It was dull gray and delta winged, bulbous and squat in utilitarian ugliness, and resting on five landing treads sunk a few centimeters into the brittle, cracked soil. He paused, raising a fist in the air and sinking to a knee. The motion sent a signal to the HUDs of the other members of his team and they followed his example, coming to a security halt.

"Katya, Wole, I want you to circle around to the left, make a wide arc around that thing and get the lay of the land. Scan for any thermal hot spots, let me know if you see any other movement out there. Once you get within fifty meters of its portside wing, set up an overwatch position and Emil and I will move in and board her."

"Roger that, Bear," Katya replied brusquely. He was glad they were friends again. They'd had a fling two years ago and it had been touchy for a while after it ended.

Hell, it's been six years. Almost everyone has been involved with everyone else by now.

He thought about going prone, but the mineral deposit mounds springing up every few meters between them and the plain where the shuttle had touched down would have made it impossible to keep it under visual observation while the other two moved, so he stayed on one knee and watched Katya and Emil head off to the left at a quick jog. They covered the distance in less than a minute, sacrificing stealth for speed, and disappeared from his line of sight as they went around a calcite deposit large enough to be called a small hill. Katya took her time scoping out the aerospacecraft, and he was getting antsy enough to jiggle her elbow when she finally called in.

"I'm not seeing any activity," she reported. "Cold on thermal, engines are shut down and haven't been powered up for at least a couple hours. Belly ramp is closed..."

"I can see the utility airlock from this angle," Wole interjected. "It's open. Inner and outer hatches, both; but I can't see inside from here. No interior lights visible."

"Okay, stay there, we're coming up." Ross used the butt of his rifle to push himself to his feet. "Emil, get on my six, we're circling around right. Keep your eyes right, Katya and Wole will watch our backs."

Ross followed his own advice, keeping his Gauss rifle and his attention focused off to the right. It seemed counterintuitive when they were here to clear the shuttle, but he was worried that whoever had been crewing the thing might have headed off that way to set up an ambush for anyone who came looking for the bird. The dim, reddening light of the setting primary threw everything into sharp relief, and Ross began to imagine cartel soldiers in every shadow, but his helmet optics were better at spotting threats than he was, and they were showing nothing.

He and Emil took longer to get into position than Katya and Wole had; they circled all the way around the shuttle, and Ross let Emil keep a lookout into the badland wilderness while he scanned the exterior of the bird. It hadn't taken any damage that he could see: no burns, no ablated shielding, just a few patches from hard use, which made sense if this was a cartel spacecraft. He did notice some ragged edges around the utility airlock, right where a universal docking adapter might be, like she'd been attached to something and pulled away without bothering to retract the umbilical.

Ross hugged the shuttle's hull and sidled up to the open airlock, trying to get a look inside from two meters below. It was no use; all he could see was the overhead. He crouched down and waved Emil over to him.

"Give me a boost," he told the Marine, slinging his Gauss rifle to free up his hands. "I'll take a quick look; if it's all clear, I'll open the belly ramp for you."

"You sure about this, Bear?" He couldn't see Emil's face through the visor, but the man's voice sounded pretty dubious. "They could be waiting in there for you."

"They could be," Ross admitted. "But I'm not getting any noise or heat sources from in there. I'm thinking they took off.

Either way, though, someone's gotta go in. Since I'm in charge, I say it's me. Now, give me a boost."

Emil didn't argue with him, probably because he realized it was useless. One of the good things about working with like same people for so many years is that they got to know you. He moved underneath the open airlock and got down on a knee, cupping his hands at hip level to accept Ross' boot. Six years ago, the Corporal mused, he could have made the jump without help, but this long living and working in half a gravity had weakened him to the point where he couldn't take the chance. He stepped onto Emil's hands and was boosted upward as the man stood abruptly.

He grabbed the edge of the airlock and yanked himself up over the side in one, smooth motion, rolling onto his shoulder and coming up to a kneeling position as he pulled his rifle around to the front and scanned for threats. What he saw there, in the dim shadows of the shuttle's interior, was blood and lots of it. Blood spattered the walls in abstract, almost artistic patterns, and pooled on the floor, gathering at a low point near the spacesuit locker.

The source of the blood was lying slumped against the far bulkhead, just this side of the cockpit. He was a young man, maybe in his mid-twenties if you took into account that he was from the Pirate Worlds and wouldn't have access to anti-aging treatments. He had a shock of blond hair and blue eyes that had been vacant and lifeless for hours now. His chest had been ripped apart, the ribs splintered and broken and yanked out through the skin.

Ross felt bile rising in the back of his throat and fought to keep it down, the fierce desire not to puke inside his helmet overriding the sheer shock and terror of the sight that confronted him...and worse, the memories that it freed from years of successful suppression. They floated in his vision like ghosts, blotting out the darkness of the shuttle with the obscenely bright lights of the *Metaurus* and the vivid red of oceans of blood orbiting the mutilated corpses of the crew. He felt it again, that inescapable, unrelenting, claustrophobic panic of being trapped on that ship with the creature, unkillable, implacable, unstoppable.

He didn't remember making the decision, just suddenly found himself tumbling to the ground beneath the airlock, hyperventilating, feeling as if he couldn't get a full breath. Desperate, he yanked the quick-release toggles of his helmet forward and twisted it off. The air was bitterly cold and as thin as a mountaintop back on Earth, and it slapped him in the face, finally breaking him free of the bonds of mindless terror that had taken hold inside the shuttle.

"Bear!" Emil was shouting at him over his own helmet's external speakers, leaning over to grab his shoulder. Ross scrambled backwards, eyes wide, staring at Emil but barely seeing him. "Bear, what the hell's wrong with you?"

"It's back," he gibbered. "It's here, Emil. It's down here with us..."

"What are you talking about?" Emil demanded.

Ross pounded a fist on the ground, trying to get himself back under control. He sucked in a couple of deep breaths, then grabbed his helmet and settled it back into its yoke, watching the HUD flicker back to life. Katya was transmitting at him, trying to find out what was wrong, but he ignored her.

"Gunny, do you read?" he called over the net they'd established before he'd left on patrol. "Gunny, this is Ross, do you read me?"

"I'm here, Corporal," Kamara answered. "Have you reached the shuttle?"

"The bird's intact, only one occupant, I think it's the pilot, and he's dead. Been dead for hours, maybe ever since he landed." He heard his words and realized he was talking fast, almost manic. He tried to calm himself down, concentrating on his breathing. "Gunny, he was ripped to pieces. He's all over the inside of the shuttle. It's back, it's here. It came down with him."

Kamara didn't respond immediately, and Ross wondered if the man believed him. Cursing, he tapped the wrist controls for his helmet 'link and uploaded the video feed from his helmet camera to the line, sending it to Kamara.

"Shit." The word was an exhale, involuntary. Ross knew the Gunny had seen the same thing he had, had come to the same conclusion. "Ross, get your team out of there, get back to base immediately. Do you copy that? Get out now."

Ross couldn't remember ever hearing the Gunny sound scared, but he sure as hell did now.

Good, he thought. *That means he understands the situation.*

<hr>

Ash saw Commander Busick's hand shaking as she tried to bring the glass of water to her mouth. Finally, she gave up, setting it back on the conference room table and clenching her hands into fists to stop the shaking.

"It would have been better if you hadn't found us," she said, her tone fatalistic, her eyes flat and hopeless. "It would have just stayed up there, asleep or hibernating or whatever."

"We'd have starved in another year." Kamara pointed out. "Less."

He wasn't sitting; he seemed too keyed up to sit, his eyes travelling back to the display screen fixed to the wall, where the IFF transponders from the Marine patrol were slowly moving across the map back towards the base.

"If it's here," Weaver asserted, "it's going to find this place. You know how intelligent it is." The Chief of Boat was calm, businesslike, treating the whole situation like it was just another day at work. His coffee cup steamed patiently in front of him, but he ignored it.

"Hold on a second," Fontenot interrupted, raising a hand to pause the conversation. She'd changed out of her vacuum suit as well, but all they'd been able to find in her size was a sweat suit from one of the science crew, with the logo of a university on Hermes emblazoned across the chest. "Tell me something. This...hybrid, you called it? This thing was supposed to be a weapon to use against the Tahni, right?"

"That was the plan," Busick confirmed. "That's what we were told."

It was just the five of them in the makeshift conference room, another of the base's repurposed storage areas that Busick and her crew had commandeered. There were only twenty-one of them in all, Ash had found out. Out of a crew of two hundred on the *Metaurus*, less than two dozen had made it onto the shuttle and down to the surface. Kamara, two squads of his Marines, Busick, Chief Weaver, the corpsman they'd met earlier and two docking bay technicians they'd grabbed up during the evacuation.

"So, it had to be in some kind of cage or something," Fontenot surmised. She was pacing slowly back and forth in front of the conference table. "How did it get out?"

"It was supposed to be in hibernation," Busick said, eyes a bit unfocussed, voice haunted with the memory. "They sent it to us in some kind of freezing chamber that was supposed to keep it asleep."

"It was like a coffin," Weaver told them, making the shape with waves of his hands. "Like a big, damned coffin, all metal with a liquid nitrogen tank attached to it. We were supposed to put it in the hold and make sure it was attached to the power feed in case its batteries failed." He grimaced. "It never made it to the hold. I don't know what happened. Could have been a battery problem, could have been a nitrogen leak maybe."

"It could have been," Kamara interrupted in a tone filled with cold fury, "that one of those damned Frankensteins fucked up."

"We're never gonna' know," Weaver pointed out. "Either way, the thing broke loose between the docking bay and the hold. Captain Schofield contacted the base here, and Dr. Nagle told him that the thing was going to try to take control of the ship's navigation, and that he couldn't let it, or the creature would head straight for Earth."

"What?" Ash blurted, straightening in his seat. "This hybrid can fly a damned Fleet cruiser? And why would it head for Earth?"

"I'm telling you what Nagle said." Weaver shrugged. "He was pretty adamant about it; whatever else we did, we couldn't let the hybrid get control of the ship."

"We tried everything we had time for," Busick murmured, and Ash could see the memories washing over her like a tide, carrying her further away from the conference room. "We tried sealing off sections, tried setting up ambushes, but we couldn't track it on the security systems. It just wouldn't show up. Everything we did was too slow. But we could tell from the reports that it was heading for the bridge. Captain Schofield sent me and the Chief with Gunny Kamara and his Marines to take one of the shuttles and sabotage the other."

Her jaws clamped down for a moment and Ash sensed she was fighting back the emotions rising with the memories.

"He had everyone left from Security make a last stand with him on the bridge, and he had the Engineering crew disable the Teller-Fox unit. I know the hybrid went to Engineering after it killed...after the bridge. We were gone by then, heading for the surface."

"Commander," Ash said slowly and carefully, finally finding a time to voice a question he'd had since he'd arrived, "you've been here six years. There can't be that many of the researchers and none of them are fighters. Why haven't you taken control of this base?"

Kamara glanced at him sharply, and then just as sharply at Busick, and Ash had the sense that the Gunny had suggested they do just that on multiple occasions.

"Aside from the fact that I would have been court-martialed if we were ever rescued," she pointed out tiredly, like she'd had this argument before, "it was suggested to me not so subtly by Dr. Sanchez that there were certain safeguards in place in an installation like this, with the sort of incredibly sensitive, incredibly secret work they were doing. Safeguards that would bring the whole base down on top of us if she didn't actively prevent it on a regular basis."

"Come on," Fontenot scoffed. "These eggheads can't all be willing to kill themselves just to stay in charge here."

"All of them?" Busick repeated. "No. But Sanchez is a fucking maniac. I could believe she'd do it. I *do* believe she'd do it."

"Are you going to tell them it's here?" Ash wanted to know. "They might have some way of taking it out."

"I already did," she said, running her hands over her face. "Nagle said he'd be up in a few minutes."

"C'mon, Bear," Kamara muttered, looking at the IFF signals on the map screen. "Hurry up."

CHAPTER THIRTEEN

JOHN ROSS TRIED TO KEEP HIMSELF FROM LOOKING BACK. It wasn't necessary; the helmet had rear-facing cameras that projected a small image on the right side of his HUD, but it was deeply-ingrained instinct, and he couldn't shake the feeling that they were being followed. Darkness had fallen, and even with the computer-enhanced night vision of his helmet trying to simulate full daylight, things looked artificial, like he wasn't seeing the whole picture, like there was something missing.

He tried to banish the atavistic fears and concentrate on the map. They were only a couple kilometers from the entrance; they just had to circle around a cluster of hills and then it would be a straight shot. Katya went over a rise that put her out of visual observation for a moment, but he could still follow her IFF transponder. He could have accessed her helmet cam feed, but there was just so much you could fit inside a HUD projection without tripping over your own feet.

He noticed Wole spreading out a bit far to the left, nearly thirty meters out from the center front where Katya was walking point and he frowned.

"Wole," he transmitted, "tighten it up."

"Sorry, Bear," the man responded. "Got too far out walking around a sinkhole."

Ross grunted acknowledgement. Those were a constant hazard out here near the thermals, and they'd had people injured before when the ground crumbled beneath them. He turned his attention back to Katya...and her IFF was gone.

"Katya!" he called, trying to bring up the feed from her helmet cam. Nothing. He started to sprint forward to get her under visual observation, but forced himself to stop and think for a second, to go with his training. "Shit!" he hissed, going down on one knee, bringing his rifle to his shoulder. "Wole, Emil, bring it in, Ranger file behind me, now!" He switched frequencies. "Gunny, do you have contact with Katya?"

Ross scanned the terrain ahead of him, gritting his teeth as he waited for a response. It was a lot of nothing. Crumbling soil, dotted here and there with ancient volcanic rock, and a slant of a hillside that just blocked off the route Katya had taken.

"Negative, Ross," Gunny Kamara answered. "I'm not picking up anything, no IFF, no health readings, no camera feed. Do you see anything?"

"Give me a second," Ross told him, switching frequencies. He saw Emil and Wole closing up behind him, only ten meters apart. "We're moving. Stay close and do *not* get out of direct visual observation of me."

He felt his hands shaking as he got back to his feet and gripped his rifle's stock tighter, trying to keep himself steady, trying to pretend this was just another training scenario. They were going to round that corner and Katya was going to be fine. It was just a helmet malfunction. Things like that happened; all their equipment was getting old.

He'd almost convinced himself of that until he saw her forty meters ahead of him on the trail. *Parts* of her were forty meters ahead. The rest was strewn across the white and yellow mineral deposits that lined their route, staining it red. Bits of ribcage littered the ground around what was left of her body and her head was missing, along with the helmet. The attack couldn't have taken more than two or three seconds, the time he'd spent talking to Wole, yet she looked as if she'd been through an industrial threshing machine.

Ross dropped to a knee, mouth dry, barely able to breathe.

"Oh, Jesus Christ!" He thought that was Emil. The other Marine was making retching sounds and the only reason Ross wasn't nauseous was that he was numb with shock. Wole said nothing, but both of them had stopped when he had.

They probably thought he was being tactically correct, staying put and assessing the situation; but the truth was, he couldn't move. He was paralyzed by disbelief. This couldn't be happening again, not down here. They'd got away from the thing; he remembered how guilty he'd felt that he'd survived and the others hadn't, but over the years, the guilt had turned to a profound gratitude. Now, everything was being replaced by fear.

They had to get back, that one thought penetrated the haze and terror. They had to get back and they had to stay together. He took several deep breaths before he was confident he could speak without gibbering.

"Emil, Wole," he said, amazed his voice could sound so calm and steady when he was on the edge of sheer, mindless panic, "we are going to stay within arm's length of each other. No straggling. And we are going to run like hell. Don't fall behind. Tell me you both understand."

"Got it," Wole responded. His voice cracked slightly, but Ross thought he was going to be able to hold it together.

Emil didn't answer.

"Emil," Ross said sharply, turning on his knee to face the man. "Do you understand me?"

Emil had been the last in line, only ten meters back from Wole. He was gone, without a trace.

"Go!" Ross yelled, pushing himself to his feet and running.

He didn't remember dropping his rifle, but his hands were empty and he felt the weight shifting on his side as the retractable sling spooled the weapon in to its spot on his backpack. He'd never run this fast before, not on track back in school, not in Boot Camp, not even when he'd been in combat against the Tahni during the war. Even in combat, you held something back, kept from going at your absolute top speed, because you didn't want to go out of control. You had to watch your foot placement and keep focused on your surroundings and look out for the enemy, and your brain never quite let your body go all-out. There was no reason for any of that now. There was no way to fight this, no safe cover to hide behind that would stop this thing; there was nothing to do but run.

He felt himself go off-balance and threw his weight forward, stomping into the ground to keep his footing, feeling the jolt reverberating upward through his legs and lower back and knowing it would hurt like hell later. If there was a later.

He didn't bother trying to watch for the thing, because he knew he wouldn't see it in time. Emil had been *right there*, only twenty meters away. He should have seen it...he should have at least noticed a hint of motion in his rear camera. He'd been focused on Katya's body, swallowed up by fear for just a few seconds, and he hadn't caught even a glimpse of when it had grabbed Emil. How could anything move that fast?

"Ross, what the hell's going on out there?" It was the Gunny. His voice was harsh, more with fear than anger. "Where are Kingsford and Dumont? I'm not seeing anything on your video feed but bare ground! What are you running from?"

Ross didn't attempt to respond. He couldn't spare the breath or the attention, and there was nothing Kamara could do for him, anyway. He wouldn't send troops out, not with that *thing* out here. He'd be killing them to save people who were already dead. Was Wole still behind him? He didn't want to turn his eyes even a centimeter aside to check his HUD for the man's transponder. Any distraction would mean death. He was convinced of it, convinced that his only hope was to get back inside.

He was three hundred meters away. He could see it now, could see the twin bumps of the hills that were the landmark he always looked for. It was the closest entrance; not the main one, not the tunnel. That would take too long, using the ID plate and waiting for clearance. No, he had to get to the emergency hatch. He'd memorized the location even though they never used it; everyone had when it became clear they were going to be here for a long time.

It had been magnetically sealed when they'd first arrived, meant to be used only in case of a cave-in or a fire, but the Gunny had taken Ross and Chief Weaver one night and rigged it so that it would open manually from the outside, but the base's systems would still show it as locked. He wanted a way in if the Frankensteins got too pushy and tried to lock them out. And Ross figured that this would be as good an excuse as any to try to lock him out.

"Bear!" Wole screamed. The word was full of terror and agony and despair and Ross forced himself to shut it out, to not look back.

It had got him. It had taken down Wole and he was next. His breath was deafening inside his helmet, his chest burning, his legs dragged down by lead weights, but he ran faster, ignoring fatigue and pain and everything but that juncture of the two hills drawing nearer and nearer. Just another hundred meters, but it might as well be on the far side of the gas giant. He was never going to make it...

And then he was there, and the hatch was there, barely big enough for a full-grown male, sheltered from view under the overhang of a calcite deposit, tendrils of moss-like fungus drooping down over it. He lunged at it, yanking the manual locking lever downward, and then throwing it open. It was a twenty meter drop inside, with a narrow, metal ladder the only way down, but Ross plunged in headfirst, grabbing at the ladder with one hand and trying to slam the hatch closed behind him with the other.

His legs swung down behind him and he was sure he was going to fall and break his neck, but he managed to catch himself, fingers cramping as his full weight yanked down on them. He scrabbled wildly, his legs flailing, and felt his right foot bang against one of the rungs. He got it into place just as it felt that his fingers were about to fail him, felt his weight shift to his legs as he found a resting spot for his left boot, then he hugged the ladder, hyperventilating and exhausted.

"Oh God..." he moaned, resting his helmet against the side of the ladder. "Oh, dear God."

There was a wrenching, scraping sound from above and light began to filter downward from the opening as the hatch five meters above him began to creak slowly open.

Oh Jesus, it's coming...

Ross looked down. He was five meters down the ladder, and below him all was inky blackness, illuminated only by the infrared lamp on his helmet. In the green-tinted haze of the IR filters, he saw nothing but volcanic rock stretching downward in a narrow cylinder until it dropped out on a tunnel so far down that the lamp couldn't reach it.

He heard a sound deep in his throat, something inhuman, something a trapped animal might make just before it began to gnaw off its own foot. He kicked free of the rungs of the ladder and began sliding downward, gloved hands lightly grasping the sides. Hazy, green-tinted darkness blurred by him and his stomach crawled into his throat as he realized how fast he was falling. He tried to tighten his grip just slightly, to slow himself, but he was too exhausted and too insane with fear for that sort of precision.

His arms were jerked upward as his palms grabbed far too tightly, and pure, raging agony blossomed in his shoulders as both of them dislocated, and he fell.

The fall seemed to take forever, took longer than senses and instincts evolved for one gravity expected, and that lighter gravity was the only reason the impact didn't kill him. His back bounced off the volcanic rock tube of the tunnel and his faceplate cracked and splintered as it impacted the ladder, and then he hit right-leg first and felt pain that made his separated shoulders seem pleasant by comparison. There was a crack that sounded like a tree snapping in a high wind, and the only reason Ross didn't scream was that the breath was driven from his lungs when the rest of him slammed down hard on the tunnel floor.

His vision swam in schools of dancing lights as he was swallowed up in the utter darkness at the bottom of the ladder. He was in an unlit, unused corridor, narrow and barely two meters tall and couldn't have seen a damn thing even if his sight wasn't clouded with agony. His helmet's visor was broken and useless, the HUD and night vision filters gone.

"Help..." He tried to yell the word, but it came out as a barely-audible gasp. No one else heard. Even if his helmet comms were working, he was too deep underground and there were no signal repeaters out in this isolated part of the installation.

Something heavy thudded into the stone floor beside him. He tried to move, despite the pain and the shock and the injuries, tried to scoot away from the vibration and the scraping, scratching sound, but he couldn't. His strength was gone, burned away in his desperate flight to die here, alone, in the dark. He managed to roll over onto his side, and there was just a hint of light filtering down from the hatch, enough to notice when it was blocked out by something big and black.

Death stared him in the face, its jaws parting to show rows of scimitar-shaped teeth.

———

"They're gone," Kamara murmured, staring at the display in shock. "They're all gone."

Ash was on his feet, glancing around the room uncertainly, waiting for Busick to say something. She pushed herself up from the table, putting a hand on Kamara's arm. He looked over at her sharply, as if he had forgotten where he was.

"Corporal Ross...he was trying to get in the emergency hatch, I think. That's the area he was in when his transponder went dead. Do you think he made it?"

"If your man led the hybrid to the hatch, then it's in here with us now."

Ash turned at the voice and saw Nagle looming in the doorway, looking strangely out of place here away from his lab. He was surprisingly calm, not seeming at all alarmed or dismayed, but instead intrigued. Ash almost thought he was being unfair, attributing clichés about mad scientists to the man; but no, his flaccid, puffy face seemed alive now, filled in and lightened up by keen interest.

"Why is it coming in here?" Fontenot demanded. She was shuffling back and forth, fingers clenching and unclenching, and Ash saw something in her eyes that he hadn't ever seen before: fear. "You said it was intelligent. It has to know we don't have a starship here, assuming it hasn't found the *Acheron*. What does it want from this place? Revenge?"

"It is intelligent," Nagle agreed, stepping inside, looking at the map display. "But it's not an entirely human intelligence. It has conflicting needs, from the different sides of itself." He raised his right hand and turned it over demonstratively. "The human side wants to go home, wants to return to Earth." The left hand balanced the right, parallel to it. "The side that is a hive mind from an alien race that was probably extinct hundreds of thousands of years before the pod crashed here wants to perform its purpose: to kill and destroy any technical civilization it comes across...and to reproduce."

"Oh, shit," Ash blurted, and his eyes widened. "It wants to get back to the pod. It thinks it can reproduce there."

"And more than reproduce," Nagle agreed. "It thinks it can repair it, if it provides enough raw material...maybe even instruct the pod's nanite factories how to make its own starship."

"Why are you telling us this?" Busick wondered. The question was almost rude in tone, skeptical. She stepped closer to the researcher, almost nose-to-nose. "We've been here six years and you haven't said a damn thing. Why now?"

"I don't want to see any more people hurt," Nagle said, and Ash thought he meant it. "You can't stop the hybrid; it will kill all of you if you get in its way." He cocked an eyebrow. "So, get out of its way. Evacuate the installation, go take that shuttle that landed and find Commander Carpenter's ship. Let the hybrid have what it wants."

"You just said it could reproduce!" Kamara snapped, shoulders hunched as if he was about to lunge at the older man. "You said it could build a fucking starship and take it to Earth! And you want us to let it?"

"I said it *thinks* it can do all that," Nagle corrected him, calm and unaffected, either by Busick's skepticism or Kamara's outrage. "I've learned a few things about the pod in the years I've studied it. I'm confident that if I get the hybrid back into the lab, I can reverse the process that blended the human volunteer with the alien organism."

"The human volunteer?" Ash repeated, slowly, enunciating each word. "Someone...a *person* volunteered to do that to themselves?" He had been backing up unconsciously, stepping away from Nagle like he was afraid he'd catch something from the man, and he didn't realize it until he felt the edge of the table bump against the back of his legs and he put a hand back to steady himself.

"It was wartime," Nagle said. His voice lost some of the confident detachment it had displayed earlier. This part wasn't as impersonal to him, Ash guessed. "We were being pressured for results and..." He shrugged. "We had already been here a long time, working on a black budget, with no results. The DSI agent in charge of the project was insistent that we produce a weapon, or we would be shut down."

"Whatever it is now," Busick said, "it's not human anymore. It'll kill you."

"I'm willing to take that chance."

"I'm not." Her tone was flat and decisive. "This is a military emergency and I'm taking control of this base. Gunny, this thing won't take the elevators. It's going to try for the emergency stairwell on level six, at the end of the ramp. I need you to hold it off there as long as you can."

"Aye, ma'am." He nodded and took off at a sprint, and Ash could hear his voice as he called to the rest of his troops over his 'link as he ran. He looked relieved to have something to do, Ash thought.

"Chief." The XO turned to Weaver. "Take Jandreau and Ashef and get to the old construction storage locker down on level eight. Remember the inventory we did two years ago?"

"The blasting charges left over from boring the tunnels," Weaver said, nodding.

"You're going to take that down to the Pit and bring the whole place down on top of that thing when it comes for the pod."

Nagle's mouth opened, and Ash could tell he wanted to object...but instead, he closed it and said nothing.

Maybe he's not as crazy as I thought, Ash considered grudgingly.

"I could help with that," Fontenot offered. "I have experience with combat engineering." She sniffed. "Among other things."

"Happy to have you along, Ms. Fontenot," Weaver accepted, motioning to the door. She preceded him out and Ash could hear their steps turn to a jog out in the corridor.

"Dr. Nagle," Busick went on, "you need to get your people evacuated to the surface just as quickly as possible. Take them to the cartel shuttle and wait for us there. You should be safe travelling out there, with the hybrid here inside, and you'll be out of the weather."

"I'll go see to it myself," the man offered, turning and heading out of the room.

"What do you want me to do, Commander?" Ash asked her as Weaver and Kamara ran off to their assignments.

"Get on the horn with your friends, Carpenter, and find out how soon they can take off." Her expression was grim. "Before we blow the shit out of this installation, it would be nice to know we had a way out."

CHAPTER FOURTEEN

"OKAY, I think that's got it," Sandi yelled into her 'link's pickup over the whine of the turbines. She felt the rush of hot air begin to subside from the portside stern vectored thrust nozzle, and she saw the pool of meltwater it had created beneath the belly of the *Acheron* immediately start to freeze over again.

It was getting dark again, and with the dusk came bitter, nearly unsurvivable cold. The test run of the third nozzle they'd repaired had warmed her up briefly, but even her cold weather gear couldn't keep out the slashing, icy knives of the north wind.

"That was only a quarter thrust," Kan-Ten reminded her from the ship's cockpit. "Are you confident the replacements will hold at full power?"

"If they don't, we're stuck here," she pointed out, "so we may as well find out as soon as possible." She eyed the setting primary doubtfully. "No use pushing it, though. We're losing the light; we'll install the last one in the morning."

She circled around the quickly-solidifying oval of ice and scrambled up the ramp, letting out a relieved breath as the warmth of the ship's interior enveloped her again. She'd been outside for over three hours, most of that with Kan-Ten helping her install the nozzle before she'd sent him to the cockpit for a low-power test.

"Sandi, it's Ash." She heard his voice in her 'link, relayed over the ship's intercom from the main communications board. "Can you read me?"

"Go ahead, Ash," she responded, unwrapping her scarf from around her face as she headed up to the cockpit.

"How close are you to getting the *Acheron* in the air?" he asked, and she could tell by his tone that it wasn't just idle impatience.

"We just finished installing the third of the four replacements. I was planning on waiting till tomorrow to try the last one and do full power testing. Why? What's going on?"

There was a hesitation, long enough that she thought he might be talking to someone there with him at the base.

"Any chance you might be able to get the last one in tonight, Sandi?"

The question was strained, like he knew what he was asking of her and hated the words even as he said them. She frowned, leaning against the back of the pilot's acceleration couch. Kan-Ten had spun the copilot's seat around to face her and was watching her end of the conversation with an unreadable visage.

"It's getting pretty damned chilly outside, but I guess I can try. What's the situation?"

"The thing is down here," he admitted and she felt her stomach sink out from underneath her. "It rode the shuttle down with Singh's pilot, then killed him. It's inside the installation, down in the emergency access tunnels, and we think it's heading for the pod...the hive, whatever you want to call it. The artifact. It wants to use it to reproduce, maybe even to build a ship. Commander Busick is going to evacuate everyone and plant charges to bring the roof down, but we can't all fit in the cartel shuttle. We need the *Acheron* or we won't last a night outside."

"I got you. We'll get it installed as quick as we can. I'll let you know when we're prepped for takeoff."

"Thanks. And be careful...once you get the ship over here, you need to keep it sealed, weapons armed until we get on board. There's only one thing the hybrid wants more than the artifact: it wants to get back to Earth, and the *Acheron* is the only way off this rock."

———

Gunnery Sergeant Alvin Kamara felt incredibly exposed standing in the center of the corridor intersection; it ran counter to every bit of tactical training he'd ever received. But that training was for fighting Tahni, or maybe humans, against an enemy that struck from a distance and worked in teams. This was less of an enemy soldier that he faced and more a predatory animal, though with human-level intelligence. It probably did have the capacity to use a gun, he decided, but it didn't *want* to. It had never picked up any of the loose weapons on the *Metaurus*, hadn't bothered.

It's taunting us, he realized. *It knows it can kill us with its claws and its teeth. It knows that will make us more afraid.*

This formation made sense. He had a squad and a half, twelve men and women, to cover this intersection and the stairway door at the end of the hallway; he'd thought about just layering everyone down at the door, but they'd be effectively blind if they did that. The thing could shield itself from cameras, somehow, so they couldn't count on the security monitors to give them a warning. His half-dozen here at the intersection would spot it first, he was sure, and they'd engage it first. If they needed to, they could fall back to the stairway door.

They were in a circle, Gauss rifles pointed outward, with him in the center to be the spotter, to scan for it and direct fire. Where they stood, they didn't have a direct shot at the stairway entrance, so every direction was a free-fire zone. It was perfect.

"We're in place, Commander," he called to Busick. "We'll hold it off until the Chief gets the charges set."

"Roger that, Gunny." Her voice wavered slightly. She was scared. He knew it because he was, too. "If you can't hold it, if it..."

"Kate," he interrupted her gently, "we *will* hold it. We'll give you the time you need."

He thought she'd signed off, but then he realized he could still hear her breathing.

"I'm sorry it didn't work out, Alvin."

He felt a brief, intense pain somewhere in his chest. He hadn't thought about their relationship in months, had managed to put it behind him as something short and ill-advised, something brought on by stress and isolation, but the words brought it back full force. Maybe he shouldn't have been such a prick about the difference in their ranks; it wasn't as if it was going to matter now.

"Make sure you get out of here," he said, his voice soft, almost wistful. "If you don't, I'll feel like I didn't do my job."

"Aye-aye, Gunny."

And she was gone. He breathed out, long and emptying, imagining himself expelling distractions and regrets and memories and focusing all his attention on the present. It was a technique he'd learned in martial arts classes on Aphrodite, long before he'd enlisted in the Marines, long before the war. He'd been in trouble with the local cops, in trouble with his family, heading down the wrong road, when he'd found the Way. It had been more than just learning to fight; he'd already *known* how to fight. No, the Way had taught him how to focus, how to concentrate, how to rid himself of the extraneous.

The corridor was silent, motionless, his Marines as still as statues, waiting. He wished he could have said with confidence that it was their iron discipline that kept them frozen, but he suspected it was just as much abject terror. Seconds crawled by, stretching out into minutes, and he heard the scrape of a combat boot on cement floor, the rasp of a weapons sling against an armored vest as men and women scanned back and forth.

The thing had to come this way, he knew it. There was no other way down; the ventilation ducts were too narrow for something that big, so it was the stairs or the elevator. When it came up the corridor, they could pump it with tungsten slugs, and Kamara couldn't believe that even this thing would be able to survive that sort of punishment. They just had to keep their eyes open.

The lights went out.

The infrared lamps in Kamara's helmet snapped on automatically, and the on-board computer enhanced the image with a rendering based on thermal, infrared and sonic sensors, but the view in his visor went from the crisp, three-dimensional delineation of visible light hitting the human eyes to something softer and less real. Kamara leaned back instinctively to look up at the light panels in the ceiling but they were still intact, just darkened and dead.

"What the hell's going on?" someone asked over the platoon band, echoed by a chorus of confusion and the slight motion of IFF transponders on his display as Marines began to shift from their positions.

"Shut up and hold your stations," Kamara snapped. Their chatter died to nervous silence and he listened intently. It was hard to notice the low, humming hiss of the ventilators when they were running, but the absence of them was painfully obvious. It wasn't just the lights. He hit the control at his wrist to change frequencies. "Commander, we've lost power down here. Do you read?"

Nothing. He cursed inside the privacy of his helmet. It made sense. Their 'links wouldn't be able to penetrate the walls of the base without signal repeaters, and without power...

"It's coming," he warned the others. His voice was steady, confident, professional. "It must have hit a power junction or the reactor itself, somehow. It's not as smart as it thinks, though; we don't need the lights."

Except the hybrid doesn't need them either...

There was a dark blur, something out of the edge of his field of view, something he wasn't quite sure was there. But he knew, he was sure. He spun on his heel and swung his rifle around, firing at the vaguely defined shape despite the fact that his helmet targeting systems didn't seem to register it. Tungsten slugs smacked into the far wall, propelled at 2,500 meters per second, sending splinters of volcanic rock erupting outward in clouds of dust, but the thing had moved; it was already meters away and running too fast for him to react.

"Shoot it!" he bellowed, voice finally betraying him, showing his panic.

But the words trailed the motion and the motion was blindingly quick. The Marine next to him was Sergeant Shan, the First Squad leader, a good man who'd left behind a wife and child on Inferno six years ago. In the time it took for Kamara to look to his right, Shan was gone, jerked backwards without as much as a scream and slammed into the wall behind them. Red-black liquid that defied clarification by his helmet's optics splashed away from Shan's body and his head rolled loose of his torso with a clatter of metal and plastic.

Gauss rifle muzzles swung around recklessly and Kamara could hear the snap-crack of the rounds breaking the sound barrier just ahead of the explosions of floor and ceiling material, and two Marines died in the time it took him to turn his head, their bodies ripped apart with a wrenching of jagged talons that seemed to take the barest effort. But there was another sound, something that pierced through the rending of metal and flesh and the screams and the discharge of Gauss rifles. It was a smack, a solid thump of a hyperaccelerated tungsten slug into a material qualitatively different than anything man had made, and Kamara saw a hesitation in the creature's fluid movements, thought just maybe he saw a ragged, fibrous rip in the thing's chest.

And then it was gone, blurring back around the corner, but perhaps just a bit more slowly than it had come, and Kamara's gunfire chased it along the wall in pockmarked ruptures of the rock.

"Back to the lift station!" the Gunny yelled, grabbing the rescue handle on the back of one of the downed Marines and hauling him along as he retreated. Not that the man could be saved, but he knew he'd need the weapons and ammo and this was the easiest way to bring it along.

"Gunny, what the hell's going on?" That was Sgt. Longley, Second Squad leader, just spotting the remaining three Marines backing toward them at a double-time pace from the intersection.

The five others there arrayed with him around the lift banks and the emergency stairwell entrance shuffled side to side, their Gauss rifle muzzles scanning back and forth in a hemispherical pattern as if they expected the hybrid to be crawling across the ceiling. He dragged the dead Marine over against the wall about two meters from them, trying not to look at the wreckage where the man's chest had been. A trail of dark crimson blood marked his passage around the curve of the hall and he tried not to look at that too much, either.

"Get set in your positions," Kamara ordered, trying to make his tone harsh enough to not be questioned. "The thing is here and it already attacked us once. I want you aiming for a spot two meters closer than the farthest you can see with your infrared illuminators, but keep your eyes on the curve in the corridor. The minute you notice anything there, even if it looks like a shadow or a trick of the light, open fire." He ducked down between the ranks of the six Marines Longley had been commanding, motioning the other two survivors with him to take up spots there, down on one knee among the others who were standing straight.

"I think I hit it, Gunny," Private Caminero said breathlessly. "I think I hit the fucking thing."

"I think you did, too," he agreed with her, trying to sound encouraging. "And I'm pretty sure that's why it took off. It'll be back, but now we know we can hurt it. We just have to keep our heads and hold our ground. Are all of you with me?"

"Hoo-rah, Gunny,' Longley enthused, along with a murmuring of agreement from the others. Caminero and Maathai, the two who'd been with him, just waited in subdued silence.

I don't really blame them, he thought.

They'd seen the thing...they knew better.

———

"How far is this place?" Fontenot wondered, eyeing the narrow walls of the corridor doubtfully. They seemed to get closer to her shoulders with each curve in the hallway and she was pretty sure they'd walked two kilometers around the perimeter tunnels that ringed the installation.

"They didn't exactly want to store HyperExplosives near

the workspace," Chief Weaver told her, not bothering to look back.

Weaver was walking quickly, purposefully, knowing exactly where he was going, but the two former docking bay technicians with him were struggling to keep up. Jandreau and Ashef, she remembered their names were, a skinny, elfin woman who looked as if she'd grown up on a low-grav world, and a shorter man with bushy hair well beyond regulation after so many years away from anyone who cared. Their utility fatigues were patched and worn, not as well-kept as the Marines' or Busick's or Weaver's, and Fontenot had the sense that they wouldn't have been the first choice to bring along.

"It's just right of the next intersection," Weaver told him a moment later, and she had the sense that he hadn't remembered exactly himself until he'd seen it.

The lighting out at this level was old and sparse and had never been that extensive from what she could tell, but over the reinforced bare metal of the storage room door a single panel glowed brightly. It shone down on a sign with the universal symbol for danger and the words "NO ADMITTANCE" in capital letters ten centimeters tall stenciled across it. Weaver yanked open a security seal and touched an old-fashioned magnetic key card to the pad beneath it, and a green light blinked to life together with the unmistakable clunk of a magnetic door lock releasing.

"Okay, be careful in here," the old Chief of Boat cautioned, hauling the heavy door open with a grunt of effort. "There's a lot of shit lying around, and most of it isn't safe."

As the door swung open with a creak of decades-old hinges, an automatic switch set the interior lighting panels flickering to life. They were as dim and past their replacement dates as everything else out here, and the room inside was gloomy with the shadows of tall metal lockers and squat plastic storage crates, turning the construction equipment scattered around the concrete floor into looming monsters.

Jandreau and Ashef hung back, and Fontenot scowled as she passed them by, following the Chief. She was only a couple steps behind him when the lights faded and the storage room and the corridors outside were plunged into total darkness.

"Oh, what the fuck?" Jandreau exclaimed. "How the hell are we going to get back out of here now?"

Fontenot had infrared lensing in her cybernetic eye, but even that needed ambient light to show her anything, and down here there simply was none. She stood stock still, not wanting to knock anything over by accident, and wished she still had her vacuum suit with its equipment belt; there'd been a flashlight on that belt.

"Calm down, everyone," Weaver sighed. A small light flared to life, impossibly bright after the absolute darkness, waving with the movements of the Chief's hand. "Some of us weren't stupid enough to wander around without a flashlight. Just stay still and I'll get the blasting charges."

He turned away and darkness blanketed the others as the light turned with him, but now there was at least enough ambient glow from his flashlight that Fontenot could see. The image was flat, and two-dimensional and tinted green; her vision processors were older and lacked the sort of computer enhancement that modern helmet systems included. But she could see well enough to make out the bulky, massive lines of the storage locker, again marked with skull and crossbones and a prominent red circle with a slash through it.

Weaver used the same magnetic card on the security pad placed at chest level on the two-meter-wide locker and pulled it open, revealing mostly empty shelves, except for three large, polymer cases. Each also sported the ubiquitous danger warnings and a government inventory label that stated they contained ten kilograms of HyperExplosives.

Which was, Fontenot reflected, a shitload of HyperExplosives.

Yeah, she thought, swallowing hard, *that'd be enough to bring this whole place down if you plant it just right.*

It was funny how living this long made a girl appreciate not dying. She hoped Weaver knew what he was doing, because she sure didn't trust Jandreau and Ashef to handle it. The thought of them messing around with that that much destructive material made her glance back askance at the two of them, which was why she was looking their way when a swathe of coruscating laser pulses sliced through both of them in a spray of vaporized blood.

Fontenot could move pretty fast; beyond just the added power of the bionics, she'd had a century to get used to them. She'd grabbed Weaver around the shoulders, slammed the storage locker shut and was across the room behind the cover of an industrial boring laser before the shooter could adjust their aim and put a burst through the space she'd just been standing in.

Weaver crashed into her chest with a grunt of pained breath, and grimaced at her plaintively, with a look of incomprehension in his eyes, like he hadn't realized what was going on. He figured it out when another blast of coherent light and ionized air passed just over their heads, some of it splashing into the other side of the machinery and sending up a shower of flashing sparks. He'd dropped the flashlight and it was still spinning slowly on its metal casing, sending a parade of shadows over the walls.

Fontenot cursed, realizing she didn't have a gun; the Marines had confiscated her weapons at the escape pod and things had been so hurried before that they'd never got around to giving it back. Weaver had a sidearm, though, and she saw him yanking it out of its hip holster, holding it in a confident, two-handed grip that told her that he'd at least taken it to the range a few times.

"Where are the others?" the Chief yelled in her ear, though he needn't have bothered; her cybernetic audio pickup was very sensitive.

"Dead," she told him, gesturing back toward the door before she realized he probably couldn't even see her. The flashlight beam was shining against the far wall and most of the room was bathed in shadowy gloom.

"Who the fuck is shooting at us?" Weaver bellowed, pitching his voice to carry across to the entrance. "What the hell's wrong with you?"

"There's no need for anyone else to die here, Chief Weaver."

Fontenot didn't recognize the voice, but it was female and sounded confident and in charge.

"Sanchez?" Disbelief was strong in Weaver's squawked reply. "You fucking bitch! What the hell? Are you fucking insane?"

He leaned around the edge of the machinery and blasted a shot in the woman's general direction despite not being able to see much of anything. Fontenot grabbed his arm and yanked him back behind cover as the answering volley flashed around them in flares of vaporized plastic and metal.

"It's 'Dr. Sanchez,' if you please," the woman insisted tautly. "Throw away your gun and come out with your hands up if you want to leave this room alive. I don't want to kill you, I just want those explosives."

"Dr. Sanchez?" Fontenot demanded. "She's that hard-ass that works with Nagle?"

She hadn't met the woman, but she recalled her name from

Commander Busick's earlier conversation with Ash, and while the way they'd talked about her made her sound like a real ass-kicker, Dr. Sanchez was probably the last person she'd expected to find behind a pulse carbine.

"I'm not giving you any fucking explosives!" Weaver yelled back, enraged; Fontenot had to grab his shoulder to keep him from jumping up again. "You just *murdered* two of my people! I'm going to rip off your fucking head and shit down your throat!"

"I've been stuck in this Goddamned hole for the last twenty fucking years!" the researcher screamed at them. She fired another burst over their heads. "I'm not going to let you Goddamned Fleet morons destroy everything I've worked for!"

Fontenot put a hand on Weaver's arm to keep him down, then jumped out from the other side of the laser borer and took a look back toward the door. The researcher, Sanchez, was standing in the door, in front of God and radar as her old Marine Drill Instructor had liked to say, looking incongruous with her baggy civilian clothes and a wicked-looking pulse carbine pouring heat out of its cooling vanes, her face screwed up with rage and determination behind a set of thin, civilian enhanced-optics glasses that would give her night vision and thermal imaging. She had a shoulder bag that Fontenot was fairly sure had spare magazines.

Sanchez turned quickly towards Fontenot and shot off another short burst, but the cyborg was already back behind cover before the researcher's finger had touched the trigger pad, and the white-hot pencils of ionized air dug harmless craters in the far wall. Fontenot steadied herself back behind the borer, then turned to Weaver. The man was blinking, squinting, trying to see anything in the worthless gleam of the fallen flashlight.

"Give me your gun," Fontenot said to him in a flat tone that brooked no argument.

"What can you do with it that I can't?" Weaver demanded, a bit petulantly.

"See," she answered simply, snatching the pistol out of his hand.

His mouth worked as if he was going to object, but she was already in motion. She crouched with her feet underneath her and jumped out into a clear corridor of cement floor between the borer and the locker with the explosives. She skidded across the floor on her right shoulder, the pulse pistol held outstretched in her left hand. The good thing about both arms being cybernetic was that she was just as proficient with either one, and the bionic eye was on her left.

The view from the ocular wasn't ideal for shooting; there was no depth perception and everything was a hazy shade of green. But she'd done it before, so very many times, too many times. It was just too damned easy now.

She touched the trigger for just a fraction of a second, feeling the tactile feedback through the sensors in the hand, feeling the HyperExplosive charges igniting inside the combustion chamber of the handgun, their heat energy pulsing through the lasing rod and out the focusing crystal. It was a three-round burst, and the ionized air traced a line through the room, connecting the focus crystal to Sanchez' chest just long enough to form an afterimage across her natural eye.

The researcher jerked backwards, trying to scream; it came out as a choked, wet gasp. She stumbled out of the doorway, putting one hand out to steady herself and letting the pulse carbine fall clattering to the floor. Fontenot pushed herself up on her right hand, getting her legs under her and rising quickly, keeping the gun trained on the other woman.

Sanchez came up against the wall opposite the doorway, leaning into it with her right shoulder. She shuddered with a hacking cough and blood sprayed out onto the bare concrete.

Fontenot walked up to her with long, slow steps, kicking the carbine away as she passed it.

She wanted to say something sarcastic, wanted to tell Sanchez that for someone so smart, she was so incredibly stupid. But the researcher's eyes were unfocused and she was slowly choking to death on her own blood, so Fontenot just back-handed her across the temple and crushed her skull. Sanchez slid down the wall, leaving a dark smear across it.

Behind her, she sensed more than saw Weaver clambering out from cover to retrieve his flashlight.

"You get that bitch?" he asked her.

"The bitch is gotten."

She pulled the shoulder bag off Sanchez' corpse and slung it around her neck, then stepped back to where she'd left the carbine. Weaver was checking the two docking bay technicians, and seeing what she already knew, that they were both dead.

"Damn it," he muttered, spitting on the floor next to them. "They weren't much as far as crew goes, but they didn't deserve to go like this." He shook his head. "I gotta' get the charges. We have to get back and get them in place while Kamara is still holding out."

"Yeah, about that," Fontenot said, "given that the next part of it depended on the cooperation of Nagle and the researchers, well…" She gestured at Sanchez' body. "Somehow, I don't think things are going to go according to plan."

CHAPTER FIFTEEN

JAGMEET SINGH KNEW THAT SOMETHING HAD GONE WRONG. He'd heard the commotion of the Marines moving through the corridor outside the medical clinic, then more footsteps heading off a different direction; that had been the first clue. Then the lights had gone out.

"Oh, well, that's just great," the corpsman muttered from the table where he'd been sitting. He'd been reading from a hand-held tablet and the glow lit up his face in the sudden darkness. "What now?"

"I take it this isn't something that happens on a regular basis?" Singh asked. He nearly chuckled at his own sudden curiosity. What did he care?

The Fleet medic looked at him sidelong, like he was wondering whether he should talk to a prisoner.

"Naw, man," he finally answered. "This place has a fusion reactor and all the wiring is inside the fucking walls. How the hell is that gonna' shut down?"

"If someone shuts it down on purpose, I imagine," Singh suggested easily, and the corpsman's eyes went wide at the idea.

A flashlight beam floated in through the open door, followed by Ashton Carpenter. He was wearing a gunbelt, a pulse pistol in one hand and the light in the other. He stopped by Singh's bed, staring down at the bounty hunter with judgement weighing in the balance on his face.

"Things are in the shitter," he said. He had one of those nondescript voices, unremarkable, like a sales manager at a fabricator plant. He was trying to sound serious, but it came out like he was reporting a bad quarter to his employees. "The creature from the *Metaurus* is here, inside the base."

"What?" the corpsman blurted, fear strong in his voice. They both ignored him.

"One of two things can happen now," Ash went on. "The medic and I can leave you strapped in here and you'll die, or you can help us try to get out of this and live to kill me another day." He shrugged. "We don't have a lot of time."

Singh knew what he should do. It shouldn't have been a question. He would lie to the man who killed his wife, tell him that, of course, he was ready to help. Then he would wait for the first chance to kill him, and make his way out to kill the other, Sandi Hollande.

"All right," Singh said. "Let me out of this shit and I'll do what I can."

Was he lying? He could see Ash trying to decide it, but he found himself wondering the same thing, and he still hadn't made up his mind when Ash reached down and shut off the neural restraints. Feeling returned to his body, as did control of his bionics. Just a jab of that hand, a chop to Ash Carpenter's neck, and he would have avenged Freya.

Instead, he pushed himself up and stood before Ash. The pilot reached into the waistband of his borrowed fatigue pants and pulled out a second pulse pistol, handing it butt-first to Singh. The bounty hunter extended his natural hand and took the gun, checking its load instinctively, then nodding.

"Where are we going?" he asked.

Ash's mouth quirked as if he found some sort of humor in all this.

"Where we both belong," the pilot said. "The Pit."

———

"What the hell is *he* doing here?" Fontenot demanded, levelling her pulse carbine at Singh's chest one-handed, the other grasping the carry handle of a blasting charge.

"We're really not in any position to turn down help," Ash told her, moving quickly to step between them.

Busick had dug up some emergency lanterns from a storage closet and the subdued glow gave the operations room a conspiratorial atmosphere, full of flickering shadows. Fontenot and Weaver had arrived while he had been busy retrieving Singh and the corpsman, and all five of them were gathered near the doorway. Weaver seemed pretty doubtful about Singh's inclusion as well, but he and Busick were occupied with running a check on the electronic timers for the other two charge containers. They'd been down in that storage locker for a long time, and only God knew how old they'd been before the DSI contractors had stowed them away.

Fontenot lowered her weapon, scowling.

"You don't think he's going to backshoot you the first chance he gets?"

Ash started to deny it reflexively, but paused with the words unformed. Yeah, he was fairly sure that was exactly what was going to happen.

"I'm hoping," he replied, trying to be a bit more honest with his friend, "that he waits for a more convenient time for all of us."

"The detonators are functional," Busick announced, looking

over at them as if she hadn't heard any of the interplay. "Let's get down there and get them planted."

"The elevators aren't working," Weaver reminded her. "We're going to have to pass right through Kamara's defensive position."

Ash could tell that the Chief was holding himself back from finishing the thought: What if Kamara and all his Marines were already dead and the hybrid was in the Pit?

"Ms. Fontenot," Busick said, ignoring the comment, "if you wouldn't mind handing off that blasting charge to Commander Carpenter, I'd like you walking point. The three of us carrying the explosives will be next, then you," to the corpsman, "then Mr. Singh." She eyed the bounty hunter, just the azure gleam of her eyes visible above the shadow the lanterns threw across her face. "If you're going to abandon us," she said to him, "this is the perfect chance to do it, but if you attempt to take a shot at Commander Carpenter, bear in mind he's carrying enough explosives to bring down a hundred meters of tunnel."

She pulled a pulse pistol from her holster and held it at her right side, the case for the blasting charge hanging from her left hand.

"Let's go."

Ash took the case from Fontenot a bit gingerly, feeling an irrational fear that he might drop it, even though he knew it was way too stable to go off from just an impact. It was solid and massive with ten kilos of explosives and another five or so of the case material, but with only half Earth-normal gravity, it wasn't too cumbersome. Fontenot seemed happy to hand it off to him, and she also didn't seem at all upset about walking point. He could only guess she felt better having her fate in her own hands and having both those hands free to fight.

"Don't I get a gun?" the corpsman asked plaintively, shuffling into line just ahead of Singh, and staring with obvious discomfort at the bounty hunter's weapon.

Ash fell in behind Busick, and caught the look of disdain that Weaver gave the medic.

"We're fresh out, son," he told the young enlisted man. "If that thing comes after the rest of us, just run like hell." He pointed upward. "That way."

Ash had walked the path to the lift banks only hours ago, but it could have been a totally different planet in the dark. Fontenot's carbine had an integrated weapon's light, and the pulse pistols accepted military-issue flashlights on their accessory rails, but having the lights attached to their weapons meant they couldn't point them at each other. Circles of illumination danced around as they all tried to cover a section of the corridor, but each of them was encased in their own personal sheath of darkness and Ash felt a thin sheen of unreality over everything.

Maybe he'd wake up any second and find out this was all a nightmare, he thought, or maybe he'd never actually made it to the escape pod on the *Metaurus* and this was actually Hell. It had all the signs of it: trapped underground with other lost souls, separated from Sandi, hunted by something that could very easily be the devil himself...except that Nagle had called the hybrid a her.

On second thought, maybe it was a good thing Sandi wasn't here; at least she was outside, relatively safe compared to the rest of them. Except he knew her, and once she repaired the ship, she'd burn right over to the installation and then she and Kan-Ten would head right in after them. Sandi wouldn't abandon him. If she could have, she would have done it back in the war. And if he could have abandoned her, he would have done it when she'd shown up and yanked him out of his boring, comfortable life and pulled her into a world of cartels and bounty hunters.

They fell into a kind of pattern as they walked, a constantly-shifting back-and-forth scan that let each of the armed members of the party monitor every part of the hallway at least once as they passed it. Ash thought it was probably Fontenot who initiated it; she had more combat experience than probably anyone alive, he estimated. There were other people as old, of course---the gossip streams back in Trans-Angeles were constantly ooh-ing and ahh-ing about how many execs in the Corporate Council were over two hundred now---but most of them were rich enough that if they'd ever seen a day of service in the military, it was over a hundred years ago.

He could live that long, he realized. He'd had the treatments because he was a military officer; it was one of the reasons he'd gone to the Academy, after seeing all the truly *old* people back in the projects. All he had to do was avoid getting killed in the next few minutes, and then somehow avoid dying in one of the crazy jobs they kept taking, or while running some errand for Fleet Intelligence like this...

Concentrate, he chided himself. He kept letting his thoughts drift away, losing focus. It was too easy down here, too easy to do without a ship's interface bringing all the data to him in a single, coherent picture. Here he had to piece it all together himself.

"Gunny," he heard Busick say, presumably into her 'link pickup. "Do you read?"

We must be getting close, he realized. Close enough that Busick thought the 'links might work without the signal repeaters. *But is there anyone left to hear us?*

"Roger that," she said, responding to a transmission he couldn't hear. "We're coming in. Don't shoot us."

One final curve, and he started to see the bodies. There were way too many of them, Kamara's Marines, their armor torn apart, some of them with their heads ripped completely off. Bits of bone were scattered around the corpses, still sticky with blood that looked black in the low light. Other things, things Ash tried not to look at too closely, were splattered across the walls. Something roiled in his stomach and he forced himself not to close his eyes.

Looking back, he saw Singh stooping to relieve one of the bodies of its Gauss rifle, swapping out a full mag spilling from a torn-open chest pouch for the empty one it had contained. He stood and held the rifle in his cybernetic left hand as if it weighed nothing, still using the pistol in his right for its flashlight.

Then they were past the intersection and approaching the lift station. There were more bodies scattered there, but there were also three Marines left standing. Ash couldn't shine a light at them directly, not without pointing a gun at them, but the ambient glow of the weapon's lights let him see enough.

One of them was leaning against the wall by the lift door, blood soaking her left leg from three deep gashes across her thigh, deep enough to penetrate the armor plates there. The armor's medical systems had probably stopped the bleeding, but she wouldn't be able to take much in the way of painkillers as long as she was still in combat. The man next to her looked basically untouched, but the muzzle of his rifle was jumping around nervously and Ash thought he must be pretty close to complete panic.

Kamara was steady, despite the ragged slices across his chest. They hadn't quite penetrated the thicker armor there, but it had been a near thing.

"We're going to set the charges," Busick told him. "Keep it out long enough for us to get them in place."

"I don't know if we can take another attack," Kamara admitted, speaking to her over his external speakers. "We've slowed it down a little, but it's still pretty damned fast and hard to hit."

"I'll stay here and help," Fontenot offered.

She looked around until she found an intact Gauss rifle on the floor, then retrieved it and a fresh mag, handing the laser carbine and the shoulder bag full of magazines to Ash. He holstered his pistol and accepted them, slinging the bag over his shoulder then tucking the carbine into his hip so he could hold it one-handed.

"Are you sure about this?" he asked her, shaking his head.

"I'm not suicidal," Fontenot replied with a humorless chuckle. "I'll still be here when you get back." She turned and eyed Singh. "What about you, pretty boy?"

"By all means," Singh assented, stepping over to join the three Marines. "This would certainly be an interesting way to die, if not the one I'd imagined."

"Hurry," Kamara urged Busick. "We'll give you what time we can."

She nodded and went to the stairwell door, waving Chief Weaver forward. The Chief of Boat pulled out a set of magnetic key cards and laid one against the door's security plate. It apparently wasn't on the main power circuit, because a green light flashed on the plate's display and there was an audible, metallic scrape as the bolt withdrew into the door.

"Where'd you get the keys?" Ash asked as Busick pulled the door open. Inside it was the blackest dark he thought he'd ever seen, and stale cold air rushed out of it to send a chill down his back. "I can't see Nagle or Sanchez handing them over."

"Found them in a leftover tool locker from when they built the place," Weaver told him, snorting a sharp laugh. "Didn't think the eggheads needed to know."

Busick brushed past Weaver and headed downward, the light from her pistol showing nothing but an endless row of stairs descending in a tight spiral. Ash followed Weaver and whispered a curse; the rock walls were close enough that a deep intake of breath could make his shoulders scrape against them, narrow enough that he thought Fontenot might have gotten stuck between them if she hadn't stayed behind. He wasn't claustrophobic---they didn't let claustrophobes into Fleet pilot training---but he also wasn't enamored of the idea of being buried in a stairwell hundreds of meters underground after they set off the charges.

Ash had always pictured himself dying in space, not collapsed under a pile of rubble in a cave. He didn't know why it made a difference, but it did. He tried to banish the fear, tried to concentrate on finding each stair and keeping his footing. He had to point the carbine upward because to point it down would have meant sweeping Weaver with his muzzle and to sling it over his shoulder would have meant being completely in the dark. That meant he couldn't see where his feet were going, and simply avoiding a neck-breaking fall should have been enough to keep his thoughts occupied, but it wasn't.

Somehow, despite the distraction, and the weight of the case of explosives constantly trying to throw him off balance, and the corpsman running into him twice when Busick slowed down and nearly pushing him head-first down the stairs, he made it to the bottom without falling. Weaver and Busick stopped at the exit door on the final landing and Ash could hear them working the security plate and throwing the locking bolt, then heard the creak of hinges as it swung slowly open.

There was the slightest glimmer of light from somewhere on the other side, and Ash felt a surge of excitement that maybe the power wasn't off down here. He ducked through the narrow doorway on the heels of Chief Weaver and followed the sweeping cone of Commander Busick's light out of the cul-de-sac of the research level lift bank through the yawning gate of the first security seal. The glow he'd seen was coming from the battery-powered locking plate beside the hatchway, blinking yellow with a warning that main power was dead, and the lights were still out in the personnel sections of the research lab. The offices were dark, the magnetic seals on the doors ajar and there wasn't even the cold comfort of a chemical striplight to show them the way. The chemical emergency lights were standard in military facilities, but there hadn't been one to be found in the whole installation.

Ash couldn't recall much of the layout of the place from his one, brief visit, but he knew they'd have to pass through the central break room. It took longer than he'd thought it would, but eventually the glare from the weapon's lights reflecting off the white polymer of the hallway diffused into the larger space of the open chamber. Busick halted abruptly, in mid-step, and Ash nearly collided with Weaver when the Chief stopped just as short. The corpsman stumbled into his shoulder and Ash turned and glared back at him.

"Sorry man," the medic said, raising his hands. "I can't see shit back here."

Ash sighed, then slung his carbine, yanked the pistol from his belt holster and shoved it back at the man. The medic took it gingerly, but with a hint of a smile.

"Keep the light on and keep your damned finger off the trigger," Ash warned him.

He turned back to where Busick and Weaver were moving into the break room, looking at something he couldn't see, blocked from his view by the bulk of the recycler. He stepped past it, keeping the light from his carbine pointed downward, and sucked in a breath when he saw the body. He'd seen the man before; it was the red-haired one who'd been coming out of one of the sealed rooms when Sanchez had been walking him through to meet Nagle. His face had been red and flushed the last time Ash had seen him, but now it was ghost-pale in death, his green eyes open and clouded. There was a hole through his chest the size of a fist, and his blood had pooled beneath him, soaking the floor around the tables.

Two more of the researchers were crumpled on the floor just past him, an older man with a head wreathed in bushy, dark curls and a look of horror frozen on his face forever, and a thick-shouldered woman with a matronly face and long, auburn hair. Both had multiple entry and exit wounds, their mingled blood staining the rest of the break room floor a dark red.

"That monster didn't do this," Weaver declared with clinical detachment. "Someone shot them."

"Commander Busick?"

Four laser weapons snapped around at the words, and a tall, skinny man with brown dreadlocks raised his hands over his eyes at the sudden, blinding flare of light, cringing backwards. Ash thought he must have been hiding in one of the offices; he saw the door yawning open just off the break room.

"Don't shoot, please!" he begged, palms up, head down. The lights shone on his white, long-sleeved shirt, illuminating a stylized cartoon image of a little, blond girl dressed in some sort of battle armor, holding a sword longer than she was tall.

"Mercier," Ash remembered. "David Mercier, right?"

"Yeah, that's me," the geologist said, nodding desperately. "Please don't hurt me."

Ash lowered his carbine, then glanced back and pushed the medic's pistol down with the palm of his hand. The corpsman nodded, abashed.

"What happened here, Dr. Mercier?" Busick wanted to know.

"It was Susan," Mercier told her, looking back up now that the lights were out of his eyes. He kept his hands up, though, which was smart, Ash thought. Busick and Weaver held their handguns at low port, not pointed at him, but still ready. "Dr. Sanchez. She had a gun, I don't know where she got it. She told us that you guys were going to blow the place up." He eyed the cases with the blasting charges in them, blinking uncertainly, but then went on. "John..." He motioned towards the body of the red-head. "Dr. MacTaggart, he tried to talk her down, tried to argue with her that we weren't soldiers, that we couldn't fight anyone. She shot him down where he stood, and when Joiner and Muller tried to get her gun, she shot them, too."

His voice wavered, and Ash thought he might be about to cry.

"Dr. Nagle was yelling at her, but she told him to go back to the Pit, that she would take care of everything" he concluded, wiping a sleeve across his nose.

"Kenner," Busick said to the corpsman, "can you stay here and keep an eye on this guy?"

"Sure," Kenner said with a nod, then corrected himself. "Sorry, I mean, aye, ma'am."

"You two, with me," Busick said to Ash and Weaver.

It wasn't that much farther. If the rest of the walk had seemed almost endless, this was surprisingly abrupt. They reached the final security seal in less than a minute, even keeping an eye out for any more bodies or survivors. There were none; there was no sign anything was amiss other than the lack of power. But the seal was shut, locked down...and the security plate's indicator light was a steady, glowing red. Whatever had cut the power to the rest of the installation hadn't affected the Pit.

Commander Busick touched the call button on the intercom panel set in the hatch. She waited a moment, then cursed under her breath and jammed it down for about ten seconds before she let up again.

"Answer me, Nagle!" she shouted, leaning over the audio pickup. "I know you're in there!"

"I'm very sorry, Commander." Nagle's reply was soft,

distant, as if he was meters away from the microphone. "I know you think you're doing the right thing, but I can't allow you to destroy this lab. I've spent the last six years searching for a way to bring her back, and I know I can do it, given the chance."

Busick gritted her teeth and was about to snap back a reply, but Ash stepped forward and spoke before she could.

"Who is she to you?" he asked. Busick glared at him, but he raised a hand to quell her. "You said someone volunteered for the procedure. Who was she to you?"

There was a pause, and Ash thought for a moment that he'd blown it, that Nagle had cut the connection, but he could still hear background noise, hear Nagle or someone else moving around, hear the rasp of shoes on the metal grating.

"Her name," the response finally came in a voice wistful and close to breaking, "was Ophelia Dimas. She was responsible for the effort to decipher the language of the pod's biological computer systems. And she was the only woman I have ever loved."

"Shit," Busick murmured, slumping against the hatch.

"She didn't tell me what she intended to do," Nagle went on as if he hadn't heard her. "Susan Sanchez helped her; she told me that she knew Agent Atumi would force us to do it eventually, if Ophelia hadn't volunteered. She was afraid I would be the one to do it, and she said the project couldn't continue without me." Another long pause. "I think, perhaps, Susan felt a jealousy at our relationship; but in the end, I was too late to stop it."

"I'm very sorry for what happened to Ophelia," Ash told him, and was surprised to find that he meant it. However batshit crazy they both were, Nagle had obviously loved the woman and blamed himself for what had happened to her. "But we can't let her get to that hive. God only knows what she'll be able to do with it if she can get it to work. You have to realize that."

"I can bring her back," Nagle insisted, stubbornness in his tone. "I'm sure of it. If I can get her here, I know I can. Just get out of her way and let her through. Get to your ship and get away."

"I know you believe that, Doctor," Busick interjected. "But what if you're wrong? What if she just uses the hive to make more like her, then makes her own starship? You said it yourself: she wants to return to Earth, and she also wants to kill everyone and destroy every trace of a technological civilization. How can we let you take that chance with hundreds of billions of lives?"

"You don't have any choice, Commander. I'm not letting you through that door, and if you stay, she'll kill you." He sighed heavily, a burst of static over the speaker. "If it comes to it, if I think she's not going to let me help her, I have the codes to the fail-safes. I promise you, if need be, I will bring the whole facility down myself."

The light showing the connection went dark. Nagle had cut it. Busick closed her eyes, still leaning against the cold metal of the hatch.

"What are we going to do, ma'am?" Weaver asked quietly. "Maybe we could use the charges on the hatch?"

"That hatch could survive a shot from a proton cannon." Busick shook her head. "It's stronger than the fucking rock around it..."

Ash felt the hair on the back of his neck rise as a thought flared to life like a supernova in the darkness and he felt a smile spread across his face.

"We need to get back to the others," he declared. Busick and Weaver glanced at him curiously. "There's a back way out of this place, and we need Mercier to show it to us."

"Why?" Busick asked. "What do you have in mind?"

"Plan B, Commander," he told her, casting a meaningful glance back at the intercom and shaking his head. "Plan B."

CHAPTER SIXTEEN

SHE FELT PAIN. FOR THE FIRST TIME IN YEARS, SHE FELT what it was like to be hurt.

Had she *ever* felt it? Yes, she realized, part of her had. The part that had once been human, had once been a woman named Ophelia, she had felt it. She'd felt it during the transformation, when that human thing had combined with the form of a Skrela warrior to make something new, something that had never been seen before.

The hybrid, they called it. She remembered hearing them say it, remembered the fear in their voices, the fascination. The others had felt fascination, the ones in the lab...not the man, though. The man named Adam had felt only sadness and desperation, not for himself, but for her. She remembered being sorry, remembered the regret. There was none of that now, no feeling, no regret, only pain and an overwhelming need to get to the womb. The womb could fix everything, the womb could fill the need, could make her more than she was, could get her home.

All she felt was the need, and all these humans blocking her way felt was fear. They'd hurt her, even with their primitive weapons...pitiful things shooting bits of metal. If she could get to the womb, she'd show them the power of a Skrela plasma cannon; all she had now were her claws and her teeth and the strength of her body. That would be enough, she was confident. She'd been coming in faster than they could follow, picking them off one at a time. One more pass, maybe two, and nothing would be in her way.

She unfolded from the nook in the ceiling, where the air vent was set into the rock, and lowered herself silently to the floor. Already, the ragged holes in her side were filling with the viscous biomechanical sludge that would begin to repair her chitin, and in a few hours, she would be whole once more. She felt the claws on her feet dig into the rock floor as she ran, going faster than the human eyes could follow.

"It's coming," Kamara announced, his voice a murmur in Korri Fontenot's audio receiver. It was built into the cybernetic ear replacement along with a transceiver that could work with her 'link or on its own, a handy thing that had saved her life more than once.

She wasn't sure if it was going to be enough this time.

She could hear the thing, too. The scrape of its claws on the rock, faster and faster, coming from around the corner near the intersection. She trained her Gauss rifle on a section of wall just past the curve in the hallway and waited, slaving her trigger finger to her bionic eye; it would be faster that way than making the decision consciously.

It still managed to surprise her when the stock recoiled back into her shoulder. There was no discomfort, of course; her shoulders were both metal, though covered by synthskin now. But the pressure sensors embedded in the skin carried the feeling to her brain and she felt it as if someone had shoved her. The third tungsten slug out of the rifle smacked into the wall, but she knew the first two had hit, and she could see the dark green blur slow and solidify into something large and two-legged and menacing.

Hers were the first shots to hit, but not the last; Singh and Kamara and the two other Marines were firing now, taking advantage of the damage from her rounds slowing the hybrid down. She could see the impacts jerking the creature to the side as it ran, spalling bits of chitin off of its biomechanical armor, and spraying some sort of black goo out when the rounds pierced through. She dared to let herself hope for just a second that they'd done it, that they'd killed the thing.

But it didn't stop, not even when a heavy metal slug shattered the right side of its nightmare jaw, sending fragments of its wickedly curved teeth flying through the air. Instead, it curved its run at the last second, ducking low and swiping its claws right through the armor over one of the Marines' lower torso. The armor ripped apart, something she'd never seen happen before, and organs spilled out through the gap along with gouts of blood, and the man inside the armor sagged, dead on his feet and too shocked to realize it.

Fontenot knew instinctively that she couldn't shoot the thing; it was too close, and there was too great a chance of hitting one of their own. The Gauss rifles were heavy and sturdy and useful for butt-stroking an enemy, but the thing was too fast for that. She swung her left fist in an almost convulsive backhand, connecting with the hybrid as it went for the next Marine in line. The blow shook her, vibrating down her fist all the way into the spinal reinforcements that anchored her bionics, but it slammed into the side of the creature's head near the wound to its jaw and sent it reeling backwards.

Fontenot was fairly certain she was going to die in that

moment. The thing was too fast for her to get in another blow before it recoiled and lashed out at her. Then Singh lunged in from just a meter away and crashed his huge, metal left fist into the other side of the hybrid's head. His punch slowed it down long enough for Fontenot to jam the muzzle of her Gauss rifle against the thing's massive shoulder and pull the trigger.

At this range, the round punched right through even the heavy, segmented armor of the shoulder, and a spray of black ichor exploded out the back of it. Then the thing was running again, still too incredibly fast to get a bead on with human reflexes, and in a second, it was around the corner and gone. Fontenot gasped in a lungful of air, suddenly realizing she'd been holding her breath. Kamara was down on a knee, checking the vitals of the eviscerated Marine, but Fontenot knew the man was as good as dead. If they could have thrown him directly into an auto-doc, he might have been saved, but the nearest one was a ten-minute walk away right past the hybrid, and it didn't have power.

There were only four of them left: her, Singh, Kamara and a short, stocky female Marine with a wounded leg. They'd hurt the thing, maybe hurt it bad, but Fontenot wasn't sure if they'd be able to finish it. She glanced up at Singh. On infrared, he looked like half a man, his bionics dark and fuzzy.

"Thanks."

"You are as dangerous as I imagined you might be, Fontenot," he responded. "It has been a memorable experience to fight beside you instead of against you."

"You sure know how to sweet-talk a girl," she cracked, grinning lopsidedly.

The door to the stairwell banged open behind them with a flare of a flashlight that washed out her night vision, and she nearly shot Ashton Carpenter in the face before she realized who he was.

"Jesus, Ash," she hissed. "You could have knocked."

"Get downstairs now," he said, not bothering to apologize. "All of you, hurry."

Kamara looked up from the dying Marine, his face invisible behind his visor. Fontenot didn't have to see it; she knew that pain from past lives. He detached the man's rifle from his retention sling and handed it to her.

"Cover our backs," he told her. Then he grabbed the woman with the wounded leg under her arm and began helping her back through the stairway door.

Fontenot saw Ash eyeing Singh carefully. The bounty hunter grunted a hoarse laugh, then stepped past the pilot to head down the stairs in front of him.

"Go," Fontenot said, nodding toward the door. "I'll be right behind you."

Going down the narrow stairwell backwards and in the dark was challenging, but her cybernetic legs came complete with internal gyroscopes to help her maintain balance, and though there had been plenty of instances when she'd regretted the injuries that had forced her bionics onto her, this was not one of them.

Maybe that's why I've lived my life out on the edge, she thought, her eyes fixed on the top of the stairs as she edged back down them, *so I keep getting into situations where I appreciate what I have.*

"Where are we going, Ash?" she shouted back to the pilot, hunching her shoulders to avoid scraping them on the rock walls.

"There's a tunnel to the emergency exit down on the lab level," Ash explained, his voice muffled and echoing through the narrow stairwell, sounding a hundred meters away. "We're heading up...after we head down."

"Are the charges planted in the Pit already?" she wondered, confused.

"No," he admitted. "There's been a slight change in plans..."

———

Adam Nagle leaned against the control panel and watched on the security monitors as the last of the *Metaurus* group disappeared into the entrance to the emergency evacuation tunnel, led by Mercier.

He was alone. The Pit loomed behind him, the alien hive calling to him as it had since the first time he'd seen it. This time, he wouldn't answer. He stepped away from the security station and went to the engineering control panel, finding the sequence to reverse the shutdown Susan had programmed earlier. Power from the reactor surged back through circuits she'd bypassed and the lights began to flicker back to life outside the lab.

Nagle strode quickly and purposefully through the security seal, feeling a chill pass down his back as he stepped into the dimly-lit, claustrophobic corridor outside. A touch on the lock plate sent the hatch lumbering downward, faster than its upward journey and yet still tortuously slow. Nagle watched its descent, hands shaking, mouth dry. He hadn't been lying to Busick; he had no intention of allowing the hybrid to reach the hive unless she agreed to let him help her. Susan was a fanatic, and undoubtedly a dead one at this point; but he had no more emotional investment in this place, not since the DSI had forced Ophelia into giving herself up to the hive.

The only reason he'd kept working was for what he'd thought was a vain hope of bringing her back. But now he just might actually get the chance.

And I'm scared shitless, he admitted to himself.

Was he scared that she would kill him, or was he scared that he'd let her down again?

The hatch sealed shut with an ominous, weighty finality. The sound of metal on metal was still echoing down the corridor when he saw her. She moved slowly, slower than he'd ever seen her since the transformation, and he could tell she'd been damaged. He wouldn't have believed that even the Gauss rifles the Marines carried could penetrate her chitinous armor, but he could see the jagged holes the slugs had punched. The black ichor was bubbling up inside the wounds, repairing her even as he watched; but for now, she was limping, in pain.

She paused as she came within a few meters of him, and now he could see the twisted ruin of the side of her face. The reflexive chittering of her jaws was conspicuous by its absence, the repair gel freezing them in place while it did its work. He felt a stab of sympathetic pain, feeling an urge to reach out and touch the wound but restraining himself.

"Ophelia," he said softly. "It's me, Adam. Do you remember me?"

———

It was the man, the one called Adam. After all this time, yet still he was here, still he looked the same. He spoke to her, but the words seemed to run together, beyond her comprehension, all except one.

"Ophelia," he called to her. It was her name. It had been her name, that part of her that had been human.

The name brought back images and thoughts of places the human Ophelia had been: of clear, blue ocean and scrub grass and hardy little trees sprinkled over hills and ancient buildings and a city called Elounda, as ancient as those stone structures. The thoughts brought back memories of the language Ophelia had once spoken, and the jumble of sounds Adam made began to unscramble in the shared neural network that had once been a human brain.

"Ophelia," the man repeated. "I can reverse the transformation. I can bring you back. If you'll agree to wait here with me until the others can leave, I can heal you."

The words made no sense. She understood them each individually, but strung together, the concepts they represented seemed totally alien to her.

Why would she want to reverse the rebirth? Why would she want to change what she was? She wanted to ask the man these things, but her body wasn't suited to human speech and even if it were, she would be unable to move her mouth until the damage was repaired. She could manage a gesture though, and she made one towards the hatch. She wanted it open, and she hoped he was smart enough to understand.

"Before I bring you inside," the man said, raising both hands palms outward, "I need to know you're going to let me help you. I can't let you into the hive, Ophelia, not the way you are now. Please tell me you'll let me bring you back."

The words were irritating, and with the pathways that brought her understanding came a greater experience of the pain. It hadn't been so bad before, filtered through the consciousness she shared with the systems that regulated this hybrid body; but now the arrangement of thoughts and concepts which had once made her human began to feel the pain in the manner a mortal being might, as an individual. And with that experience came fear, for the humans associated the pain with death, and they seemed to fear death more than anything else.

She motioned again, more urgently this time, wanting inside. Inside, she could reconnect with the womb, and it could soothe her fear, make her less this human thing and more what she longed to be, a Skrela warrior drone. Drones felt no fear, felt no pain, knew no limitations.

More irritating words, words that made her feel pain, and fear, and anger.

"I can't, Ophelia. Let me help you, please." The man's face twisted in some emotion she might once have been able to read. "I love you."

That word, it made the pain spike in her face, in her chest, everywhere, and she felt herself jerk back, claws curling.

"What is it, Ophelia? I do still love you, I swear!"

The word again, causing pain and a cloudy confusion in her neural network. She struck out at the pain, just a casual swipe of her claws. The man named Adam vanished in a spray of arterial red, his body slumping forward while his head bounced against the closed hatch and rolled across the floor.

She watched the body fall, and the pain and confusion in her thoughts seemed to fade with the human's life. Things were clearer now. There was only the need. The need conquered all other thought. He'd said the others were trying to leave. One of them would be able to open the hatch. And if not, they might have a ship. A ship could take her home.

Her sensors tasted the air and picked up the scent of humans leading through a doorway across the chamber. She turned away from the thing that had once been Adam Nagle and followed their trail.

CHAPTER SEVENTEEN

Sandrine Hollande tried to make her hands work despite the tingling numbness of her fingers and the nearly uncontrollable shaking. She wondered how Kan-Ten was able to show so little reaction to the cold; she knew Tahn-Skyyiah, his homeworld, was, on average, hotter and wetter than Earth, and that the major Tahni cities were clustered in tropical areas. He was swaddled in layers of clothing, topped by a cold-weather jacket with warming coils, just like she was, but she knew that it wasn't enough to keep the savage, bitter wind from slicing through her and she knew it would be even worse for him.

He soldiered on, though, which was enough to keep her from complaining about it, except inside her own head. At least it wasn't completely dark. It never really got dark on this moon from what she could tell. The arc of the gas giant filled the night sky, reflecting enough of the system primary's glow to create a constant twilight, bathing the rolling hills in an otherworldly purple glow; but the temperature difference was significant.

I should have just put on the damned vacuum suit, she thought, gritting her teeth to keep them from chattering.

But she'd spent the last two hours with her head tilted backwards, standing on a folding ladder as the two of them worked the replacement nozzle into place and bonded it with the engine assembly, and trying to do that in a suit would have been nearly impossible. Doing it in the cold without a suit was only highly improbable and utter agony.

"God damn it," she muttered, transferring the bonder from her right hand to her left and trying to shake some feeling back into her arm. The hose connecting the bonding tool to the tank resting in the snow under the belly of the ship was already coated with a thin layer of ice.

"Just another ten centimeters," Kan-Ten comforted her, conspicuously not taking advantage of the opportunity to stretch out his shoulders, despite having held the housing in place for nearly an hour. Maybe his shoulder joints worked differently than a human's, she thought sourly.

"Yeah, yeah," she replied, flexing her fingers a few more times before she took the bonding tool back into her right hand.

I can always pop into the auto-doc later if I wind up with frost-bite...

"Sandi, we're on the surface."

The voice on her 'link's ear bud sounded so much clearer and more distinct than Kan-Ten's, since it didn't have to make its way through layers of hood and scarf, and she easily recognized it as Ash. Sandi remembered to pull her scarf away from her mouth before she replied.

"We're still a few minutes from being done here," she told him, feeling her lips dry out and crack under the assault of the wind. "Did you get the charges planted?"

"Nagle shut us out of the Pit," Ash explained, and she could hear the frustration in his tone. "We're going with another idea. The Pit is built into the original crater the hive made when it impacted the moon, and they had to do a shitload of reinforcement to keep it open down there. I talked it over with

Commander Busick and Korri, and we're pretty sure if we plant the charges at the right places up on top, directly over the Pit, that we can cause a cave-in that'll bury it permanently. That way, even if Nagle lets the thing inside, it won't be able to get back out."

"I'm finding that idea highly dubious, lover," she admitted. "Stay warm, I'm on my way."

She pulled her scarf back up and reactivated the bonding tool, holding it carefully in place over the seam of the nozzle.

"I can hold it from here, Kan-Ten," she said to the Tahni, placing a hand near where his had been supporting the assembly. "Go on inside and get the reactor warmed up and get ready for a thrust test. We're running out of time."

————

"I'm beginning to believe I didn't think this through."

Ash stared down at the bowl-shaped depression between the hills, buried under ten or twelve centimeters of snow, suffuse with the muted glow reflecting from the face of the gas giant, and wondered how they were supposed to find the stress points to set the charges on that blank white slate. It had been a three-kilometer hike from the emergency egress hatch, and the only cold-weather gear they'd been able to grab were some all-purpose jackets kept in a locker next to the tunnel entrance back in the lab, and those weren't nearly enough.

He glanced back at the others, feeling a twinge of guilt at dragging them out here. Fontenot and Singh stood apart, while Kamara and the Fleet corpsman leaned over the wounded Marine, checking her condition on the readouts from her armor. The scientist, Mercier, paced back and forth, hands tucked into his armpits for warmth. The cold didn't seem to bother either of the cyborgs, and the Marines body armor had heating systems, but Kenner, the medic, was visibly shivering, and Mercier looked like he wanted to crawl into a hole and die.

"It's okay, son," Chief Weaver assured him, blowing a warm breath into his hands before he picked the polymer tote with the blasting charge back off the ground. "I've been here six years and there hasn't been a hell of a lot else to do but dream about blowing this place up." He waved a hand. "Follow me, both of you, and I'll show you where to plant the bombs." He nodded deferentially to Busick. "If you please, ma'am."

"At this point," she said, shaking her head as they trudged down the hillside, digging their boot soles into the frozen ground, "I'm ready to let you take command, Chief."

"Ma'am," Weaver spoke up above the whistle of the wind, "I don't know anyone else who could have kept us all sane and reasonably well-organized this long. Anyone else in charge, we all would have killed each other, or sure as shit killed those damned scientists long before now."

"One thing I don't get," Ash admitted, "is why the DSI never came back out here. I understand that the Fleet probably didn't know anything about this place, but Nagle said there was a DSI agent in charge of this operation."

Busick and Weaver shared a look.

"His name was Atumi, and he was on the *Metaurus*," she explained. "If I know the DSI, this whole thing was compartmentalized enough that there might have been two other people in the whole agency that knew about this, and even *they* might not have known everything."

"You don't know how many times we had that conversation," Weaver said with a chuckle. "How many nights we spent wondering if one of these days, the DSI might come out here to check on the installation and whether or not they'd kill all of us for seeing too much."

"Chief, not even the DSI...," Busick began, but the Chief of

Boat waved her off and pointed to a patch of snow that looked just like the others to Ash.

"Put one of them right here," he directed. He scowled. "Ideally, we'd want to dig maybe two meters down, but this ground is pretty frozen..."

"Let me try something," Ash offered. He handed his case of explosives off to Weaver and waved him and Busick away, then unslung his laser carbine.

"Is that a good idea, sir?" Weaver wondered.

"Probably not."

He aimed the laser's emitter straight down, covered his face with his left arm, and pulled the trigger. An almost overwhelming heat washed back over him, like leaning into a sauce pot full of boiling water, and he closed his eyes against the stinging, burning hail of superheated bits of soil as the laser pulses vaporized the snow and dug into the ground beneath. A warning vibration in the grip let him know the magazine was empty and he lowered his arm, realizing with a start that his jacket sleeve was smoldering.

"Shit," he murmured, patting at it until the spark died.

He blinked away afterimages and saw that the magazine-draining burst had dug a cavity about ten centimeters across and half again as deep. He shrugged and swapped out the empty from the shoulder bag Fontenot had given him and was about to try again when a gloved hand closed over the receiver of the carbine and pulled it gently away from him. Ash looked from the hand to the visored helmet of Gunny Kamara; he realized, with a flush of embarrassment, that the Marine must have run over immediately when he saw a Fleet pilot doing his best to get himself killed.

"Let me," the NCO said, tapping his visor demonstratively.

Ash handed the weapon and shoulder bag over a bit sheepishly, and stepped back, retrieving his blasting charge from

Busick. Kamara was enveloped in billowing clouds of smoke, and flashes of vaporizing dirt and rocks sparked up around him, but he stood statue-like, unaffected. He tossed an empty mag on the ground behind him, and went through one other before he turned back through the curtain of smoke and steam and motioned the others forward.

Weaver knelt down beside the laser-excavated hole and popped open the catches of the case he'd been carrying, pulling out a bright yellow metal cylinder and lowering it carefully into the hole. Ash watched with what he knew was an irrational anxiety; he knew the charges were safe to handle, but still, that was a *lot* of HyperExplosives...

The Chief of Boat placed the charge, then looked back at the others, frowning.

"We don't have a remote detonator for these things," he said, as if just realizing it. "I can use the timer instead." He scanned the edges of the hollow, shielding his eyes from the biting wind with the blade of his hand. "I'll give it thirty minutes. Shouldn't take even half that to place the other two charges, so that should give us plenty of time to clear the area."

Half an hour seemed awfully short to Ash, but he figured the Chief must know what he was doing.

"All right," Weaver said, hopping up from the hole, still wreathed in smoke. He grabbed the charge cases from Busick and Ash, holding one in each hand as he nodded to Kamara. "This way, Gunny."

Ash shrugged as the two of them headed off across the hollow, feet sinking deep into the snow with each step.

"Guess we're not needed," he said to Busick, stuffing his hands in his jacket pockets now that he no longer had to carry the blasting charge or the carbine. "Maybe we should start getting everyone else moving away from here."

"I wonder how far is safe," she mused, trudging along beside him as they leaned forward to climb back up the hillside. "Half a kilometer, maybe?"

"I'm thinking the other side of that," Ash opined, pointing at the highest of the surrounding hills, climbing up perhaps a hundred meters in elevation from the hilltop where the others were gathered, a good two hundred above the hollowed out bowl where the charges were being set. "It's a bit less than five hundred meters straight-line, I think, but the height should shield us from blast and debris."

Busick was nodding as they approached the rest of the group, and Ash saw Kenner, the corpsman, looking at them imploringly, as if his commander could do something about the weather.

"We're moving out," Busick told them, indicating the hill Ash had picked. "Ms. Fontenot, can you and Singh carry Private Caminero? We need to get that hill between us and the blast area within the next twenty minutes."

"Hold this for me," Fontenot told Ash, shoving a Gauss rifle at him. She'd still been carrying two of the weapons since covering them all on their descent down the stairwell to the tunnels.

Ash hefted the weight of the thing, trying to get used to the feel of it. He'd gone through a familiarization course with it in the Academy and that was the last time he'd fired one.

I'm a pilot, he thought for maybe the thousandth time since all this had started. *How the hell do I keep winding up as ground troops?*

"I'll take point," Busick declared. "If you wouldn't mind watching our backs, Ash."

He shot her a thumbs-up, teeth beginning to chatter as standing in one place for too long allowed the cold to begin traveling up from the ground through his boots. He was even looking forward to the climb, since it would bring up his core temperature...as long as he didn't start sweating. That might be fatal out here.

He thought he heard Busick transmitting something to Kamara and Weaver over her 'link pickup and he guessed she was telling them where they were headed. He peered out into the depression where the massive crater had been eons ago and saw two indistinct figures in the perpetual dusk, bent over another smoking hole in the ice and snow about fifty meters from the first one.

When he looked back, he saw that Busick and the others were already moving out, quicker than he'd thought, and he had to jog to keep up.

———

The trek back through the tunnels and up the ladder had taken her much, much longer than the reverse route had, only hours before. Her injuries were being repaired, but the damage to her shoulder joint slowed her ascent; she'd had to be careful of a slip that could undo the progress the gel had made with an impact on the cement floor below. Now, finally, she pushed open the hatch and stepped through into the wind-swept night.

Snow had powdered the ground since she had last come this way, but the clouds had blown over with the north wind, and the sky offered a clear view of the planet around which this moon orbited, uninteresting to her as it harbored no life and thus offered no targets. She knew the other humans had passed through before her; she could still sense the chemical traces they'd left behind. One had been wounded by her hand, and the blood left a particular scent, sweet and somehow addictive. That one would slow them down, and perhaps she could still catch them before they reached whatever ship they intended to use to leave this place. The ship would take her home, back to that blue water and green hillside, where all those kind, smiling people lived.

She would kill them all. She would tear their civilization down around them and drink in their screams as they died, she would...

There. The footprints in the fresh snow led off that direction. It surprised her; she'd expected that they would run for the shuttle, but instead they were moving away from it, toward the foothills. She tested her limbs and felt a resurgence of energy; the repairs were nearly complete now, her full mobility restored. She loped with long, bounding strides, eating up meters with each step. On this ground, the humans were only minutes ahead of her.

Featureless, snow-covered plain blurred into lichen-encrusted calcite and thermal pools belching steam into the night sky, then turned seamlessly into low, rolling hills. Snow and soil and strands of lichen and the powdery remains of weathered rock exploded from under her clawed feet and one bit of ground was much like another. She followed the tracks when there were tracks, followed the scent when there were none, and three kilometers flashed by with no real sense of the passage of time.

And suddenly she knew exactly where she was, as if there was a homing beacon somewhere in her brain that had led her back to the place. The hills squatted around the hollow bowl shape, and part of her that was much older than Ophelia Dimas recognized where the womb had impacted this barren place, back when she'd had a real purpose, back when *they* had been here.

They had infested the galaxy with their version of life, with what they considered their mission. They'd spread their sin from one end to the other, building their cities and their zoos and their preserves and tampering with the very fabric of the universe in their hubris. Their stain still infected this place, this nearly perfect place. Their insidious, cancerous growth made its atmosphere and encouraged it to wear itself down with each cycle of growth, and made it a place where the humans could live.

The humans were nearly as bad as the ones they called "the Predecessors." Their arrogant pride forced them to tamper with things they would have been wise to let be, things like the womb. The womb was below, nearly directly below, and part of her that had the capacity for curiosity wondered why they would come here. The rest of her, the part that only felt the need to destroy what the Predecessors had built, to destroy their progeny, saw the two men walking across the snow-covered depression, white spray stretching out with each step, and wanted to go rip them apart.

Wait, the part of her that had once been human cautioned. *Wait for their ship to come. Wait and seize it when it lands.*

No.

The balance shifted so abruptly that the hybrid nearly tumbled off her feet, staying upright mostly through momentum. The human part of her had been struggling for control with the drone programming since the very beginning, and even more since she'd awoken aboard the *Metaurus*. She'd been fighting the drone's need with needs of her own, with the desire to find a working ship and go home, and the fight was over, it was lost.

She was no longer a *she*, she was an it, a drone warrior and no longer even partially human. It had no fear, had no pain, had nothing but need, and what it needed now was to kill those two humans. Its jaw worked again, and the teeth began chittering as it ran at them.

———

Ash was trying to walk backwards, uphill, in the dark, through the snow without falling over when he heard the jets screaming by high overhead.

"It's Sandi," he yelled, head whipping around, looking for the *Acheron.*

The others were about twenty meters farther up the hill and he thought he saw them pause at his shout, but his focus was on finding the ship. He glanced back the way they'd come, downhill toward the hollow, thinking she might fly in from that direction. He almost missed the black blur, moving along the crest of the hill faster than any human ever could, would have missed it if a patch of fresh snow hadn't reflected the light from the gas giant just right.

It was the hybrid, he knew it in his gut.

"Korri!" he yelled, remembering to touch his 'link so she would hear him above the roar of the wind. "It's going for Kamara and Weaver!"

He took off running, knowing he would never make it in time, unsure if he could even hit anything with a rifle he he'd fired once, ten years ago, but unable to do anything else. He had made it just a few meters when Fontenot blew past him, her bionics churning ground faster than he ever could.

"Gunny," he tried Kamara's helmet radio. "Gunny, can you hear me?"

Nothing. He didn't know if he had the right frequency, didn't know if the Gunny's helmet had taken damage, but there was no answer and he didn't have the breath to keep yelling. He tried to keep an eye on Kamara and Weaver, but the trail down the hill went into a dip and he lost sight of them and the creature. Then he was back up on top and could see the thing, could see it closing on the two men and Fontenot closing with it, and he knew she wouldn't be fast enough.

Fontenot slowed just slightly and he saw the creature break

stride, jerking to its right, and he could guess that the cyborg had fired her Gauss rifle. The hybrid didn't stop, though, barely slowed. It was closer to them than she was, just too close to stop it in time, and she couldn't shoot again without hitting the others. Kamara had seen it, but it took him precious seconds to bring his rifle around; he was too late.

The thing hit Weaver, slicing into his chest with a single, devastating slash and the Chief went flying, spinning away, and Ash felt as if he'd been punched in the gut. The old man was dead, just like that, in half a second. Ash was less than a hundred meters away now, and of all of them, he was the only with a clear shot. He threw the rifle to his shoulder, using the manual aiming reticle in its optical sight, and started firing even before he had the thing targeted.

Miraculously, he hit it square in the chest and it stumbled backwards, giving Kamara just enough time to get off a shot. Tungsten slugs the size of a man's little finger tore into the thing, and it lunged towards the source of them, towards the nearest target, the Gunny. Fontenot risked a shot from behind it, even though it was directly in line with Kamara, but the hybrid ignored the impacts on its heavy back armor and swung a wild backhand at the Marine. Its claw tore the rifle from his hands and sent him sprawling three meters away, tumbling head over heels.

Ash wanted to shoot again, but Fontenot was moving into his line of fire and he cursed, running toward where Kamara had gone down instead. The hybrid was taking rounds from Fontenot, some of them penetrating its chitin, but one gun wasn't enough to bring it down, and it plodded toward her, advancing with two-meter-long strides. He could hear the insane chittering now, though the light was too dim and he was too far away to see the jaws working.

It was going to get her, Ash knew it, and he was too far away and at the wrong angle to do anything about it. He knew in his gut that this was it, that Fontenot was going to die, and he and Kamara would follow soon after, and there wasn't a damned thing he could do about it. He was torn in just an instant between trying to help Kamara and throwing himself at the hybrid to try to save Fontenot, knowing that either action was pointless.

His chest rumbled with the roar that filled the night, and glaring light played across all of them, blinding and yet revealing every obscene detail of the hybrid, every unnatural melding of human and alien. The thing turned away from Fontenot, looking upward, and so did Ash, unable to help himself. It was the *Acheron*, hovering on columns of superheated air only thirty meters above them, so incredibly huge, like a mountain hanging over their heads, looking so much larger than it did from the inside. Its landing lights glared down at the creature, harsh and accusatory.

The hybrid screamed. Ash hadn't thought it could make that sound, that it could make any sound except the mindless chittering, but it screamed, a ululating howl that pierced even the bellow of the cutter's engines. The thing tried to leap at the ship, clawing at air, and came much closer than Ash thought it would. It was still on its upward arc when the proton cannon fired.

Ash wasn't looking directly at it, which was the only reason he wasn't completely blinded. The blast of charged particles ripped apart the night with the harnessed energy of a fusion reactor, ripped apart the very fabric of reality; and the hybrid ceased to exist, finally, vaporized in the coherent heat of the heart of a star.

The concussion slammed Ash to the ground, the super-heated air sucking the breath from his lungs and searing his skin like the worst sunburn of his life. Afterimages danced over his vision, and he barely retained consciousness. And the one thing that remained in his battered brain, the one coherent thought that cut through the haze was: *The bombs.*

Something grabbed him by the arm and he saw Fontenot's face swimming through a kaleidoscope of light and haze and smoke. She hauled him to his feet and pushed him ahead of her, and somehow he was able to run, stumbling blindly, digging in with his toes, pushing himself up the hill. They had seconds, he was sure of it, seconds until the timers...

The charges blew and the world exploded with them. Ash was rolling downward, ears filled with a shrill whistle, brain weighed down with tons of soil, the pain a hammer that had slammed into his body, a shoe dropping from the sky to pound him flat. He was tumbling, out of control, clawing at dirt and rock and feeling it collapse under his fingers, feeling the vibration through the very ground that he knew was the Pit collapsing in on itself.

He would be buried along with the ancient secrets here, a mystery of his own to be discovered by travelers in some distant eon and puzzled over.

Did this strange, fossilized alien create the hive? Was he one of the ancient ones who settled this world and built these strange ruins?

He might have laughed if he'd had the breath or time.

He was falling and he knew it was the last fall, the one that would end with him lying broken under thousands of tons of rubble, and then his hands finally caught something, something hard and unyielding that gouged at his fingers. He reveled in the pain and lunged toward it, grabbing with both hands.

He was, he realized as he blinked dust and dirt out of his face, clinging at the jagged end of a BiPhase Carbide support rib, stronger than the rock and dirt that had collapsed around it and extending back all the way into the side of the hill. Part of it had been twisted away by the incredible weight it had tried to support, and what was left was cutting into his hands; he could feel the blood welling up and he knew he wouldn't be able to hold on long. He tried to kick his legs upward to lock them onto the thing, but the pain was too great and he nearly let go.

He had seconds before his fingers gave out and he knew it.

"Sandi," he croaked, wishing he could talk to her one more time.

"No, just me."

He blinked, thinking he was hallucinating at first. Jagmeet Singh stood balanced on the narrow strip of BiPhase Carbide that formed the anchor of the support beam. Ash could feel it shaking, see it swaying, but the big man stood perfectly still, his natural hand thrown out for balance, the other, the flat black metal one, reaching down to grab Ash around the wrist just as his grip failed. All of Ash's weight yanked him down against that unyielding hand, and he felt his shoulder jerk in its socket, but Singh still stayed upright.

"What a perfectly poetic way for both of us to die," Singh declared, his voice clear and ringing above the rumble of the collapsing rock and dirt, his natural and cybernetic eyes visible even through the clouds of smoke and dust. "It would be so easy, just to let everything end."

With a slight grunt of effort, he lifted Ash up and threw him over his shoulder. Ash felt mildly nauseous from the violent motion, and he wheezed painfully as the cyborg's metal shoulder jammed into his gut. But they didn't fall, and wavering, unsteady metal gave way to crumbling rock and dirt, and then to solid ground, and Singh tossed him to the ground, Ash's shoulders smacking hard against the cold and unyielding dirt.

"I'm afraid neither of us gets off quite that easy." Singh laughed, the sound nearly as strange and alien as the hybrid's chittering. "People like us never do."

CHAPTER EIGHTEEN

Captain Richard Fox turned the crystalline data spike over and over in his fingers, regarding it as one might an ancient jewel pried from some golden idol. The morning light glinted off of it enticingly, reflecting polychromatic flares onto the café's white, plastic tables.

"No survivors, huh?" Fox repeated, closing his fist over the spike, then tucking it away in a shirt pocket. The shirt was bright red, decorated in purple sun-flowers and worn untucked over baggy shorts. "That's a shame."

"The hybrid got most of them," Sandi confirmed, keeping her voice and eyes flat. "Dr. Sanchez killed some. The last couple who tried to get out died when the Pit collapsed."

"I was damned lucky to get out of that alive myself," Ash put in and she flashed a glance at him, wishing he'd shut up. He wasn't nearly as good of a liar as she was.

It was a beautiful morning in Dollabella, clear and warm and still, and the sky was a deep blue that Sandi had half-thought she'd never see again. It felt incredible just to be outside again, somewhere there wasn't snow and freezing wind at mid-day in summer, felt transcendent to have room to breath and sprawl out after spending so many hours crammed into every available space on the *Acheron* with nine people in a ship designed to hold two comfortably and redesigned to hold four with a little hot-swapping of beds.

It had helped that Ash and the female Marine---Sandi still couldn't remember her name, even after spending all that time on the ship together---wound up taking turns in the auto-doc for most of the trip. Ash had been healing up from a collapsed lung, second-degree burns, sliced tendons in his hands, three cracked ribs, a burst eardrum and retinal scarring, and he hadn't let her forget that most of that was from her firing the proton cannon only a hundred meters away from him.

Singh had stayed locked in a storage closet in the hold most of the trip, and only Ash arguing his case had convinced her not to space him. She fought against a scowl as she remembered the bounty hunter walking down the belly ramp in an empty field out in the middle of nowhere on Andalusia, days before they'd finally arrived back on Sylvanus.

"We should have killed him," Sandi had grumbled, slapping the control to raise the ramp.

"I have to believe people can change," had been Ash's reply. And then he'd hugged her and damn it, how could she argue?

"I'm not sure I believe you," Fox admitted in his casual, off-hand way that still managed to let you know he could kill you at any moment without breaking a sweat.

Sandi tensed, and next to her, she could see Fontenot's mouth thinning into a hard line. Ash's eyes narrowed, the muscles of his forearms flexing on the padded arms of the outdoor café's chair. Kan-Ten was silent and immobile, but she knew him well enough now to see that he was ready to fight or run, if need be.

"Fortunately," Fox continued with a shrug, "it doesn't really matter. You accomplished the mission I assigned you; everything else is your business."

Sandi hadn't quite been holding her breath, but she hissed out a little sigh anyway. She saw Ash relax almost imperceptibly.

"The funds are in your accounts," the Fleet Intelligence officer told them, waving a hand dismissively. "All payments have been made as agreed. I'll get in touch when I have another job."

"Hey Fox," Ash said as the man pushed his way up from his chair. At the officer's inquisitive look, he went on. "Why did we have to meet at the same café again?"

"I like the coffee here."

And then he was gone. Sandi waited a few minutes, watching the crowd in the street around the café and nursing her espresso. They'd run out of coffee on the ship after the first hundred hours, and the caffeine withdrawal had been hellish.

"Do you think the others will be all right?" Ash wondered, toying with the remains of a croissant.

"They can't go back to the lives they had," Fontenot mused, "but at least they have a chance to start over. And we spread them out on different colonies, I doubt anyone's going to find them, as long as they keep their mouths shut."

"It's a shame about Weaver and Kamara," Ash said and Fontenot nodded agreement.

Sandi hadn't met either of them, but she'd been there to witness Commander Busick's devastated reaction to Gunny Kamara's death. The Marine had come so close, but he'd been caught on the edge of the explosion, and no one had been near enough to help. The collapsing ground had swallowed him up as if he'd never been.

"Kate Busick seems like a very strong person," she offered

hopefully. "And we left them all as much money as we could afford."

"The one that worries me is Mercier," Fontenot said, her fingers clasped on the table in front of her. The synthskin made them look so real, you could easily forget that they could break a man's neck with a single twist. "He could try to sell what he knows to the Corporate Council or the DSI."

"Kenner could be a loose cannon too," Ash admitted, a bit morosely. "But with the hive buried, the hybrid gone and the *Metaurus* destroyed, how much could anyone do with the information? None of them could prove any of it, and if Kenner or Caminero say anything, they could be charged with desertion."

"What are we going to do now?" Kan-Ten asked. The Tahni had been fairly silent; it had been a bit awkward spending all that time on board ship with humans whose last experience with the Tahni had been a war that they hadn't known had ended.

"Is there a beach anywhere around here?" Sandi asked, leaning back in her chair and sighing longingly, grateful just not to be cold. "I really want to go to the beach."

———

Jagmeet Singh stood frozen in the street outside the clinic, afraid to go in. He couldn't remember the last time he'd been afraid, but the idea of stepping through the doors scared him worse than death. The foot traffic around him was polite and no one tried to shove him out of the way or cursed him for blocking the road; this was one of the posher levels of Belial, away from the fleshpots, and the bare-knuckle fighting, and the Virtual and robotic and real prostitutes. The lights were bright, the colors solid and professional and the clientele was rich. His clothes were a concession to his surroundings, his arm covered by a long jacket, metal hand gloved, and a cap pulled low over his face to hide the metal half.

The treatments performed in the medical facilities in this section weren't cheap, but the doctors and technicians who staffed them were the best, attracted by the money and the atmosphere. Singh had the money; he hadn't spent it on anything else in quite some time. But he didn't fit in with the other patients, and he could feel the stares. People came to clinics like this for restruct surgery, to perfect or change or radicalize their look into something more fashionable. Few came here to have limbs regrown or injuries repaired, but this place seemed safer than any of the medical facilities available to him in the Pirate Worlds, which was worth the extra cost.

But going inside, getting this done...it felt like he was abandoning Freya's memory. He'd carried his scars, carried these artificial parts to remind him that he'd failed her, that he hadn't been there for her and hadn't been able to avenge her. Removing them, moving on, leaving the scars and the bionic replacements behind, was that the same as leaving her behind?

Where would he go? What else could he do? His reputation as a bounty hunter might survive this, but he could never work for Jordi Abdullah or any of the cartel bosses again. They didn't take well to betrayal.

"No great loss," he mumbled to himself, still staring at the front entrance.

He heard the commotion behind him, heard someone scream and he moved by instinct, throwing his left arm around just in time to take the blade across the metal of his wrist and deflect it from its target, his neck. The man holding the knife was big, bigger than he was by four centimeters and ten kilograms, and Singh sized him up almost immediately by his face and his clothes. He had the rough, weathered look of a man who'd grown up away from Earth or the Core colonies, a man who'd never seen an anti-aging treatment or a nanite injection. His jacket was ribbed with lamellar armor, as were the backs of his gloves, and he held the monomolecular-edged combat knife as if he knew how to use it.

He stood out in the upscale crowd like a whore in church, and that, along with the clothes, told Singh that the man wasn't a professional. He wasn't a bounty hunter, or at least not one who'd been on the job long, and Singh had him pegged as cartel muscle.

The cyborg bounty hunter jumped back with surprising agility for his size, noting the clean slice through the vat-grown leather of his jacket and the matching white score across the matte black of his bionic arm. That knife was serious business, no matter how professional its owner was.

Singh ignored the crowd; some were running, some were screaming, others were frozen in place, watching with eyes wide from shock or perhaps salacious curiosity. None were threats, none were allies, and that was all that mattered at the moment. He focused on his opponent's stance, the movement of his feet and the set of his shoulders. He knew how to use that knife...and Singh was unarmed. Well, except for his arm.

The next attack came in low, sweeping in an arc that would have disemboweled him had it landed. Instead, he caught the wrist in his metal grasp and jerked it upward sharply, snapping both of the bones in the forearm. The big man screeched, a high-pitched sound that belied his bulk, the sound continuing unabated until Singh yanked him into an elbow strike that caught him across the bridge of his nose. The knife hit the ground about the same time as the big man's shoulders, and Singh followed the would-be assassin down, planting a knee across his chest, his bionic hand going to the man's neck and squeezing just slightly.

His eyes bulged with fear and pain and disbelief, as if he couldn't understand how he'd arrived in this position.

"Who sent you?" Singh asked, softly but clearly.

The big man croaked something and Singh sighed, letting loose the grip on his throat just slightly.

"Jordi Abdullah," he hissed out. "You stole his ship, the *Gitano*." The big man gasped a breath past the pressure of Singh's fingers. "He's got a price on you..." He grinned past a grimace of pain. "I just got here first. You can kill me, but..."

"Thanks, I will."

The man's neck snapped with a twist of Singh's hand and he went still. The onlookers who hadn't fled seemed to gasp collectively in chorus with the last breath rattling out of the assassin's mouth. Singh stood, regarding the body, considering what it meant.

The clinic would have to wait, as would his spiritual journey, wherever it might have been leading him.

He had unfinished business.

WHOLESALE SLAUGHTER BOOK 1
WHOLESALE
SLAUGHTER
RICK PARTLOW

ABOUT RICK PARTLOW

RICK PARTLOW is that rarest of species, a native Floridian. Born in Tampa, he attended Florida Southern College and graduated with a degree in History and a commission in the US Army as an Infantry officer.

His lifelong love of science fiction began with Have Space Suit—Will Travel and the other Heinlein juveniles and traveled through Clifford Simak, Asimov, Clarke and on to William Gibson, Walter Jon Williams and Peter F Hamilton. And somewhere, submerged in the worlds of others, Rick began to create his own worlds.

He currently lives in central Florida with his wife, two children and a willful mutt of a dog. Besides writing and reading science fiction and fantasy, he enjoys outdoor photography, hiking and camping.

www.rickpartlow.com